Edward Hogan was born in Derby in 1980 and now lives in Brighton. He is a graduate of the MA creative writing course at UEA and a recipient of the David Higham Award. His first novel, *Blackmoor*, won the Desmond Elliott Prize and was shortlisted for the *Sunday Times* Young Writer of the Year Award and the Dylan Thomas Prize. His second, *The Hunger Trace*, was shortlisted for the Encore Award. *The Electric* is his third.

Praise for Edward Hogan

'A writer of great energy and fearsome powers of observation' Hilary Mantel

'What with coming of age, a love triangle or two and the discovery of family secrets over a fifty-year timeframe, there is a lot going on, and Hogan manages it elegantly. He has a knack for giving us just the right amount of detail' *TLS*

'Hogan excels at tracing unspoken drama between characters, catching the shifts in temperature' *Literary Review*

'Hogan is clearly a writer to watch' *Independent*

Also by Edward Hogan

Blackmoor
The Hunger Trace

The Electric

Edward Hogan

JOHN MURRAY

First published in Great Britain in 2020 by John Murray (Publishers)
An Hachette UK company

First published in paperback in 2021

1

A CIP catalogue record for this title is available from the British Library

Paperback ISBN 9781473669574
eBook ISBN 9781473669567

Typeset in Adobe Garamond by Hewer Text UK Ltd, Edinburgh
Printed and bound in Great Britain by Clays Ltd, Elcograf S.p.A.

John Murray policy is to use papers that are natural, renewable and
recyclable products and made from wood grown in sustainable forests.
The logging and manufacturing processes are expected to conform
to the environmental regulations of the country of origin.

John Murray (Publishers)
Carmelite House
50 Victoria Embankment
London EC4Y 0DZ

www.johnmurraypress.co.uk

1949–51

Daisy rinsed her hair over the kitchen sink in the station house. It was one of those July nights when the shapes outside the window darken, but the sky never does. Robert was out, checking the licensed premises in the village. The straps of Daisy's summer dress hung halfway down her arms and she had a towel across her shoulders. From a jug she poured the steaming water down over her black hair and into the basin. She unpeeled her feet from the lino.

When she heard the sound of boots on the path outside the front door, she paused with the jug half-raised. She listened to the muffled exchange: Robert's firm, policeman's tone, and a younger voice, untroubled. Probably a drunk, Daisy thought.

She flinched at the knock on the door. Quickly, she scrunched her hair with the towel, shrugged on the straps of her dress, and walked down the hall. When she opened the door, Daisy saw Robert cuffed to William Jarrod, the youngest son of a local farmer. A difficult family. William was sixteen, but tall. With his arms wrenched behind his back, his body looked narrow. He smiled at her, his teeth surprisingly straight and white. A lick of hair hung over his forehead.

'What's happened?' Daisy asked her husband.

Beneath his helmet, Robert's face shone with sweat, and he would not meet her eye. 'Breaking,' he said. 'Let's call it that, for now. Him and his brother got into Geoffrey Watson's place.'

Daisy squinted into the shadows, but could see nobody else. She knew of the absent brother: a simpleton. She felt the water cooling on her neck.

'We need to get this one locked up. Is the cell ready?' Robert said.

'We haven't used it for so long. There'll be no bedding.'

'I'm not sleepy,' the Jarrod boy said with a smirk.

'Just keep quiet, you,' Robert said, as they crossed the threshold.

Daisy felt William Jarrod watching her. He looked at the towel in her hand.

'Would you get the door, Daisy, please?' Robert said.

She opened up the office at the front of the house, and turned on the light, illuminating two chairs and a desk, on which sat Daisy's Corona portable typewriter and a neat pile of documents. In the corner was the village's only telephone. The room smelled of cigarettes and paper. All three of them crossed the office, and Daisy pulled the bolts on the black wooden door of the old cell, which contained a stool, and a low, bare bed. These days, Daisy used the cell for storage: her dolly tub stood in the corner.

Robert detached himself from William Jarrod and pushed him inside. 'I'll have your brother here, soon,' Robert said. 'And then a divisional car will be on its way to take you both in.'

'Tell them not to hurry,' William said. 'These quarters are very pleasant.'

Robert slammed the door, and ran the three bolts home.

'He hasn't a light,' Daisy whispered.

'It won't be for long.'

'It's pitch dark in there.'

Robert nodded. He took off his helmet. His fair hair was sodden at the front, but dry and wispy at the crown. He pulled down the cover on a small eye-level hatch in the door. Light seeped into the cell through a metal grate. 'That will have to do, for now.'

Robert telephoned county headquarters to request a car. 'I know. I will explain later,' he said into the mouthpiece, before ending the call.

'Where's the brother?' Daisy asked.

'Still at Watson's farmhouse,' Robert said.

'Well then, you must go back there and get him,' Daisy said.

Robert put his hand on Daisy's bare shoulder, and moved her away from the cell. He dropped his voice. 'I don't want to *leave* you here. With him.'

'He's locked in, Robert. I've looked after prisoners before.'

In the two years since Robert's first promotion had taken them from the city to this one-man rural beat, they'd housed the occasional Sussex farmer who needed to sleep off the drink. Those men were always so sorry, so polite, at breakfast the next morning.

'This one's different,' Robert said. 'Perhaps I could stay here, and the divisional car could stop by the farm on the way.'

'You can't leave the Watsons holding Thomas Jarrod,' Daisy said.

'I know.'

They'd recently had the downstairs wired for electric light, and in that stark brightness, Robert looked young. He glanced up at the clock. 'Just lock the office door and keep to our rooms, Daisy. I will come back as fast as I can.'

He kissed her forehead gently. William Jarrod sniggered inside the cell, and they both glanced over at the hatch in the door.

'I'll be fine,' Daisy said.

Robert put on his helmet, and he and Daisy went back into the hallway. As he opened the front door and stepped into the night, Robert turned. 'Don't talk to him,' he said.

In the kitchen, Daisy boiled the day's remaining water on the range and dried her hair. She worked out the distance to Watson's farm: about half an hour, there and back. The divisional car would take longer. Across the road from the station house lived their only neighbour, George Makeney, an ancient widower. Beyond Makeney's house it was a fair trek to the village. Daisy thought of the many thrillers she had watched as a teenager at the picturehouses back in town. In her film scrapbook, she'd kept a list of rules for dealing with an intruder. *Keep something heavy to hand in the bedroom. Know your home in the dark. Use of mirrors.*

As she took the kettle from the range, she recalled a recent visit to the grocers. When she'd walked in, she'd heard the women in the queue talking about the older Jarrod boy, Thomas. They speculated about what was wrong with him. One woman said that as a child he had fallen into a pit of dead pigs.

'Is that why he looks the way he does?' another woman said. 'I mean his face?'

When the wives caught sight of the policeman's wife, the conversation ceased, as it always did. The women went blank,

4

fanning themselves with their ration books. The grocer called Daisy forward. 'Do come to the front, Mrs Seacombe.'

'No thank you,' Daisy said. 'I will queue.'

But the grocer insisted and the other women stepped aside. *It's just respect*, her husband always said, though it didn't feel that way to Daisy.

When she left with her tinned meat and dried eggs, Daisy saw a woman standing rigid by the open window down the side of the shop. It was Emma, mother of the Jarrod boys, and she'd heard everything. Her blonde hair hung in a long plait, and her face looked weather-beaten. She narrowed her blue eyes, scowled at Daisy, and then fled.

Now, in the kitchen, Daisy heard William Jarrod calling from his cell. 'Ex*cuse* me,' he sang. 'Ex*cuse* me!'

Daisy had left the office door open, and could hear him clearly. She walked back down the hall and stood in the door-way, watching the hatch. 'Are you all right?' she asked.

'Oh,' said William. 'There you are. It's very dark in here.' He spoke well, for a farm boy. He had a certain confidence.

'I am sorry about that,' Daisy replied. 'But it won't be for long.'

'There isn't a toilet, is there?'

Daisy cursed under her breath. They had an earth bucket for prisoners, but she'd left it in the garden shed. 'I'm afraid not. You'll have to wait.'

'Were you bathing?' he said. 'Did I interrupt you?'

'Don't you worry about that,' she said quietly.

'I need to—'

There was a clanging noise from inside the cell, and a brief cry.

'What happened?' Daisy shouted. 'Did you fall?'

There was no answer, and the house took on that deep quiet. When they first moved out of town, two winters ago, Daisy had sometimes woken in the night and thought she'd lost her senses, so dark and silent was their bedroom. Back home, the street lights and car engines and the white noise of the sea had comforted her. You couldn't hear the sea from this place.

'I said, are you all right?' she called again.

Nothing. She hesitated, but then crept across the office, and stood before the black door. Suddenly, William Jarrod's mouth was at the grate. 'I need to cut you,' he said. 'I need to cut you until they can't tell you're a woman no more.'

Daisy turned away quickly and her hip slammed into the desk. She called out in pain, and then ran from the office. She closed and locked the door behind her. Her right leg was dead and she thought she might be sick. After a second, William Jarrod began to scream – a high-pitched, mocking impersonation of a frightened woman.

Daisy thought about leaving the house, and putting as much distance as she could between herself and William Jarrod. But an image came to her mind of the road to the village, as it plunged into the tunnel of trees. She had a duty to her husband, and the Force. Jarrod continued to wail. Daisy ran into the kitchen and pulled a carving knife from the drawer.

The noise stopped. As much as she'd hated his pretend screaming, the silence which followed was worse. Being near to William Jarrod seemed somehow safer. So, with the knife held before her, Daisy walked back down the hall.

A bang on the front door. 'Who is it?' she shouted. 'Robert? Robert, is that you?'

'Yes. Open up,' Robert said.

When she first opened the door, she saw only Thomas Jarrod, the older brother, his face stretched and almost feature-less. One of his ears was malformed, and blood smeared his lips. Daisy tightened her grip on the wooden handle of the knife.

'Daisy, it's all right. I'm here,' Robert said, emerging from behind his prisoner. 'I came as quickly as I could.'

Thomas Jarrod wore no handcuffs. He said nothing, just tongued a cut on his lip and winced. His age was somewhere between eighteen and twenty-five. Daisy thought of what the woman in the grocers had said: *a pit of dead pigs.*

'The other one?' asked Robert.

Daisy glanced towards the office.

'I'm sorry, Daisy,' Robert said, stepping inside and guiding Thomas into the hall. Softly, Robert put his hands over Daisy's and took the knife away. 'Why don't you go upstairs? I can handle this now.'

'No,' she said. 'I'm not leaving you.'

Thomas Jarrod gave them no trouble as they escorted him into the office. He was huge, and the hems of his trousers did not reach his boots. Daisy felt instinctively tender towards him, and the feeling surprised her. He sniffed the air. There was a warm, sulphurous stink in the office now. All three of them looked at the cell door.

'Tom, is that you?' William called from the cell, his voice perfectly calm.

'Yes, William,' replied the older brother.

'Did they hurt you, Tom. Those Watsons?'

'Only a little,' Thomas said, pressing his fingers to his lip.

'Not surprising. It was a sin, what we did,' William said. 'But we'll be home soon.'

'Home and dry,' said Thomas, sadly. 'What will mother say, William?'

'I can't imagine.'

Daisy took disinfectant and a sheet of cotton wool from the cupboard. She held the items up to show Robert, who nodded. Thomas Jarrod seemed not to see her as she approached him. He just leaned against the desk and stared at the black door.

'I'll clean that cut for you, if you like,' Daisy said.

With his large, dirty fingers, Thomas rolled down his bottom lip to reveal a shining red gash. Daisy removed the lid from the disinfectant, covered the opening with cotton wool, and tipped the bottle. Firmly, she pressed the cotton wool into the cut. Thomas flinched. A tear formed, and he blinked it down his cheek.

'Well done,' Daisy whispered.

Robert took off his jacket, arranged his braces and rolled up the sleeves on his white shirt. He looked at the clock, and then the window. A blue eye appeared at the hatch in the door. Daisy felt an urge to press her fingers through the grate.

'Tom . . . are you not handcuffed?' William said.

'The policeman said I wouldn't need the handcuffs if I was a good boy.'

'So, you're free to go then,' William said.

'He most certainly is not free to go,' Robert said.

'Constable, look at the size of him. Do you really think you could stop him, if he wanted to leave? Your wife would have more chance.'

'Be quiet.'

'Tom?' said William.

'Yes.'

'You can go whenever you want,' said William.

'That's enough!' Robert shouted.

In Thomas's tired eyes, and the long, fair lashes, Daisy saw something of his mother. He sat on the edge of the desk, frowning, deciding. He never looked away from the cell door. Daisy didn't know whether the stench from the cell had faded, or she'd just got used to it.

'Tom?' said William.

'I said shut up!' Robert shouted. 'Nobody is going anywhere until the divisional car arrives.'

William laughed. 'And when will that be, Constable?'

'Soon.'

'You know, I had a lovely talk with your wife, while you were out.'

Robert glanced at Daisy, and then gestured towards the hall, but she couldn't leave now. That was what William wanted.

'We had a lovely chat, didn't we, *Daisy*?' William said.

Robert twitched, struggling to control his temper.

'Didn't you tell her to lock the office door?' William said. 'You were quite clear about that, as I remember. *Don't talk to him.* That's what you said.'

'I'm warning you,' said Robert.

'She disobeyed you, Constable. A bad sign, that. She came right up to this door. Very concerned, she was. Very concerned for my health.'

Robert strode across the room towards the cell. Thomas stood up from the desk. Daisy took her husband by the wrist, and he stopped. Robert turned to her. His eyes were wide, his right fist clenched. Daisy gently rubbed the soft tangle of veins and ligaments on the underside of his wrist. Robert looked away. 'Keep your mouth shut,' he said to the cell door. 'Do you hear?'

William did not reply.

A few minutes passed. Daisy let her shoulders drop. Then came the sound of boots on the stone floor of the cell, followed by a thump against the door. After a brief silence, William charged the door again. Then again. Nobody spoke. Robert didn't even tell him to stop. After the first few slams, the old oak frame began to judder, and a little dust came off the bare bricks above.

'Robert?' Daisy said.

'There's no way,' Robert said. 'Not in a million years. That door's been there forever.'

Daisy knew all about the age of the place, and it gave her no comfort. The house was riddled with a damp that turned the wallpaper to mush. In the winters, a white mould formed on the back of the sofa, and woodworm had wrecked half of the cupboards. Things fell apart here.

As William continued his rhythmic ramming of the door, Thomas Jarrod scratched the back of his neck. His breathing became ragged. Daisy couldn't tell if he was excited or upset. A small split appeared in the door frame. Bread-coloured wood showed through the old black paint. Daisy turned to Robert and saw his hands clasped behind his back, holding the carving knife she had taken from the kitchen.

The door creaked on the next thump, and then the headlights of the divisional car raked across the window. 'They're here!' Daisy said. She ran from the office and dragged open the front door. Two officers stepped out of the small squad car and walked up the drive. They slowed when they saw Daisy standing in the light of the doorway, and from their expressions, she knew she looked wild.

Daisy stood aside while Robert and the two officers took the Jarrod boys – both in cuffs now – out of the house. William Jarrod stared at her as he passed, but Robert reached out, grasped him by the jaw, and turned his head away. They loaded the brothers into the back of the car. Daisy leaned against the door frame, and parried away the furry moths, which were soft against her fingers.

After watching the tail lights of the squad car disappear, Robert came back to the house and closed the door behind him. He held Daisy so tight she could hardly breathe against his damp shirt. 'I'm sorry you had to see all that.'

'I'm fine, Robert. It's nothing.'

'I should never have left you here with him. Damn the police. Damn the Watsons.'

'No. You had to go. What did they steal from the Watsons' house?'

'Nothing,' Robert said. 'They didn't steal anything. It was some sort of. I won't talk about it. Nobody was harmed, physically.'

Something seemed to occur to him. He went into the office, took up his lamp and shone it into the dark cell. He sniffed and swore.

'What is it?' Daisy asked.

'Don't come in,' Robert replied. He walked through the house and out the back door to the shed. He came back with a garden spade and a metal pail filled with water.

'Daisy, where do you keep the soaps?'

'Do you need me to clean something?'

'No, you shouldn't have to.'

'I've dealt with plenty.'

'I'm going to do it,' he said.

Daisy talked him through the ratios of water to bleach, and he told her to go upstairs to bed.

When he joined her, Robert brought tea – the good stuff sent over in food packages from America. They kept the candles burning. Robert's hands were red and cold from the water. They tried to talk about other things, but couldn't. 'I think of their mother,' Daisy said.

'God only knows what goes on in that house,' Robert said.

'The big one. Thomas. It must be hard, growing up with William for a brother. It's enough to make you feel sorry for him.'

'Well, don't,' Robert said.

He turned to her, half of his face in shadow. 'Daisy, was it true, what William said?'

'What do you mean?'

'He said that you went to the cell door, while I was gone.'

'He pretended he'd hurt himself, Robert. I didn't know what to do. Any other prisoner, I'd have gone in there to help him.'

Robert winced. 'What did he say to you?'

Daisy thought of William Jarrod's mouth at the grate. She studied her husband, and saw a man who suffered with nerves. A man who woke in the night, crying out, and could supply no reason for it.

'He just said he was going to escape, that's all. He said the cell was old, and it couldn't hold him, and he'd get away across the fields.'

They fell silent for a moment. Robert looked at her carefully. The temperature had dropped, and the house tightened around them. The wood and the plaster ticked and creaked. Daisy found it difficult to believe that William Jarrod was gone from the place.

'Are you angry with me?' Daisy said.

'Of course not,' Robert said. 'You did everything properly, just like always. I wouldn't have got through it without you. But a woman shouldn't have to hear what you heard tonight.'

'But I'm all right.'

'People like him can leave a mark on a woman. They can ruin her.'

'What?' Daisy said.

But Robert just shook his head, and stared at the wall.

Daisy had met Robert in Brighton, after the war, at the dance hall above the Astoria cinema. He was lean and wiry, his shoulders lost in his jacket. His father had been a bricklayer before he died, and Robert clearly felt nervous with the daughter of an accountant in his arms. Daisy enjoyed his unease. He had joined the Force, and a policeman was a decent catch – a stable wage at an uncertain time. Robert told her he liked her black curls, the almost violet shade of her lips, and her slightly crooked front teeth. He loved her whole mouth, he said, although he sometimes felt powerless to stop the words coming out of it.

She insisted he take her to the Gaiety cinema, on the edge of town. The building itself looked like something from science fiction – a drum-shaped art deco space station, with a neon letter of its name on each of the vertical concrete fins at the front. In the lobby, there were fountains, caged birds and a black ceiling studded with lights.

'I'd rather dance,' Robert said, as they walked into the auditorium. 'All this American pap: it's just fantasy.'

'But you have to find a way to get your girl on her own in the dark, I suppose.'

She loved it when he blushed. They came in halfway through a thriller, watched the ending first, and then waited for the programme to start again. During the news broadcast, the audience noticed a cat in the cinema. It scrambled under seats and bounded across the bottom of the screen, to hoots of laughter. 'The moggy did it!' someone shouted, when the film restarted. But Robert shifted uncomfortably, crossed his long legs.

'What's wrong?' Daisy asked.

'Nothing,' he said.

'Are you afraid of cats?'

He kissed her then, squeezing her arm so hard that the red marks of his fingers remained on her pale skin the next day.

'I'm afraid,' he said, between kisses, 'that I might not be good enough for you.'

But she thought he was.

Officially, the five-year marriage ban for new police recruits had been lifted, but Robert continued to live in the section house at Preston Circus. Daisy listened to his complaints about missing her, but secretly she found the separation exciting. It gave their meetings – at dances, on night-time walks, at the ice rink – a charged tension. Their desire opened up the city – they sought the cover of alleyways and the seafront arches. Later, she thought of the length of his forearms, and inhaled the spicy scent of him from the fabric of her dress.

Eventually, an inspector visited Daisy at home, in Kemptown. He was a tall old man with a notebook and a raw shaving rash on his neck. Daisy followed him through the rooms as he silently examined the bookshelves and the cooking range and the cupboard where her mother kept towels. In the hallway, he pinched his trousers and lowered himself to a squat. He put on a pair of soft, white gloves and ran his fingers along the top of the skirting board. He examined the glove tips and then stood.

'You have known Constable Seacombe for two years, is that correct?'

For a moment, Daisy didn't recognise his name. 'It feels like much longer,' she said.

'It is not. You work . . .' the Inspector consulted his notebook, '. . . as a telephonist at the exchange. That's good. The Force welcomes competent women.'

'But I would have to leave the job, if I married Robert, wouldn't I?'

'You would not be idle,' the Inspector said.

He left his notebook on the kitchen table when he went to examine the outhouse. Daisy carefully lifted the cover and glanced at the section headings on the first page: FAMILY OCCU-PATIONS, ADDRESS, COMPORTMENT. At the bottom of the page, the Inspector had written three question marks, as though reaching for another category.

Shortly after they married, the Force gave Robert the single-beat in the countryside. Daisy felt proud of him, although the promised chemical closet never arrived, and after two years they still drew their water from a well. She dealt with correspondence, typed reports, cleaned and cooked, and manned the only telephone for five miles. She worked hard, and for no pay, but she didn't mind because she and Robert did it together.

After the affair with the Jarrods, she received a brief letter from the chief constable, praising her 'dutiful actions'. But the encounter knocked Daisy off balance and she asked Robert for news of the boys.

'It's out of my hands, Daisy. William is too young for jail and I don't know what they'll do about the other one. There's a rumour the whole family will move north. In any event, I can't see those boys coming home.'

He was right: they never saw William and Thomas again.

Robert's night troubles were nothing to do with the Jarrods. Once, Daisy heard him trying to scream in his sleep. He scrambled to his feet, and opened his mouth, but his cries came out as a trapped animal moan. Daisy tried to comfort him, but he shrank from her touch. 'Robert?'

'Where is he?' Robert said, and then woke.

'Who, Robert? You were having a dream.'

He looked at her, in the grey light of the early hours, and then he climbed back into bed and slept, without a word.

*

Later that summer, Daisy took Robert's bike and cycled into the village with the outgoing mail. Either side of the lane, the wheat rose high, and the pollen made her lungs rattle.

The post office desk was in a corner of the grocers. Two women fell silent as Daisy walked in. She took the mail from a satchel and handed it to the counter clerk.

'Ah, yes, Mrs Seacombe,' he said. He reached beneath the desk and produced an envelope. 'This came for you, care of the office.'

The clerk raised his eyebrows. One of the women behind Daisy tutted. Daisy quickly shifted the letter into the empty satchel, and left the post office, waiting for a moment until the conversation within started up again.

Nearing home, she noticed a rich green smell in the air. Its earthy power grew as she cycled closer to the garden of her neighbour, George Makeney. The scent filled Daisy with an odd hunger, and she got off the bike and propped it against Makeney's hedge. She had eaten poorly for years, and so it took her a while to recognise the smell of fresh tomatoes. She could almost feel the stiff vine between her fingers, taste the sharp flesh. She had to stop herself from running as she followed the scent. Over Makeney's gate, she saw the greenhouse behind his cottage, and the tangle of vines and bright fruit pressing against the glass. How had old Makeney managed such a thing? It seemed to Daisy like a miracle.

She closed her eyes and breathed in the odour. Perhaps Robert would be able to get a pound of tomatoes from their neighbour. There had to be some benefits to the job. Shaking herself from the trance, Daisy walked back to retrieve the bicycle, but a woman stood in the middle of the dry country road.

It was Emma Jarrod, mother of the boys. She remained motionless long enough for Daisy to note the changes in her appearance. Her hair was cropped unevenly short, her eyes red-ringed. A bloody cut streaked along her shin, and chalk dust covered her sandalled feet. She had come from the direction of the police house, and stood now between Daisy and home.

'Good afternoon,' said Daisy.

Emma Jarrod walked slowly by, throwing one bitter glance in Daisy's direction. Her blue eyes looked stark against her sunburnt face. She said nothing.

When she had gone, Daisy cycled home quickly, full of foreboding. But she found her husband back from his beat, cheerfully clipping the edges of the front lawn. He smiled and she went to him. She could smell the meaty sweat on his body, the soil on his hands. Everything seemed too close today, too real.

'Did anyone visit?' she asked.

'No. Is something wrong?'

'I feel strange.'

He put his hand on her back. 'You *are*, my love,' he said.

She went to bed early that evening, and woke at dawn, nauseous. Downstairs in the kitchen, she tried not to wake Robert as she vomited into a bucket. Only when she had cleaned out the bucket did she remember the letter.

The satchel was in the office. She took out the envelope, and opened it at the table. The envelope contained another, addressed simply to Daisy Birch – her maiden name. Inside, the letter was written on paper with a faint blue tinge. The return address was St Claude, Manitoba, Canada.

Dear Daisy,

Guess who! First three don't count. It is me, your good friend Paul Landry, formerly of The Princess Pat's, and the Electric Theatre Picturehouse. Also formerly of every cheap 'pub' in the city of Brighton. How are you, Dee? I hope you remember me.

I know this letter, if you even get it, comes out of the blue. A lot of time has passed since we knew each other, but I can't seem to forget you. I also remember every name of the 1932 Olympic-winning Winnipeg hockey team, but I don't have the same feelings for those fellows. Not <u>really</u>.

I am staying on the family farm for a while, because my mother is sick. The weather is scalding now, but this winter it was 28 below. My village is a little dull. It is famous for having the world's second largest smoking pipe. No, honestly, this pipe is as big as a house! You can find a picture of it in a book called 'Big Things in Manitoba', available from your local public library. I wish you were a Big Thing in Manitoba.

How are you? You said you planned to go to night school. Did you? Do you see any of those other gals? Have you seen any good pictures lately? Did you catch 'I Was a Male War Bride'??? I wish I could go see a picture with you again.

Maybe you're wondering why I'm writing this, well the last thing you said to me was 'send me a letter, Paulie!' I guess that was 1944. I am a slow writer, but a man of my word. I would sure love to hear from you and hope we can correspond. I better call this good, for now.

Paul Landry

Daisy sat blinking in the office. She did remember him, of course, but her memories of the war were like some old film she'd seen. Like a different universe. She had been wild, back then.

Paul Landry. Billeted in Brighton and Uckfield. She remembered a good ice skater, who called his skates 'tubes'. Cigarettes he called 'smoke poles'. His real name was Jean-Paul, and his father, who died young, had been French. His mother was of English descent, or maybe Irish or Scottish. Daisy had kissed him once. Many of her telephonist friends had taken the transatlantic boat to Canada in 1946, some with children.

Robert came into the office in a vest and blue pyjama trousers. His hair, still clumped with yesterday's pomade, stuck out at the sides. 'Working already, darling?'

'Not really.'

'You look pale. Did we get some bad news?' He nodded to the letter.

'No,' she said, putting the missive back into the envelope. 'In fact, I might have some *good* news . . .'

Robert's eyes widened. 'Are they coming to install the toilet?'

Daisy stood. 'I think I may be pregnant, Robert.'

'What?' Robert wrapped his arms around her, but then pulled away. 'Oh God! I must be careful with you!'

'We can still touch,' she said. 'Anyway, I don't know for sure. We shouldn't get too excited yet.' She'd miscarried, a couple of years before.

He held her gently, and they danced in the office. As they slowly spun, she saw the black cell door, and then the letter on the table.

'We have to celebrate!' Robert said. 'What shall we do tonight?'

Daisy thought for a moment. 'I miss the pictures,' she said. 'Can we go into town? To the cinema?'

Robert looked taken aback for a moment, but then he smiled. 'Anything you want,' he said.

It took Daisy a long time to reply to Paul Landry's first letter. She toyed with the idea of not responding at all. When the war started, she'd been a child, but she was a woman by the end of it. She had hardly touched a drink since VE Day. To write to Paul was to remember her wild, wartime self. It meant remembering the house of her cinema-going friend Maureen Williams, torn apart by the raid of May 1943. The ARP men had dug down into the rubble, looking for Mo's body, while her bed had stood on top of the pile, the red blanket neatly folded, exposed to the fields of Rottingdean in the middle of the afternoon.

But it was proper to write back.

Dear Paul,

How nice to receive your funny letter. Of course I remember. It has been a long time, and much has happened here. I am married, to Robert, who I met after the war. I am Mrs Seacombe now. You will probably laugh and make remarks, but my husband is a police constable. We work hard, so no time for night school.

If you see Stephane or Tony, please say 'hi'. I hope your mother gets well soon, and I wish you health and happiness for the future.

Yours sincerely,

Daisy Seacombe

He didn't write back, and she supposed that was the end of it.

Robert first proposed the move back to town late in the winter of 1951, a year after Linda was born. He paced the front room as he made his case, waving in his hand one of his daughter's toys: a wooden staff with coloured rings. 'I feel like I'm missing opportunities out here,' he said. 'And I don't know if this is a good sort of place for a child to grow up.'

Daisy knew her husband was still thinking of the Jarrod boys, although their house stood empty – smashed-up and left to rot.

'Might it not be unsettling to move?' Daisy asked, bouncing Linda on her knee.

'When I did the training, up in London, I met this fellow, Ray. He told me about the CID. It's different to normal policing. You just disappear off, do as you please. You've got to have nous. You've got to be tough up here.' He tapped the side of his head.

Daisy smiled. She stood from her chair and kissed her husband. Linda reached out for the coloured wooden rings.

'You're not so tough,' Daisy said.

'Well, maybe you could teach me,' he replied.

She looked around the damp room and found little to cling to. She saw the caved-in plaster, from when Robert had once punched the wall after losing his notebook. The window had frozen over, and her baby's hands were blue and orange with cold. Last month, she had gone down to the cellar and found the bloodied sheets from her ferocious labour, which Robert had discarded there. The sheets had frozen solid, and stood free, so that she mistook them for a creature at first. A fox, maybe.

It might be good to move back to town.

It took another couple of years to put their plan into action. In the meantime, she received another airmail letter, addressed care of the post office in the village. She opened the letter on the bridleway, two miles from home.

Dear Dee,

I was so pleased to get your letter, which took its time to reach me, as I have moved back to the city. You write just how you speak. It was like hearing your voice again! So . . . thank you.

So, you married your arresting officer! No surprises there. We all knew they'd get you in the end. I guess there is a chance that he is reading this, in which case, 'Hello sir, you are a lucky guy'.

I myself am having a torrid affair with Molly Dalton, usherette at the Beacon. Her favorite topic of conversation is money. Kisses don't pay the bills, she quips. Like I say, it's all extremely torrid.

I know your letter did not really ask for a reply, so I don't know why I am writing this. All I can say is that I feel restful when I am writing to you, and I hold out hopes of being pen pals. Chances are slim, I know, but I have to try.

Let me tell you about things here. As you may know, the Red River burst its banks, and turned the city into a puddle . . .

And off he went, describing the train trip to Winnipeg from the little prairie outpost where his mother lived. He said that when you looked out of the carriage window, you got the feeling that the fellow painting the scenery had fallen asleep.

She liked to read about the details of his daily life. He said he could send Nescafé, if they needed it, and Eveready batteries. He could make up a package at Eaton's department store in Winnipeg. Her childhood hero, the actress Deanna Durbin, was from Winnipeg.

Daisy felt her mind filling with the words of her reply. Soon, they would move back to the city anyway. There was no harm in writing. It was only words.

1997

Mike needed milk. That's what started it all. He cruised the backstreets near the hospital, dipping his head to look out the car window for a Co-op. The September sunset glared off the glass of a newsagent's, but it had closed for the evening.

Chapel Terrace had cars parked on both sides, but he saw the man walking towards the edge of the pavement from a good distance away. Aimless drifter, head down, typical of a certain sort of Brighton bloke. He looked like a man with no responsibilities. That's what Mike would remember thinking. The man's trousers were turned up above the ankles, his fisherman's jumper covered with sparkling drops of moisture, though it wasn't raining. Impractical soft footwear. Some kind of hippy.

When the man stepped off the kerb, in front of the car, Mike pumped the brakes and turned the wheel. A decent emergency stop.

From that point, it was all one smooth movement: handbrake on, seatbelt off, hazards on. Mike opened the door and got out. The man stumbled back into the shadows of the tall white houses.

'You fucking idiot!' Mike roared. 'What the fuck! What the fuck are you doing?'

The man still had his hands out in front of him, as if to stop the car. 'I'm sorry,' he said.

'Sorry? You weren't even looking! I could've crashed! Just because you couldn't be arsed to look. Not a care in the fucking world.'

'Hey, just calm down.'

Mike lost control. He swung his fists at the man, vaguely aware of a droning noise, which could have been a plane, or could have been in his head. He landed a couple of punches on the back of the man's neck, but the first time he connected with the face it felt so good, so right, that he picked up the pace of his attack.

The man fell against the railings of a house, and slid into a squat, his arms covering his face. He said something, repeated it over and over. It sounded like an *insult*. A curse. Something about Mike's wife. Mike was twice divorced, but he wasn't about to let the man insult him. He aimed a few more kicks at the legs and flanks. The man was crying.

'Weak prick,' Mike said, and strode back to his car, the breath reaching all the way through his body to the tips of his fingers, which began to tingle with the damage.

It had happened maybe three times in his life, although never that bad. Usually, Mike avoided the intimacy of confrontation. When his mum died, a nurse had shouted at him for blocking a doorway, and he'd almost wept. At times like that, he *wanted* to go crazy, but you couldn't just decide.

As he'd hit the hazard lights on Chapel Terrace, he'd felt the relief of being lost to rage, of escaping his imperfect self.

Back at his flat, he ran his hands under the kitchen tap. A stink came up from the drain. Regret settled on him. He thought about calling his sister, Linda. She'd have known what to do, but she'd dug him out of too many holes already.

That night, too pumped-up for sleep, he paced the hallway, waiting for the phone to ring. His nephew had left a pair of shoes by the door, and Mike stared at the impression of the boy's toe in the leather. What kind of an example was he to Lucas? What would the kid think if Mike had to go to jail?

The next day, hands aching, he drank instant coffee, without milk, and then went to work. Mike sold equipment to automobile garages. He carried a Nokia mobile phone when out on calls. A lot of people had them. His stomach lurched every time the phone rang that day. The feeling in his gut was the same as the feeling he used to get as a teenager, when he saw the girl he fancied. That nervous plunge. His body and soul made no sense to him.

After a week, he could go ten minutes without thinking about it. The bruise which spread across the fingers of his right hand turned green. The police didn't call, and nothing surfaced in the newspapers.

Maybe he'd done the right thing. After all, the bloke had stepped into the middle of the road. What did he expect? Perhaps he'd be more careful now. Mike suffered no guilty nightmares. He'd never believed that life joined up that way.

Then, as he urinated in the head office toilets one Tuesday morning, the words of the pedestrian appeared with total clarity in his mind.

My wife. Please. My wife has just died.

He doubted the words at first. How could they have been buried in his mind like that? As he walked between the toilet and the washbasin, they remained senseless. *What's that got to do with anything?* Mike thought, while he washed his hands.

But as he took a paper towel from the dispenser, it became clear. Mike looked down, and it was as though the edge of the paper towel was the hospital, and his thumb, lying parallel, was Chapel Terrace, which the man had tried to cross, unable, in his grief, to lift his head.

Mike began to drive home via Chapel Terrace. The first few times, he drove quickly, staring straight ahead, but he eventually forced himself to park. He walked to the spot where the pedestrian had stepped out into the road. The only sign of the incident was the curve made by the three sets of tyre marks. Brake, release; brake, release; brake.

Windows filled with light, up and down the street. Mike imagined people coming home, switching on televisions and ovens. Families.

An alleyway cut between two of the houses, at the end of which stood the hospital, its white walls blue in the dusk. The pedestrian must have walked in a straight line from the door of the hospital into Mike's path. Mike wondered how the man had managed to get safely across Eastern Road, which was much busier. He couldn't confirm his idea that the man's wife had died on that same day, but it felt true.

Was his home within walking distance? Mike wondered if there was a link between death and living close to a hospital. Could the sight of a building filled with disease get into your body somehow? Maybe the bloke lived miles away, though. What would you do if your wife died? Take a walk, probably.

The heating in the changing rooms of the public baths was cranked way up. Mike undid his tie and top three buttons and dragged his shirt over his head. On Thursdays, he picked his nephew up from school and took him swimming, while Linda visited their dad in a care home in Hove. Linda thought Lucas needed a male influence, the boy's father being absent, and Mike happily obliged. He watched Lucas scanning the changing room cautiously, a big, broad sixteen-year-old, the cuffs of his school shirt digging into his forearms.

'You not getting changed?' Mike said. Lucas, being deaf, did not hear. He got by fairly well with the hearing aids and lip-reading, but the acoustics in the changing room were poor, and you can't lip-read when you're looking the other way. Mike tapped his arm and repeated the question.

'Might go in the cubicle,' Lucas replied.

'Please yourself,' Mike said, pulling down his trousers. 'I've got nothing to hide.'

'That's just your opinion,' Lucas said.

Some other kids peered over, drawn by Lucas's conspicuous voice. Mike scowled at them until they got the message.

'What happened to your hand?' Lucas said.

Mike looked down at his knuckles. 'Work. I fell on the stairs,' Mike said.

'What?'

'Trapped them in a car bonnet.'

Lucas frowned. 'You should be more careful,' he said.

Mike nodded. For a moment, he'd forgotten about the incident on Chapel Terrace.

'First to twenty laps,' Lucas said.

'I'm not flipping doing that,' Mike said, laughing.

'You're not fat,' Lucas said.

'What?' Mike said. 'No, I said, I'm not doing that. Hang on, do you think I'm fat?' Mike patted his belly, and they both smiled at the misunderstanding.

'Not really,' Lucas said. 'Okay, maybe a *bit*, these days.'

'Cheeky bugger. Well, let's see if it helps me float,' he said, but Lucas had already removed his hearing aids.

In the pool, Mike couldn't let himself go. He couldn't get his breathing right, and his legs felt full of acid. The rusty liquid in the poolside gutters might have been the pedestrian's blood, the tangled mass in the drains, his hair.

A couple of hours later, they sat in the Honda, red-eyed and knackered, outside the bungalow on Bramble Avenue where Lucas and Linda lived. Dusk came fast. Mike turned on the car's interior light.

'Mum wants a word with you,' Lucas said.

'It's getting late.'

'It's good to talk, you know. That's what my speech therapist says.'

They got out, and Mike followed Lucas into the house. The boy flicked the light switch a couple of times, and a few seconds later, Linda responded, flashing the lights in the living room. Their wordless greeting.

Mike slipped off his shoes on the thick carpet, but still left a scuff of grit and larch needles and snail guts. The smell of macaroni cheese made his stomach clench. He put his hands deep into his pockets.

'Hello, boys,' Linda said, striding through the hall in her jeans and sleeveless top. She embraced her son, who had grown bigger than her. He turned to wave goodbye to Mike.

'Remember, Lucas. Show them what you're made of,' Mike said.

Lucas frowned, and sloped off to his room.

'I wanted to talk to you,' Linda said to Mike. 'Next week, I can't visit Dad on Thursday, so can you take Lucas on Friday instead?'

'Got a date, is it?'

'Sod off. I'm working late.'

'About time you got out there.'

'Says you.'

'I'm swatting the birds away, me.'

'They love it when you call them birds, I bet.'

'I can do Friday, yeah.'

'Or maybe *you* could visit Dad?'

Mike sighed.

'When was the last time you went?' Linda asked.

'It's not like he knows what's going on, is it?'

'Not the point.'

'There isn't any point.'

Linda looked over Mike's shoulder, into the evening. Mike kept the door open with his heel.

'You've got to let it go,' Linda said. 'It's been ten years. More.'

'I ain't got a problem, honestly.'

'He did it out of love.'

'I just don't see how sitting there with him makes any odds. Why don't you take Lucas?'

'No. I don't want to trigger anything. Memories.'

'You're full of contradictions, sis.'

'The splendid mystery that is woman,' Linda said quietly. 'Will you stay for dinner?'

'Nah, better not. Lucas reckons I need to lose some weight anyway.'

Linda smiled. 'Hang on.'

She went to the kitchen and came back with a glossy old book featuring an eighties woman in a leotard and headband, soft-focus. *Callanetics Countdown*. Mike took the book and flicked through, hiding his bruised fingers beneath the spine. He grinned at the pictures.

'In thirty days, you too could have a body like hers,' said Linda.

'The things I'd do with it,' Mike said.

Finally, he saw the man again, as he drove to work one morning. It hadn't occurred to him that the pedestrian might exist in places other than Chapel Terrace, and at other times of day. He recognised the shape of his head, and the trousers, one leg rolled down now. The same weird canvas boots. The limp confirmed his identity.

Mike didn't slow down, and the man didn't see him. It was over in the time it takes to count slowly to three. Mike got the lurch in his stomach again.

He stopped at the junction and other details filtered in: the greenish bruise on the side of his face, the strapping on the hand. The pedestrian had walked beside a sombre, olive-skinned girl of around seventeen years old. She carried a raincoat, and wore a blue suit, which marked her out as a sixth-former at a local secondary. Four weeks had passed. How long before you send a bereaved girl back to school? How long before a bruise fades from a face?

That afternoon, he left work early, drove to the school, and parked outside. Through his open window, he heard faint, tuneless voices singing. Drizzle dampened the arm of his shirt, and he buzzed the window up. He wondered if the sight of his car would disturb the man.

Buses came, and idled. Mike breathed slowly, preparing himself. The kids burst out of the gates: noise, squealing, pleas, laughter, bikes and skateboards, and then quiet.

It seemed that the man would not turn up. Mike hadn't seen the girl, either. She must have caught the bus. He felt disappointed, but not surprised. Life was like this: something hoped for seemed likely, but never came to pass. He considered leaving, but pictured his flat: the pile of unopened boxes in his bedroom, the dull brown of the box tape. He waited a little longer.

Shortly after 3.45 p.m., the girl emerged from the school. Mike saw her in his rear-view mirror. She pulled up the hood on her raincoat, zipped it as high as it would go. She looked both ways, and then ambled down the street in the direction of Mike's car. The sight of her, in the mirror, made him anxious. He'd watched many such scenes on television. They never ended well.

'Hannah!'

The voice came from further back. It was him – the pedestrian. The girl turned, gave a little wave, and waited. The man hobbled to catch up, and then leaned over, sucking in breath.

Mike watched them hug, briefly, in his mirrors. In the rear-view they seemed far away; in the wing mirror they were closer.

Eventually, they began to walk. Mike felt trapped as they neared the Honda. The coupé model was reasonably rare, but the man didn't notice. As they passed, Mike reached for the window button, stopped, and then reached again. ''Scuse me,' he said, leaning across the passenger seat.

The man allowed his daughter to finish talking, and then limped to the car, probably thinking Mike wanted directions. When he recognised Mike, he stopped, but didn't curse or gasp.

Mike spoke, to see what came out. 'Listen, mate,' he said.

'*You*,' the man said.

'Dad?' said the girl.

'I wanted to talk to you,' Mike said. 'About what happened the other week. I wanted to apologise.'

'Leave us alone.'

Trying to conceal his limp, the man walked away. He moved fast and his daughter struggled to keep up. Mike wondered what she'd been told. He imagined that day – her mother gone, her father – what, in hospital? Mike started the car and drove slowly alongside the pedestrian. His refusal to make eye-contact, the straightness of his back – it all reminded Mike of the way women get when they're angry.

'It's raining,' Mike called. 'I could drop you home or something.'

'Are you insane?' the man said. 'Do you think I would ever—'

'I remembered what you said. I didn't hear, at the time,' Mike said. 'I'd lost it. It was wrong, what I did. Seriously wrong. But I didn't understand until later. About your wife.'

The man stopped. 'Hannah,' he said to his daughter.

'What?' the girl said. 'What's going on?'

'Keep walking.'

'Dad? What's wrong?' she said.

'Just walk. I'll catch up.'

Reluctantly, the girl wandered a few metres away, and the man came back to Mike's car.

'I don't know what you think you're doing,' he said. 'But don't you ever mention my wife.'

'Look, there's got to be something I can do for you,' Mike said.

'Something you can do? Jesus. You know what I'd like? I'd like you to feel how it felt for me.'

'Can we talk about it?' Mike said.

The man stared at him, and shook his head in disbelief. He glanced at his daughter, who waited further up the street, biting her lip.

'Please,' said Mike.

'I won't do this in front of her,' said the man. 'There's a chip shop on the corner. Wait for me there.'

Mike pulled up outside the chippy. Through the plate glass shopfront, the colours shone bright in the gloom: the blues of the fish tank and insect-o-cutor, the yellows of the hot plate and Summer Bay beach on the TV. Shatter cracks radiated from a tiny hole in the glass. Mike wondered who would shoot a chip shop.

He didn't expect the man to arrive but after twenty minutes, he did. Mike opened the passenger door, and the man looked at it. 'I'm not getting in,' he said.

'It's pissing it down,' said Mike.

'Even if it was raining fire.'

'Okay.'

'I could've called the police,' the man said.

'I know.'

'I still could.'

'Look. You said you wanted me to know how it felt,' Mike said. 'We could try that.'

'What do you mean?'

'You know. An eye for an eye.'

'You're disgusting.'

'It's all I've got,' Mike said.

'That you would *follow* me. That you would wait for me outside my daughter's school . . . it's unbelievable.'

'I know I can't make things better. But I have to do something.'

The man gripped the car door but didn't shut it. He closed his eyes. His coat was slick with rain. Mike didn't know what he was thinking. He didn't know him at all.

'Once won't be enough,' the man said.

'You what?'

'Eye for an eye, you said.'

Mike nodded. 'I'm Mike.'

'No names,' the pedestrian said.

The public library where Linda worked had big old windows, and on October afternoons like this, the sun could blind you. Linda shrugged on her jacket, ready to leave.

Her colleagues, some of whom she'd worked with for many years, wanted her to go for a drink. As always, she declined. 'I'm going to see my dad.'

'What about Saturday? Will you come on Saturday? We're doing *Last of the Mohicans*,' said Suzanne, a part-timer who wore large black dresses and bright jewellery. Some of the library assistants ran a 'dress-up film club', where they watched a video at one of their houses, in themed fancy dress.

'I really can't, sorry.'

'Jim Brennan from acquisitions is going as a Native American. *Loincloth alert*, Linda,' said Suzanne.

'I'm doing something with Lucas.'

'Bring him along. He can be a soldier. God, Linda,' Suzanne said, picking at the sleeve of Linda's dark brown blouse. 'I'd love to see you in a bodice. Or even a *dress*. All this corduroy and denim!'

'You're right, you're right,' Linda said, shouldering her bag. 'I should wear more bodices.'

'You know the bit where Daniel Day-Lewis is in the waterfall with her?'

'Haven't seen it.'

'*What?*'

'I haven't been to the cinema since 1986.'

Suzanne looked pensive. 'It's true,' she said. 'There hasn't been much on, lately.'

Linda usually visited her dad on Thursdays, so she already had an uneasy feeling as she stepped off the bus in Hove, outside Cedars, the care home where he lived, on the wrong day of the week.

In the middle of the car park stood the cedar tree which had worked its way into Linda's dreams, with its weirdly obvious symbolism – the accusatory stillness, its stubborn ability not only to survive in a concrete wilderness, but also to sustain a whole ecosystem of spiders and squirrels and bird life. That evening, the cedar marked time, the trunk holding the sad orange light that tells you England will soon plunge into months of darkness. Linda edged past it, muttering curses.

She signed the visitors' book, and mouthed hello to Jenny, the young receptionist with her spray of tight curls, who was speaking on the phone. The corridor on which Linda's dad lived had a rubbery blue floor, glinting with some kind of mineral. She walked past paintings hung high on the walls so as not to interfere with the movements of trolleys and beds and wheelchairs. The paintings depicted pastoral scenes. Downland hunting.

She looked through the panel of glass in the door of her dad's room, but her fingers slipped from the handle, because there was already someone in there with him. A man in his sixties, with short grey hair, sat on a stool by the bed, reading aloud from a paperback. He wore a pressed, short-sleeved white shirt, and large, black-framed glasses, the lenses blanked out by the light coming through the big window. Every few sentences, the man looked up, though her dad, of course, gave no sign that he heard or understood. Through the glass panel, Linda couldn't make out the words, only the muffled music of the man's foreign voice.

She stepped back, but couldn't stop looking. The man's face had that sheen which comes with a close shave. Linda took in his thick forearms, the dark, woody colour of his brogues, the glint of reflected light from his watch. She recognised him. The recognition came to her gradually, and started with a physical sensation like the weakness that grips you when you realise you've cut yourself. Still smiling about something he'd read in the book, the man turned his head towards the door, and Linda stepped quickly out of view.

The edges of her vision greyed, and she could taste metal. Her fingers and her toes went cold and numb. 'Don't be ridiculous,' she said to herself.

She marched back down the corridor, went outside, took a big pull of air and waited for her vision to clear. She didn't turn back, not yet. Across the road, beyond the cedar, a light clicked on, illuminating the swinging sign of the Crown and Cushion. 'Okay,' Linda said.

The pub was smoky. On a raised platform, men in plaster-covered tracksuit bottoms and Desert Storm boots glanced up from a game of pool. Red and yellow balls slowed on the sharp-lit green of the table.

Linda's gin and bitter lemon came in a half-pint glass, which she took to the window seat, where she could watch the care home entrance. At this distance, with a bullseye window and a road between them, she figured the sight of the man leaving wouldn't cause her any hysterical symptoms.

She knew she should confront him. That's what a normal person would do. Ask him what the hell he thought he was doing there. But she knew she wouldn't. Couldn't. She had her way of dealing with things. Her life – with her son, her brother, her dad – it was a fine balance, and something like this could cause all sorts of trouble.

She didn't see him leave, but after an hour, and another ill-judged gin, she figured he must be gone by now. She left her empty glass at the bar, and went back to the care home.

'So. My dad had a visitor today,' Linda said to Jenny, the receptionist.

'I don't think so, Linda. No. Apart from you.'

'There was a man in the room with him. I saw it with my own eyes.'

Jenny frowned sulkily.

'I'm sorry,' Linda said. 'I didn't mean to snap at you. It's just that I saw a man sitting by my dad's bed. He was reading to him.'

'Ah, yes. You're quite right. My mistake. I don't think of them as visitors.'

'Who?'

'We subscribe to a charity service, where volunteers come in and read to patients who are blind, or . . . who can't read for themselves.'

'And is it always the same reader?'

'Yes. There's two or three that come, and they always read to the same patients. The charity reckons it's good to build a relationship. We do it on a Friday night because there's not many visitors.'

'How long?'

'They read to three patients, half an hour each.'

'No, how long has that particular man been reading to my dad?'

'Oh God, I don't know. We've been using the reader service for ages. If it's the same man I'm thinking of, he's been coming here for years. Linda, are you okay? Is something bothering you?'

'What's his name, Jenny?'

'I probably know it, but so many people come in and out. Oh, we could look in the book!'

She dragged the visitors' book over, and spun it round to face Linda, who ran her finger down the time column. The man had only written the name of the charity: *St Raphael's Readers*.

But she knew his name, anyway. She had seen it signed on the letter that dropped out of her mum's old *Picturegoer* magazine, when she was clearing the stuff out of the house.

'Do you want to talk to him?' Jenny said. 'I could arrange for him to come in early next week.'

'No,' she said. 'I won't be talking to him, thanks. And I'd appreciate if this conversation stayed between you and me.'

'Of course.'

'I'm going to see my dad now.'

'Okay.'

'Oh. And Jenny? He's gone, right?'

'The reader? Yes.'

By now, the sky outside the large window in her dad's room had faded to dark blue, and shadow shrouded the railway bank and untidy bushes behind the care home. Her father, as always, sat motionless on the chair-bed by the window. He wore a yellow shirt and grey cardigan, clothes he never would have chosen. The muscles in his legs had wasted, and his trousers looked like washing hung out to dry. 'Hi, Dad,' Linda said, but she didn't look him in the eye, because she thought her expression would give away what she'd seen.

An alien scent hung in the room: clean, subtle. The man's aftershave. Linda turned on the lamp, and put a Dean Martin CD on the portable stereo. Her dad had always liked the suave crooks of the Rat Pack. Linda sat down on the wipe-clean stool the man had used. The lamplight fell on Robert's expressionless face: the pink scar at his left temple, the flattened cheekbone.

'I don't usually come on Fridays, do I? So. What's been happening?' she said, but her voice sounded false. Her dad had been in this exact spot since she'd last visited, eight days before. He'd been next to this window when she went shopping last week, and when she walked along the seafront to her job at the library, and when she watched *NYPD Blue*, and every time she fell asleep.

Usually, Linda could control such morbid thoughts. Usually, she'd jabber on happily about the gossip at work, and the soaps, and Mike and Lucas. But tonight, she felt uneasy.

Dean Martin crooned about little fools who could never win. Linda reached out and turned off the CD player. 'Sod off,' she muttered.

She turned to her father. 'I'm sorry, Dad,' she said. 'But don't worry. I'll find out what he's up to. I'll sort it. I don't know how, but I will.'

An hour later, Linda got off the bus and turned onto Bramble Avenue. Opposite their bungalow, the larch trees dropped their needles, the street already half-an-inch thick with them. The rusty scatter reminded Linda of how the sink used to look after her dad had shaved off his stubble at the end of a holiday.

When she entered the bungalow, Linda flicked the lights on and off, and waited a few moments for the flashing reply from

Lucas's room. *Hello.* She stood in the hallway, closed her eyes. When she opened them, Lucas stood beside her, a glass of squash in his hand. 'Oh hi!' she said.

He smiled. His eyelashes were long like Mike's.

'What you doing?' he asked.

'Nothing. I'm okay,' she said.

There was a reason she hadn't heard him approach. As a young boy, he'd been a noisy slammer of doors and cupboards. He hadn't meant it, being deaf, or severely deaf, or partial-hearing, or hearing-impaired, or hard of hearing, or whatever the experts called it this week. Linda had responded to his slamming by re-carpeting the rooms, and putting rubber stoppers on the doors. She'd replaced the drawers with the type that closed gradually, no matter how hard you shoved them, and even the toilet seat had a slow-drop mechanism.

'How was your day, love?' she said.

'Pretty good,' he said, with a shrug.

'Get any appointments for parents' evening?'

Lucas frowned. 'How did you know about that?'

'You left the letter on the kitchen table.'

In fact, Linda had found the letter in his rucksack, which she went through periodically. She couldn't help it. She just wanted to know her son was okay.

'Right,' he said. The distant whistling feedback from his aids filled the silence.

Linda looked in the hallway mirror. For the first time, she was letting some grey come through her otherwise auburn hair. 'At work, they say I should wear more dresses,' she said, and then turned to him. 'What do you think of my clothes?'

'Aren't they your normal clothes?'

'Yes, but do you think they're boring?'

Lucas considered this. 'You could wear more bright colours,' he said. 'It's all a bit . . . *beige*.'

'I like neutral shades.'

'You look like a cup of coffee.'

'Lucas!'

'I like coffee!' he said, rubbing her arm. 'I *love* coffee.'

She laughed.

'How's granddad?' he asked.

'Fine,' she said.

Cassie first arrived in the classroom in October, and Lucas almost mistook her for a sixth-former that day, because of the dark skirt and sky-blue blouse. Sometimes the head-girl types would come and sit with him, so they had another good deed to put on their UCAS applications. He didn't mind.

This young woman looked around the room. It was English, last period, a Thursday. Amber light came in through the big windows. Her gaze settled on Lucas, and she smiled. She knew. People knew. Lucas stared down at the larch needles caught up in the laces of his shoes.

She walked over and turned the empty chair to face him before she sat down. 'Hello,' she said, clearly but without exaggeration. 'I'm Cassie. Terry is sick. I'm filling in.'

Terry was Lucas's usual learning assistant, a jovial older man who made Lucas put his hand on the baggy, sun-tanned skin of his (Terry's) neck so he could feel what vocal chords did during correct enunciation. Lucas liked him because he didn't draw any attention. But today, all the boys at the front had turned in their seats.

'Please, miss!' they said. 'I'm deaf, too!   deaf, miss!' Something like that. Duncan Youds buried his tongue under his bottom lip, to make his voice weird. To make it sound like Lucas.

Cassie ignored them. 'Do you have everything you need?' she said.

She smelled of freshly applied deodorant, even at 2.30 p.m. Lucas could see a lot of her gums when she opened her mouth, which he found unsettling. Her hair was short, blonde, and longer on one side than the other. It had a feathery quality. He didn't find her attractive at that point. He liked breasts – big heavy ones that rested on tables – and Cassie had more of an athletic build. She moved her hands when she talked.

'Oh,' Lucas said. 'I don't sign.'

'Okay,' she said. 'My brother is Deaf and he signs, so '

Lucas missed the end of her sentence. She rubbed her knuckles together when she said 'brother', and Lucas glanced around the room to make sure nobody had noticed.

'Don't sign,' he said.

He'd spent years perfecting a way to survive school. The experts had said that – with his very slight residual hearing, the right technology and hundreds of hours of speech therapy – he was the perfect candidate for a mainstream life. He tried to prove them right, and considered himself an expert at Fitting In. His method was to stay positive, and stay under the radar. If he couldn't see what a teacher said because he had a moustache that obscured his mouth, or because she turned to face the whiteboard while she talked, then Lucas read around the subject later. He knew his voice was weird, so he tried to speak as little as possible. If someone took the piss out of the way he sounded, he laughed along. He didn't chase girls; he didn't audition for the school play; and he kept a very tight rein on his temper. Generally, it worked – people left him alone. But now, this young woman sat next to him, with her powdery hair and red mouth. She studied her blouse and brushed off a fine pelt of something like dust.

Meanwhile, Mrs Finch was suddenly midway through an explanation of the English coursework, a writing exercise called 'A Life in the Day', based on the format of a newspaper feature. From what Lucas could make out, Mrs Finch was talking about breakfast.

'Don't just about breakfast,' she said. 'Think your breakfast says about *you*.'

Cassie shook beside him. Laughing, it seemed. The other kids suddenly became active, leaning under tables to get writing equipment from their bags. Lucas stared at the whiteboard, and the words 'Pop Tart'.

Cassie tapped his arm. 'So. Lucas,' she said. ' your breakfast could talk, would it say?'

'I don't know. It would probably beg for mercy,' he said.

She laughed. More heads turned towards them.

Lucas took out his pencil case and ring-binder, and saw – too late – that someone had Tipp-Exed HOMO on the front of the binder.

'Hey, what's all this?' Cassie said. 'Who ?'

'Doesn't matter,' he said. 'It's just a bit of fun.'

That sort of thing didn't happen very often, and when it

did, he ignored it. The trick was not to get drawn in. He opened the binder quickly, as Mrs Finch approached. Mrs Finch had a habit of missing off parts of her words when she spoke to Lucas. She did this to mirror his flawed speech, but it actually made lip-reading very difficult.

'Hi Luca. Do you eed some hel? You aven even pick up you penci,' she said.

'I'm fine, thanks,' Lucas said.

'Well. You got Assie to elp.'

'Yes. Thank you.'

She walked away. Cassie nudged Lucas. She took out a black notebook and turned to a fresh page of squared paper.

WHY IS SHE TALKING TO YOU LIKE THAT? she wrote.

Jesus, Lucas thought. Terry never said stuff about the teachers.

SHE IS JUST BEING NICE, Lucas wrote back.

Cassie gave him a look of comical doubt.

Lucas took a toilet break. In the brightness of the strip-lit bogs, he found himself sweating. He ran tap water over his wrists. Soon, Terry would recover, and he could slip back under the radar. Back to normal.

He coasted through the rest of the lesson, writing about his 'breakfast experience'. He thought about how his mum sometimes fell into a sort of trance in the morning, staring out of the kitchen window, furry suds dripping from her fingers into the sink. She made out she was tough, but Lucas knew better. She hung by a thread. But he didn't write that. Instead, he wrote sentences like: WHILE I PREFER WHITE BREAD, I KNOW THAT BROWN BREAD CONTAINS MORE FIBRE THEREFORE I USUALLY SELECT BROWN.

He did his best to avoid eye contact with Cassie, and as soon as it was time to go, he nodded a quick goodbye, and hastily left the building. Duncan Youds grabbed him on the way out. Youds smelled of sausages and Lynx Java. 'Hey Mario, who's   bitch?' he said. To give him his dues, Youds always looked at him when he spoke. Lucas laughed, and shrugged, his usual response.

They called him Mario after the video game character, because he'd once had curly black hair, and a downy moustache. He'd shaved and cut his hair since then, but the nickname stuck. God knows there were worse names. Rhea Nelson, in year ten, was known as Gonorrhea.

By choice, Lucas didn't really have friends. Sometimes, though, he'd have a brief conversation at the end of the day, with a girl called Iona. Iona had a deaf cousin, Nicky, who used to go to the Partial Hearing Unit with Lucas, at primary school. The three of them had spent time together, before Nicky went off to the Deaf School just outside town.

Today, however, Iona – thin and pale – gave Lucas a tight smile and hurried away as he took the crowded path towards the school exit. He soon figured out why: Cassie was walking beside him. He flinched when he realised.

'   meet you, today,' she said. 'I'll see you tomorrow.'

Lucas looked over to where his uncle's Honda waited in a haze of its own heat. 'I have to go,' he said.

He rushed across the road and got in the car.

'Who   ?' Mike asked.

'What? Learning assistant.'

They both looked at Cassie in the rear-view mirror, and then

Mike tapped Lucas's hand. '   seems   Terry's changed his hairdo,' he said.

That evening, Lucas glided through the blue, airless freedom of the swimming pool. After moderating his voice all day, he pushed down under the water, and silently screamed his heart out. But he could not outswim the image of that girl. He saw her red mouth, her sky-blue blouse, her fingers rippling like a sea plant as she signed. The visions had him breaking the surface and gasping for air.

Hours later, in his bedroom, he sat on his Michael Jordan beanbag and went through his rucksack, looking for *The Sandman: Master of Dreams*. He dragged out his English binder and tossed it on the carpet. It shed a cloud of tiny hair particles that glinted in the lamplight. On the binder, under HOMO, Cassie had written HOMINI LUPUS. A thin skin had formed on the Tipp-Ex.

He next saw her in Basic Studies. The Basic Studies room was hidden under the stairs in the maths block. The normal kids called it the Basin. Lucas went there for speech therapy. They'd tried to make the Basin homely, with comfortable chairs, butter tubs sprouting cress on the windowsills, and a photo montage in tribute to Diana, Queen of Hearts.

Cassie sat across from him, at one of the low tables. She emptied Terry's laminated cards out of an envelope and rolled her eyes. On one of the cards was written 'bear', on another, 'pear'. Cassie placed them face up.

'You know   to do, I guess.'

Lucas nodded, and she began. 'Pear, bear, bear, bear, pear . . .'

Each time she said a word, Lucas was supposed to point to the corresponding card. A lip-reading exercise. He pointed pretty much at random, and tried not to think about Cassie turning to shut the door when she came in. He tried not to think about her broad, strong hips. He'd never paid much attention to those areas on girls before, but in a way that was like *discrimination*. He didn't want to discriminate against arses.

'   ridiculous!' she said, slamming the table. '   the point of sitting here with a kid who   doing pear bloody bear.'

As she said the words, he instinctively pointed to one card and then the other. Cassie laughed.

'Didn't you *ever* sign?' she asked.

'I think I did until I was about six.'

'   happened when you were six?'

That was a very good question.

'Pardon?' Lucas said.

'Did your parents sign?'

'My mum learned, yeah, and my Nanna.'

'What, and you just stopped?'

'Look, I can't remember how to do it. The teachers said it was holding me back in school.'

'And you're doing *really well*, now.'

'I'm doing *fine*!' he snapped.

Shame rose in Lucas. *Shame and rage*. He'd spent years building a shield against those feelings. He looked away. Cassie's bag lay open on the floor. Inside was a large mobile phone, and a can of deodorant called 'Intensive Care'. Gently, she tapped his hand. Her fingers were marked by indentations from fingerless gloves.

'I'm sorry,' she said, and rubbed the centre of her chest in a circle. Lucas felt something, when she made that sign. God knows what. But the feeling was deep.

He took out his English binder and pointed to the words in Tipp-Ex. HOMO HOMINI LUPUS. 'What does it mean?' he asked.

He didn't understand her reply, so she opened her black notebook and wrote, MAN IS WOLF TO MAN.

Amen, Lucas thought.

Lucas had no memory of the time before he was six. Couldn't remember signing, or anything else. He couldn't even remember his Nanna, who had looked after him back then. There was just a big spooky black hole in his mind.

He certainly had no intention of relearning to sign. Since Nicky had left for the Deaf School, he hadn't really associated with deaf people. At this point in his school career, he figured that using sign language was the social equivalent of morris dancing, or announcing that he had a micro-penis. But every afternoon that autumn, he would watch Cassie walk past the window in a vest and cycle shorts and those shoes with the little cleats on the sole. She secured her hair with a sweatband and climbed onto a green racing bike. And he wondered if he might do anything she said.

Lucas loved the cinema. Where else could he go and sit surrounded by other people without endless awkward interactions? It was fine to sit in a cinema, alone. Cool people in polo necks did it. He liked action movies best (Jackie Chan was his favourite – no explanations required), and the European films they showed at the Duke of York's. French films had subtitles, and anyway, there didn't seem to be much dialogue.

But that Saturday afternoon, he walked out of *First Strike*, at the ABC cinema, after an hour. He just couldn't concentrate, and he pretended to himself that he didn't know why.

The bus dropped him off across the road from Ringdean's row of shops, and the hairdresser's which Cassie's mother had taken over. The place had been called 'Hair Force One' before, but Cassie's mum had renamed it 'The Cut', and introduced more of a salon feel. Cassie sometimes helped out there on weekends.

The candy-stripe barber's pole turned slowly against the blue dusk. Images came to Lucas's mind: boiled sweets, fairgrounds, hazard tape.

Through the plate-glass shopfront, he saw Cassie's mum shift her weight from one cowboy boot to the other. She discarded bits of tin foil, and dropped scissors and clipper teeth into the tube of blue disinfectant. They were finishing up for the day. The light of The Cut burned bright, and Lucas knew he was hidden from view, in the outer dark.

Cassie came from the back of the shop with a rubber-bristled brush. She swept up swatches of hair, which made the place look like the site of a bird kill. In black jumper and jeans, she leaned on the staff of the brush to stretch. After a while, both women moved towards the back door and the light went off, leaving Lucas to wait for his own reflection to appear in the glass – a great ghoul.

He sloped off to the chemist and bought two bottles of Intensive Care deodorant, which he hid in the polystyrene balls of his beanbag when he got home. This blatantly contravened his rules for Fitting In, and he knew he was done for.

During the next week's Basin session, they worked on 'idioms' for the 'A Life in the Day' project. Lucas was good on idioms, because he read so much. He once sneaked a look at his SEN report, which said '*Lucas uses reading as a form of social withdrawal*'. You couldn't win.

He glanced out of the window at the chlorinated mist hanging over the pines surrounding the outdoor swimming pool. Some kids walked by. One of them made that face at him: the big, gurning mouth. He turned away, hoping Cassie hadn't noticed, but she had.

'Right,' she said. ' tend we're on TV.'

Lucas rolled his eyes, and Cassie stuck a rubber grip on the end of a pencil for a microphone. ' viewers, I'm here with Mario Seacombe,   . Mario, how do you   about being deaf?'

'Fine,' he said. 'Can we talk about something else?'

'Humour me. I'm trying   inside your head, for the project. How   feel about your hearing?'

He glanced at his 'idioms' worksheet. 'I take it on the chin,' he said.

'You take your hearing on the chin?   may have discovered the problem, medically speaking.'

Lucas cracked. 'It's all anyone ever talks to me about!' he said. 'On and on about how terrible it is to be hearing impaired. It's not terrible. It's fine!'

'Home's *fine*. School's *fine* . . .'

'Yes! And I'm sick of people asking "how deaf" I am, or trying to explain what things sound like. I don't care! And the endless fucking tests!'

The other Basin kids stared at him, and he tried to calm down. This was exactly the kind of behaviour that would mark him out.

Cassie put a finger to an imaginary earpiece. '   remind you, Mario, that we're live on air.   to our younger viewers for the language.'

He shook his head.

'Look,' Cassie said. 'We can do speech therapy for the next hundred years, and you'll never pass for hearing. You're not *hearing impaired*. You're *Deaf.* You'll never be like them.'

'Sometimes you're not very nice,' he said.

She raised her pencil/microphone again. 'When these idiots at school   faces at you   call you names, what do you say?'

'I say "pardon?" '

It took her a while to get it. She laughed, revealing all that gum. 'Very good.'

He read from the idioms again. 'It goes in one eye, and out the other.'

'Hey, there's a sign for that!'

She taught him a couple more: an itching sign, to show you disliked someone; a putting down of the ears, as a cuss. 'This one,' she said, performing the sign, 'means, "my hands are sealed".'

He laughed, and tried to copy her. She took hold of his fingers, to help him. That was how he started to learn. No agreement, no contract. Just her hands on his.

'This,' she said, baring her teeth and claws, 'is the sign for "angry". I strongly suggest you use it.'

1953–5

Thirty houses stood on the police estate, each dwelling reflecting the rank of its inhabitant. The place was known as 'The Colony'. It had a clubhouse and a recreational area, and Divisional HQ could be seen from the windows of most of the homes.

The Seacombes first arrived late at night. Half of the lights on the terraced row still glowed. 'Why are they all awake?' Daisy asked, clutching Linda to her shoulder.

'Night shifts, I suppose,' said Robert. He put a hand on the small of her back. 'Wives waiting up. It'll be good for you to know there's people next door in the same boat.'

Later that first week, Robert encouraged her to go to the wives' sports social: a crown green bowls tournament.

'Oh no,' Daisy said. 'I wouldn't know what to wear.'

'You look lovely. Go as you are.'

She wore a homemade navy pleated skirt and a navy waistcoat over a white short-sleeved sweater.

'I'd be nervous,' Daisy said. 'I don't think it's for me.'

'It *is* for you,' Robert said, smiling. 'It's for *me*, too. Important you get along with the other wives. Good for a man's career.'

'I see.'

'You've been out in the sticks too long, that's all. You'll get back into the swing of it.'

Daisy looked around their new home. The rooms were small and the ceilings low but they had indoor plumbing and the wallpaper, with its burgundy stripes, stayed fixed to the wall. She heard her daughter climbing the stairs on her hands and knees.

'What about Linda?' she said.

'I'll deal with her.'

Walking to the bowling green, Daisy saw women, in groups of two and three, converging from the grid of streets. In the east, the sun glowered, but storm-clouds loomed in the west, giving the façades of the houses an unreal glow.

Most of the women wore jackets.

Daisy told herself this was her town. And she had once enjoyed socialising. She strode across the bowling green to a group of wives standing at the clubhouse end. 'Good morning,' she said. 'I'm Daisy.'

The group looked deferentially to a short woman in white-rimmed glasses and a grey suit. She had on white disk earrings that matched her flat shoes. 'Go on . . .' she said.

'I'm here for the bowls.'

'Who is your *husband*?' said the woman.

'Oh. Robert. Robert Seacombe.'

The woman in the white-rimmed glasses winced. '*Police Constable* Seacombe, I have to assume?' she said. There was a sigh of laughter. 'I am Mrs Clore,' said the woman. Mrs Clore identified the other women in the group, but this was information, not introduction.

'I fear we shall have to re-instigate the badges,' she said. 'Mrs Seacombe, your shoes are inappropriate. And there are no shoes appropriate to the act of walking across a bowling green, whilst not in play.'

Daisy blushed, and Mrs Clore seemed to take pity on her. 'You'll discover refreshments in the clubhouse,' she said.

'Thank you.'

'When you find the tray, Mrs Seacombe, bring it out.'

The clubhouse smelled of meat paste and orange squash. The wives in there looked different. She heard the difference in their voices: they spoke like Mrs Clore might have if she'd fallen down the stairs. Eyes flashed in Daisy's direction. Pricing her up.

'Hello, I'm Mrs Gaye,' said a woman with a cheap permanent. 'Peggy. Your neighbour. I'm afraid we all saw you talking to the brass, out there.'

'I didn't mean anything by it,' Daisy said.

'Well, if you thought that was the way to a quick promotion, God help you.'

'I wasn't even thinking about—'

'Rule number four: all anyone talks about is promotion.'

'Number four . . .?'

'I think you learned the first three rules the hard way. Footwear. Bowling green. Where you belong.'

'I'm supposed to take a tray of refreshments out to them.'

Peggy Gaye smiled. 'Not to *them*, love. You don't get to serve them for a long time. You're to serve us. Now, I think our husbands share a beat. Robert, is it?'

Another woman, young and with a body that had not yet borne a child, called out: 'Mrs Clore would like us to wear the badges. To avoid any gaffes.'

The badge had a pin, which had pierced both her waistcoat and her sweater. POLICE CONSTABLE. 'I see that I'm yet to move up the ranks,' said Robert, when she arrived home that afternoon.

'I hate this place,' Daisy said.

'I think it's all right,' Robert said. He sat in the armchair. Linda napped on a blanket by his feet. Daisy heard the rumbling voice of the wireless announcer from next door.

'It's stuffy. Everyone walks around in fear of saying something wrong.'

'You'll get used to it. You need to get out there, and make some friends.'

'Stop telling me what I need to do,' Daisy said.

She expected Robert to stand out of his chair, for his jaw muscles to tighten in threat. But he just shrugged. 'Whatever you say.' He nodded to her badge. 'You're the ranking officer.'

Daisy pulled out the pin, and ripped a hole in her sweater. 'For God's sake,' she shouted.

'Daisy, keep your voice down,' Robert said. 'We don't live in the country anymore. We have neighbours.'

'Well, it's our business. Not theirs.'

Robert shook his head. 'Not really,' he said.

He did stand now, and took Daisy by the wrist. He looked at the flap torn from her sweater, the flesh of her breast swelling over cotton. 'I'm sorry you had a bad day, but it's important that we help each other.'

'Let go,' she said. 'Linda needs to wake up.'

Robert smiled. 'We all do,' he said.

The next morning, Daisy rose early. Her head ached. She ambled down to the front door, opened it, and took several big breaths. Carefully, she looked along the terraced row. Six of the nine houses already had women outside. They watered hanging baskets, put out empty milk bottles, snipped grass back from paths, walloped rugs, and talked. Always talking, always watching.

Perhaps those women had seen her make a fool of herself the day before, but Daisy didn't care about that. She worried more about the postman. She had given Paul Landry her home address, and that now seemed like a terrible mistake. The red-faced postman chatted to one of the women at the end of the street, and appeared to Daisy like a travelling ragman during the Plague. Her husband surfaced upstairs, clearing his sinuses. She slammed the door shut and kept watch over the letterbox.

That afternoon, she went to the post office in town, set herself up with a PO Box, and wrote to tell Paul never to send mail to her house.

That was how the letters continued.

Dear Dee,

My birthday was fine, thank you for asking. I drove out in the truck and slept under the stars. Just me. It was some party! In terms of gifts, mother bought me a tiepin (God bless Mother! I haven't worn a tie since 1938), and my sister, Marguerite, a set of pencils. Clare bought me a quart of rye whisky and drank half.

My friends say, 'Hey Laundry (they call me Laundry)! All you ever talk about is this G-D Limey girl. Why don't you get some real pals? Or take up a hobby. Stop living in the past!'

So I'm taking a night-class. In history.

It's part of a bigger plan, which I will tell you about one day, but for now I go packets for the history. It all sounds like fantasy stories until suddenly they start talking about the Depression, which I <u>lived</u> through! I could write you about it, seeing how you can't get away to study. We could do the classes together. A correspondence course! With your smarts and my stationery, we may pass the test.

She ignored the mild flirting. He wrote about his social life – Clare, from the letter, was his on/off girlfriend – but he also wrote about ideas. He wrote about history and education. He wrote about how you might live your life, as if there was a choice.

Daisy replied in the same vein. She liked herself in the letters. She could be someone else on the page: a cross between her wartime self and an early Barbara Stanwyck. She wrote about the movies she'd watched, and compiled lists of her favourite scenes. A list of Bette's best put-downs. A list of the best side-eyes.

She never mentioned Robert or Linda, but she made fun of the wives' meetings and police dances, and that helped her through the early months on the colony. She rehearsed the letters as she went about her daily life – cooking meals, sewing, hanging the washing. She didn't even realise she was talking aloud until she felt the clothes pegs moving in her mouth.

'Did you have anyone before Neville?' Daisy asked Peggy Gaye.

'No. Not many after, either,' said Peggy.

They sat on stools outside their front doors, each with a glass of stout and a cigarette. They often did this, during their husbands' night shifts, chatting until neighbouring wives with men on earlies called out the windows for peace. Peggy had guided Daisy through the first year on the estate. She told her what dresses to wear at which dances, and which women to avoid. She made sure Daisy sat at the right table during the Wives' Club meetings.

'Neville wants to be CID, too, you know,' Peggy said.

'It's all Robert talks about,' said Daisy.

Neville Gaye looked up to Robert. His ears stuck out, and his hair was so wiry that Peggy said he'd given up on Brylcreem and now slopped on *shaving cream*. Robert, though, only hung around with a constable named Ray Harper. It was Harper who came over on off-days, and never with his wife.

And it was Harper who brought Robert home, that night. Unusually, they arrived outside in a squad car. The headlamps made Daisy and Peggy squint. Harper and Robert got out of the car. In summer, the Brighton bobbies wore white custodian helmets, but Robert carried his in his hands. Red smudges marked the rim.

'Robert?' Daisy said. 'Is everything okay?'

Robert said nothing.

'Go inside, and we'll tell you,' said Harper.

Daisy had disliked Ray Harper from the moment she'd met him. He was slimmer and shorter than Robert, but sharper, with a thin moustache and teeth like old Scrabble tiles.

Peggy, sensing trouble, nodded goodnight, and took her stool inside. The crimson tip of her discarded cigarette glowed in the shadows.

Inside, Robert unbuttoned his jacket. His shirt was soaked and pink, stiff where the liquid had dried.

'What's this?' Daisy said.

'Blood and water,' Robert said. He took off the shirt and let it drop to the chequerboard lino of the kitchen.

'Girl tried to kill herself. Slit her wrists,' Ray Harper said.

'Jesus, Robert,' said Daisy. 'Are you all right?'

'He's better than her,' Harper said.

Daisy scowled at Harper.

'S'all right,' Robert said, turning to his wife at last. He smiled weakly. 'She's going to be okay. The girl.'

Daisy got hold of herself. 'Right. What can I do? I'll get a bath going.'

Ray Harper laughed. 'God, anything but that.'

'It's fine, Daisy,' Robert said. 'I'll wash at the sink.'

Robert rinsed the pinkish soap off his forearms. The water ran cold. Daisy looked down at the shirt, balled at her husband's feet. Eventually, she picked it up, trying as she did so to stop her fingers from trembling.

'I'm sure a bath would be better,' Daisy said.

'For God's sake, *enough*, woman! *Enough! Just shut up!*' Robert screamed.

She froze, recognising the change in his voice, its move into that higher pitch. She never thought of his rage as part of his personality. It was more like a seizure, or one of his night terrors. She pitied him for the loss of control. Sometimes, if she kept very still, and avoided eye contact, it passed.

Like now.

Robert's shoulders sank. 'I'm sorry. The girl was in the bath, Daisy,' Robert said. 'When we found her. That's all. That's all it is.'

Even days later, he didn't want to discuss it, and Daisy had to read about the incident in the newspaper. Rita Freeman was sixteen, and due to make a full recovery. Robert received a commendation for the speed of his response, and his efforts to staunch the bleeding. The paper ran a picture of him, smiling. The photograph was a few years old, and Daisy found herself shocked by the change in his appearance.

Ray Harper had a habit of leaving his teacup in the centre of the table, and Daisy suspected he did it deliberately. She scrubbed at the circular stain. 'Why don't you ever have Neville Gaye over?' she asked her husband.

'Neville's all right,' Robert said, polishing his boots.

'Why don't you make a pal of him? Me and Peg are friends, and you both want to be in the CID.'

'Gaye will never make CID.'

'Why not?'

The powdery black polish clung to the brush ends in clots. 'He doesn't drink, for a start,' Robert said.

'Oh come on, that's no reason.'

'It's plenty of reason. And he's got no hair on his face. Doesn't even shave. He gets teased by the lads. When he eats his dinner, he has this habit of moving his plate very close to the edge of the table.'

'I hope *you* don't tease him, Robert.'

'He moves it closer and closer to the edge. Half the time, he spills it on his lap.'

'He does not.'

'The fellas take bets on it. He's odd.'

'Those CID chaps are odd. Ray Harper is odd.'

'Neville's a nervous case.'

'*You* get nervous sometimes.'

The boot brush halted. 'I will overcome that,' Robert said sternly.

'You could jack it in, you know,' Daisy said. 'The job, I mean.'

'What, and end up as some security guard at the Co-op while we all starve to death? Besides, the job is not the problem.'

'We could move back to the countryside. A one-man beat. Something more relaxed. It wasn't so miserable all the time. We worked together. It felt like we could help people. You remember the carnival they had? Just sitting out on the bales all night with a drink.'

'I don't want to think about that. About what I was like then. The sort of man I was.'

'You were happy,' she said.

'I was weak,' he replied.

He blew on the toecap of his left boot and slid it off his hand.

'*I'm* just worried about this divisional dance,' she said. 'Peggy calls it the Kneepad Ball. I don't want to let you down.'

Robert smiled. 'We'll be fine,' he said. He stared at her for a moment. 'You've got a lot going for you.'

*

She only remembered that she lived by the sea when she found mussel shells in the flowerbed. When they first arrived, she had walked around the estate with Linda, trying to tire her out. She could never seem to find the edges of the place. So she was happy to go to the doctor's, even if the surgery was only a couple of streets from the colony.

The waiting room smelled of old sweat and damp wool. Somehow, people seemed to know where she was from. A woman with bandages on her shins, under sheer tights, sneered at her.

A pale child drew carefully on an old newspaper, and when they called his name, he threw the paper down in front of her. She tilted her head to see what he had written.

PIG.

That evening, she sat outside her open door with Peggy. 'You're quiet tonight, Daisy.'

'Oh, I'm fine,' she said. She nodded at the upstairs window, through which they could hear Linda murmuring in her sleep. 'Me and Robert are hoping for another.'

'Thought as much,' Peggy said.

'How come?'

'We could hear you hoping all night, last week.'

Daisy smiled, and let smoke escape from her lips.

Neville came hustling through the dark, his shift finished. 'Hello, darling,' he said to Peggy. He leaned down to kiss her, and she tugged on his large left ear. 'Evening, Mrs Seacombe,' he said. 'How's you?'

In the street light, Daisy noticed the soft hazy fuzz around Neville's chin.

'Did Robert not walk back with you?' Peggy asked her husband.

'Oh. Robert isn't on lates this week,' Neville said brightly.

Peggy stiffened, and glanced at Daisy. 'He's probably doing one of those training exercises or something,' she said.

Daisy put out her hand to halt Peggy's offer of explanation.

In bed that night, she remembered seeing *Casablanca* for the first time, at the Electric Theatre. She couldn't remember the year, but she'd gone alone, which probably meant that her friend Maureen had already passed.

Daisy's timing had been off. She took her seat with ten minutes of the film left to run, and watched the ending first. Daisy's friends had told her it was wonderful, which set her up to dislike it. The conclusion of the film, with all its complications and too-slick dialogue, passed her by. She heard weeping – quite a lot, actually – but she didn't put much faith in audience reactions, even at the Electric.

The film finished, and the rolling programme restarted with its news items and two-reelers. When the main feature began again, Daisy heard a persistent whispering, three rows in front. She was used to the noise and conversation of the auditorium: you couldn't get a thousand people to be absolutely silent. But this regular mumbling disturbed her concentration. The whispers seemed to follow each line spoken by the actors. Dialogue, whisper, dialogue, whisper.

Ten minutes into the film, Daisy had had enough of the noise. By squinting she could make out two men on the end of the fifth row. The film, with its weird structure, had drawn her in, and she'd be damned if these men were going to destroy it with their mumbled commentary. She stood, and made her way down the aisle steps.

'Excuse me,' she said. 'Would you please be quiet? You may well be trying to whisper, but it is *not* working, and the whole thing is very distracting.'

The two men, soldiers, looked up at her with something like fear. One was slim with an uneven haircut and a big moustache. The other wore spectacles, and was short, dark, and sort of pretty. A real comedy duo.

The slim one spoke. 'Qu'est-ce qu'elle a dit? Ah, elle a dit qu'elle est degoûtée par votre odeur. Ça la rend malade.'

'Non, le problème c'est vos oreilles. Quand il y a trois acteurs sur l'écran, elle ne peut voir que celui qui est situé au milieu. Elle est belle, non?'

'Ouvrière d'usine. British Steel.'

Canadians, Daisy realised. They were staying in town. The little boys followed them around, hoping they'd drop warplane cards from their cigarette packs. 'I beg your pardon,' she said. 'Do either of you speak English?'

'I'm sorry, ma'am. I do. Picard speaks a little, but—'

'In that case, how *dare* you use French to talk about me while I'm standing here. That's incredibly rude.'

'Sit down, girl!' someone shouted. 'I can't see Ingrid's legs.'

'*You* sit down. You don't know anything about it!' said Daisy.

'Mon Dieu,' said Picard.

'I apologise,' said the short one. 'I promised to take Picard to the movies. He's young and he misses home and I wanted to take his mind off everything.'

'Qu'est-ce que vous avez dit?' asked Picard.

'The dialogue is too fast for him,' said the short one. 'I'm translating. You know, I think I've *seen* you.'

'I've *heard* you,' said Daisy. 'And I'd rather not. I'd be grateful if you could do your interpreting more quietly.'

She went back to her seat and there was a little laughter, a small round of applause from the surrounding patrons. 'For King and country!' someone said.

The whispering continued, but at acceptable levels, and Daisy's feelings softened. She had known the first batch of French-Canadians billeted in Sussex. The two hundred Fusiliers Mont-Royal had looked fine to her, marching through town to 'The Jockey of York'. But they'd crossed the Channel to Dieppe, where half of them were killed. She knew better than to get involved.

The ending caught up with her halfway through the film. The deepest part of her mind must have made the connection between the events unfolding on screen, and the conclusion she'd seen over an hour earlier. It hit her with force, and she began to cry. She tried to hold onto her emotions, partly because of the Canadians in front. She didn't want them to hear her crying. The pauses between the whispers grew.

Daisy did not need to watch the finale again, and she left early. The short one followed her out into the foyer.

'I hope you're not leaving because of us,' he said.

Daisy recalled a special opening night showing of *North West Mounted Police* at the Odeon in 1940, the ushers dressed as Mounties, the usherettes as squaws. This guy was cute enough, but no Gary Cooper.

'No,' she said, sniffling.

'It was a killer. The film,' he said.

'I thought it was . . . manipulative,' she said. A word she'd read in *Picturegoer*. 'Hard to translate, I'll bet.'

'Darn near impossible. It was way too fast. And then, after all that effort, I turned to Picard, and the poor little baby was asleep! God knows how long he'd been out.'

Daisy allowed herself a smile.

'My name is Paul,' he said. 'Actually, Picard was wondering where we might go for a drink and some warmth later.'

'Wondering in his sleep, was he?' Daisy said.

Her memory was broken, now, by the noise of the back door slamming. Her husband came up the stairs, and she listened to his breathing settle as he crept into the room. 'Where have you been?' she whispered.

'What? Work,' he said.

That year, they held the divisional dance at the aquarium. Outside, the lights rippled along the pier, and the seafront Teds combed their hair with dirty fingers, muttered curses at the police.

Daisy had made herself a green gown and a faux fur box coat. She and Robert descended into the underground aquarium with the Harpers. Ray Harper's wife was from Sardinia. Not even Ray could pronounce her name, and everyone called her Mickey. She had tight, bottle-blonde curls and a gap between her front teeth. 'I'm nervous,' Daisy told her, as they passed the blue glowing jellyfish, and turtles as big as cars.

Mickey snorted. 'You should be. Everyone here is staring at you.'

'That's not a very nice thing to say,' Daisy muttered, as they entered the dank, yellow-bricked passageways towards the dance hall. The band limbered up, strings screeching and echoing.

'The men. I mean the men are looking,' said Mickey.

'At you, perhaps.'

'Oh, God, has nobody ever told you?' Mickey said, allowing her gaze to drop down Daisy's side. She took a drink from a tray. A clear liquid in a cocktail glass. 'Here, drink this.'

Daisy's fingers stuck to the glass. Against her instincts, she knocked the drink back as they emerged into the packed hall. The programme advertised modern and traditional dancing. On one side of the hall a glass tank threw out green light. Within, Daisy saw tangles of thick eels.

That night, Robert introduced her to so many men. She could not keep track of their names and ranks. She noticed that her husband left his half-finished drinks discreetly on tables. For her part, she swallowed three more of the clear cocktails.

As she danced with one old man, she saw Mrs Clore among the women at the edge of the dance floor, watching her intently, the limp ropes of her arms visible through a shawl.

'*That*'s it,' said Daisy's dance partner, reeling her in. His face smelled of pepper. 'That's it. Nice and tight.'

She struggled away, but he pinched her, hard, above the hip bone.

'No!' she said.

He said something back. It could have been, 'Bloody cow' or 'You'll find out.'

Daisy didn't stop to clarify. She pushed through the bodies. At the dance hall doorway, she turned and scanned the room for Robert. He stared at her over his glass. She left, but he did not follow.

Outside, at ground level, the cold sobered her. The nearest cinema was the Academy, and she began to walk westward, but heard a voice behind her.

'Mrs Seacombe? Daisy?'

Neville Gaye climbed the aquarium steps, squinting through his own smoke. 'Care for a cigarette?' he asked. He made a terrible mess of the word 'cigarette'.

'I thought you didn't drink,' Daisy said, turning back.

'Well, there were still a couple of sips of alcohol left in the building when you'd finished, and I didn't like to waste it.'

They stood against the blue-green rails above the beach, and took turns performing monologues. When Neville finished, Daisy began, her eyes following the lights of the cars racing down Kings Road. 'Me and Robert used to *work together*, out in the countryside. Now he never tells me anything. Nobody does. If I hadn't had those lett—'

'You wouldn't want him to tell you *everything*, would you? I try to keep Peg away from my work. I don't come home and say, "There was this boy, half his face burned off and not six years old". I want to protect her. She'd get hard if I told her all that.'

'I wish I was hard,' Daisy said.

'We have to talk to . . . ladies of the night, obviously. Part of the job. But try telling Peg. Anytime we quarrel, she says, "Why don't you just run off with one of your whores?" You know, the inference being a sexual liaison.'

Daisy laughed.

'It's like your Robert and that tart: some of the things she'd been through. You wouldn't want to know . . .'

'What tart? What are you talking about?'

'The one he dragged out the bath. The suicide attempt. His commendation.'

71

'She was a prostitute?'

Neville tried to focus. He tried to tune in to the distant but approaching voice of his sober self.

'Neville!' Ray Harper's thin face appeared at Neville's shoulder, clear and fresh in the moonlight. Daisy saw her husband a few yards away, arm in arm with Mickey.

'You look smart tonight, Nev,' Harper said. 'And your wife is radiant, as always. Spoke to her not a moment ago, as it happens. She is always so *charming*.'

'She's looking for you, Neville,' called Robert.

Ray Harper sighed. 'Oh, she most certainly is,' he said.

'Right,' said Neville. He made an odd bow, and Daisy saw the residue of dried shaving cream in his parting. He walked stiffly away.

'Idiot,' mumbled Robert.

On the bus back to the colony, Ray Harper feigned concern for Neville. 'I hope Peggy's not too firm with him.'

'Maybe they'll get divorced,' said Mickey, looking out of the window.

'No,' said Robert. 'You can't get divorced in the police. It's career-ending.'

When the babysitter had been paid, Robert made tea in the kitchen. 'I saw what you did to Clore,' he said.

'Who?' Daisy said.

'Chief Constable Clore.'

She hadn't realised who her dance partner was. Robert tossed the teaspoon into the sink.

'You didn't see what he did to *me*, though, did you?' she said. 'His filthy hands all over me.'

'I saw him dancing with you.'

'Weren't you jealous?'

'I thought it was going well,' he said.

'I wish you were jealous,' Daisy mumbled. In *Baby Face*, Lily Powers had slept her way to the top, but she hadn't done it for her husband.

'Don't worry,' said Robert. 'I spoke to old Clore. He didn't mind. He likes a woman with a spirited mouth.'

Daisy exhaled.

'But I don't,' said Robert. He took a sip of his tea and then left it on the kitchen counter and walked past her.

'You didn't tell me Rita Freeman was a whore, Robert,' Daisy said.

Robert stopped in the hallway. Daisy watched the silhouette of his shoulders rise and fall, his shirt tugging across his back. His voice came out of the darkness. 'Did you not hear what I just said?'

The letters continued. In June 1954, she read one while sitting on a deckchair in their tiny back garden, the newspaper resting on her pregnant belly.

I am sorry I didn't write for a while. Mother has been worse. Sometimes, I feel sort of hopeless and foolish. You ever feel like that? I hope not, Dee.

We visited some of Clare's relations in Chicago, USA, and got to see this blues musician guy by the name of Bo Diddley. Clare says his songs are immoral, but he sure can pluck a guitar.

I am still working at GM, but I am finally onto the next phase of my Big Project. I'm studying aerospace engineering. It is a big wow, Dee. The first thing they tell you is that you don't even think about an aircraft for the first two months. You just think about air! How it moves, what it's made of, all that. Have you ever thought about air, Dee? These teachers get paid crazy wages for this goofy stuff!

I'm certainly spicing up the conversation during coffee break at the factory. Everyone hates my guts. I hope you don't.

She hauled herself off the deckchair and went into the house, where she hid the letter under tissue paper in a shoebox in her wardrobe, already planning her reply.

In spite of Daisy's social failings, Robert made CID that year. Ray Harper went through in the same batch, and they were initiated with a so-called 'stag night'. No wives. In his first month, they went on a shooting trip in Sussex, and Robert accidentally killed an owl. His colleagues mocked him until he lost his rag and punched a young detective's front teeth out.

As autumn blustered in, Daisy got a line on some good wool in a beautiful midnight blue. She found a pattern for a nice swing coat, ran it up quickly under the warm light of her sewing machine, and wore it over her belly. She liked being pregnant again, and listened to the urgent and sinister blood-sent advice of her unborn child. *Eat something red. Sleep on the floor.*

Michael was born in November, small and dark, and Daisy stayed in hospital for a while with an infection. On the ward, sunsets throbbed pink in the windows. Daisy felt glad to get home, although the place was a mess, and Linda seemed trau-matised and hungry after a week with her father.

A couple of days after her return, Daisy called to Peggy out of the kitchen window. 'Peg, do you want to come and see the baby?'

'Not for now, thank you,' Peggy said, hanging up the wash-ing in her yard. She went inside and turned up the wireless as loud as it would go. Daisy had heard of women not speaking because of a promotion, but she could hardly believe it. There'd be no chance to talk it over, either: no more night shifts sharing a beer and a cigarette, now that Robert had joined the CID.

There was less socialising, altogether. The CID men didn't even attend their own dances, and rarely invited their wives to the unofficial gatherings.

'Jesus, Daisy. Before, you never wanted to go,' Robert said one morning, blowing across the surface of his tea.

'I just want to know why I'm not allowed,' said Daisy. She took the flat iron from the stove and spat on its surface. It sizzled.

'It's a different kind of police work,' he said. Then he smirked, hung-over. 'Wives talk.'

She scowled at him. 'I think you just like your privacy,' she said. 'You and your little brothers.'

She tried to encourage him through the difficult early days of his new post. He would come home at strange hours, drunk and twitchy. His night terrors returned. Sometimes he laughed joylessly in his sleep.

The next year, she heard Bo Diddley's self-titled hit on the wireless at home. She danced with Michael on her shoulder, while Linda tried to sing along. The song's arrival gave Daisy the sense of a line drawn across the Atlantic, of an ocean bridged by a voice. She knew it was silly.

Later that evening, she stood on the stairs and listened to a conversation between her husband and Ray Harper in the kitchen. Robert complained that he could not make sense of his new job.

'Nothing ever goes anywhere,' he said. 'We never close a bloody case. You can't . . . you can't crack the code of this city.'

'What are you talking about, Robert?' said Harper impatiently.

'It's like looking for God!'

'Robert, *please*,' Harper said. He spoke quietly, so that Daisy could not hear his reassurances, only Robert's reply.

'Maybe you're right,' Robert said. 'But so, what are we *doing* then? What can we do?'

'We can try to get by,' said Ray. 'Make a little money out of a bad situation. We can try to exert some control . . . try to survive. You're too mystical about things, Bob, that's your problem. You think too much, and you're not very good at it.'

Daisy tightened her grip on the banister. She hated Ray Harper more than anyone she'd ever known.

'Daisy thinks I ought to go to night school, learn a new trade,' Robert said.

Harper laughed. 'Robert, you're *CID. You already know everything.*'

He suggested Robert take up a sport instead, but Robert could not think of anything he'd be good at.

'You could do owl shooting,' said Harper.

'Sod off,' Robert said.

Daisy heard the hiss of beer bottle gas, and her husband sighing. She thought about going up to bed.

'Look,' said Harper. 'Just because things are chaotic, it doesn't mean *we* have to be. An example. A lady in Brunswick. Old girl. She helps out kids in trouble. You know. Babes.'

'Abortions? That's illegal,' said Robert.

'Well then, let's have a cup of tea with her tomorrow,' Harper said. 'Tea and a chat.'

'About the law?'

'About business, Robert.'

'I don't . . . wait. What was that?' Robert said. 'You hear something?'

That summer, the Duke of York's showed *Snow White and the Seven Dwarfs* again, and Daisy took Linda. She remembered seeing it for the first time, herself. Her father had taken her, and she had marvelled at the glowing carapace of the organ rising out of the floor like some massive insect, and trays of teapots and teacakes passed along the rows. Now, the cinema was half-empty.

Linda lay on Daisy's chest, her jelly sandals planted on her mother's thighs. The neon strips on each side of the screen blinked off, leaving traces of light in the air. Daisy calmed her daughter with a kiss on the head. She recognised in Linda her own tendency to be dragged under by the illusion, and held her girl tightly when the wicked stepmother appeared. But it was the idea of a pig's heart in a box that did for Linda. She began to burn up, and when Daisy put a cool hand on her chest to check her temperature, Linda fainted.

On the bus home, Daisy made Linda suck ice cubes. She had drenched her fringe in water from the fountain. Daisy worried that Robert would be angry. *Corrupting her with fantastic stories and excitable nonsense.*

But when they arrived home, Robert dozed in the armchair, and Michael lay, star-shaped, open-mouthed and asleep in the middle of the living room floor. 'If we kiss them, will they wake up?' Linda asked.

Hours later, when Daisy put her to bed, Linda said, 'What is Snow doing now, Mummy?'

Daisy smiled. White, of course, was a perfectly sensible surname. 'The film is over, my darling.'

'Yes, but what is she doing now?'

For a child, the film goes on, like life. 'I don't know,' Daisy said. 'She's probably asleep. I mean . . . God . . . in a nice way. Resting. She is probably resting.'

Linda nodded. She slid down in the big bed. 'Mummy?'

'Yes, darling.'

'When can we go to the cinema again?'

The wind funnelled through the alleyways of the estate, and Daisy had to lean forward to get Michael's pram going. At two in the afternoon, Linda was in school and Robert at work. Returning from the post office, Daisy carried an airmail envelope in the pocket of her midnight blue coat, which she'd taken in to fit her slimmer figure. Mrs Clore held on to her headscarf as she chatted to a group of women at the corner of the road, so Daisy slipped down an alleyway to avoid them. Before she reached the house, she tore off the envelope and stuffed it through a drain grate. She threaded the folded letter between her fingers.

When she got into the hallway of her home, the wind dragged the door shut behind her, and she closed her eyes, relishing the silence of the house. With the letter still in her hand, she took off her coat.

'Is that new?' Robert said.

She spun, quickly, and saw her husband sitting on one of the stiff dining room chairs. 'I thought you were at work,' she said.

'The coat. Is it new?'

Daisy forced her hands to stop shaking, and turned to hang up the coat, slipping the letter into the pocket as she did so.

'No,' she said. 'I made it ages ago.'

'I've never seen it.'

She smoothed her grey woollen skirt. 'Well, Robert, I don't know what to say about that.'

He had a look in his eye that she'd never seen before. Blank. Dead. The way he sat made his trouser cuffs ride up, and the thick wad of his crotch was prominent. His tie hung below his belt like viscera, and the chair looked small beneath him.

'The colour of the coat is sluttish,' Robert said.

'You'd know all about that.'

'Yes, I would. I go to disgusting places, so that people like you don't have to.'

'I think you like it,' she said.

'Where have you been?' he asked.

She removed her scarf. 'What? Shopping, in the morning. Then I—'

'Where? Shopping where?'

'Western Road. Then I popped over to the Hooks' to help Iris with the christening gown.'

'Another baby for the Hooks, eh? What's that, five kids?'

'Four. What's your problem, Robert? What are you trying to find out?'

She walked over to him, away from the coat, away from the letter.

'Sit down,' he said, as he himself rose. Daisy found herself seated, even before she'd registered the command. 'Trevor and Iris Hook have gone to Suffolk, to see his family.'

'Yes. They were packing when I left. What's your *point*?'

'I am trying to account for your time.'

'I'm not one of your villains, Robert. And I have a baby on my arm all day.'

'He's not much of an obstacle.'

'Is that the nicest thing you can say about your son?'

'Don't be smart.'

'I can't help being smart,' she said. 'What's *wrong* with you, Robert? What's happened? You never used to be like this.'

'Don't say that,' he said, gritting his teeth. 'It's unkind. You're supposed to be on my side.'

He stared beyond her, and then closed his eyes, but she saw the emotion flooding back into him. He walked away, sidling past the pram, hands in pockets. 'Robert?' she called, but he opened the door and stepped out into the gale.

When she was sure Robert had gone, Daisy took the letter from her coat pocket. She began to read as she walked towards the kitchen.

Dear Dee,

I want to say two things: firstly, it was NOT me, nor any of the Princess Patricia's Canadian Light Infantry, who wrote the 'F's on all those road signs for Uckfield. I quite liked the place. Secondly, I wanted to try to explain how I feel about you.

'Oh God,' Daisy said, and rested her head against the kitchen wall.

You may say that we only knew each other a short time. I know all the obstacles, all the problems. For starters, there's about four feet of snow here in Winnipeg. I can't even get to the <u>store</u> . . .

She laughed, and as soon as she laughed, she almost cried. That had always been the way for Daisy. It was the comedies that made her weep. It had been a long time since somebody had told her a joke.

But I was thinking today about how you broke into the wine cellar of the old manor house where the boys were staying. I remember you going through that maze of dusty old bottles and looking over your shoulder at me, shoes in your hand, already mad drunk, and I thought – this girl can do <u>anything</u>. Tony said you were untameable, but I never wanted to tame you, I just wanted to see what you did next. Being around you, Dee, was like hanging on to the tail of a comet.

I don't know why, but that time seems more real to me sometimes than the day I'm living in. I guess there is a part of a person's life which just burns brighter, somehow.

I'll tell you a secret: sometimes I close all the curtains in the living room and turn off all the lights, and it's like being in the picturehouse with you again.

But then Mother walks in!

Clare and me broke up. She wanted to get married. I probably should have said yes. I guess that's what people do – settle. But how do they stand the greyness of it? What was it you always said about the movies? 'What's so great about real life, anyway?' I'd rather write to you (and sometimes get a reply, eh?).

Well, I better scram. I hope this hasn't disturbed you too much.

Paul

When she finished reading the letter, she listened to the children of the police playing in the street outside. One of the kids rhythmically knocked a house brick against the pavement while the others sang some tribal song.

Daisy remembered how, in the week after Maureen's house was bombed, she'd gone to the big storage shed in town, where they kept all the household items cleared from the blitzed houses. In the high-roofed space there stood small oases of home: an arrangement of sofa, armchair and lamp in one corner; a cutlery drawer, kettle and stack of tins by the far wall. Everyone knew the damage a bomb could do, but it could also leave things strangely untouched. Daisy had soon recognised the bookshelf from Mo's living room, and she knelt before Mr Williams' encyclopaedia set, which she and Mo had once scoured, almost heaving with laughter at the anatomy illustrations. And shining there by the foot of the bookcase, without so much as a layer of dust on the glass, was Mo's mother's pint bottle of gin.

Now, in her kitchen, Daisy was shaken from the memory by the sound of Neville Gaye urinating next door. You couldn't hide anything in this place. She looked down at the letter in her hand, and made a decision. She took the matches from the top of the cupboard and burned the letter in the sink. It could not go on.

1997

ike parked on the next street, because he worried about how the pedestrian might feel if the nose of the Honda appeared in the frame of his living room window.

Most of the buildings on the pedestrian's road were in the Regency style, divided into flats, with weatherproof plants on the balconies. But the pedestrian and his daughter lived in a block of red-brick houses. The door was a once bright yellow, but green mould now crept in from the corners. It took Mike a while to figure out that the big latex '0' pasted onto the middle of the door had once been a '9'.

When the pedestrian opened up, he seemed tired, his short hair scrunched into a peak. Mike doubted anything would happen. 'Come in, then,' the pedestrian said, limping back into the house.

By the stairs, Mike spotted the pedestrian's strange boots – the ones he'd worn when he stepped out into the road. They had a *cleaved toe*. Mike took in the cosy clutter: a living room full of books, no TV, bright rugs and bare floorboards. He'd been in houses like this once or twice before – he'd never really understood why posh people couldn't tidy up. What was the word Linda used? Bohemian.

Mike saw his own mobile number scribbled on a notepad by the phone, with the word 'Driver' written above it. They went into the kitchen. 'Can I get you a drink?' the pedestrian asked.

'Oh. Maybe just some water.'

The pedestrian went to the fridge, rather than the sink, and took out a bottle. Mike glimpsed a packet of thin, salty meats – the kind they had in France and Spain – and a jar of artichokes. Signs and wonders.

He took a sip of water and put the glass down on the kitchen table, next to a pile of junk mail. The pedestrian's name was Stephen Bentham, apparently. His daughter's homework lay open on the table.

'Your girl's out, right?' Mike said.

'Of course,' Stephen snapped.

'So. Where do you want to do it?'

'Not in the house. I've cleared my work out of the shed. It's slightly cold . . .'

On the windowsill, Mike noticed a photo frame had been turned face down. The wife, he assumed.

In the garden, Mike smelled overflowing drains. Apples from a neighbour's tree glowed orange on the lawn, and late autumn wasps did the rounds. He felt vulnerable when he saw the shed. Pieces of cardboard had been placed inside the windows. That shed seemed far from the world, far from help.

Inside, Stephen switched on a bare bulb. The place was huge – closer to the size of a garage – and didn't smell like any garden shed. No odours of grass or oil or creosote. Paint flecked the floorboards, and sketchpads were stacked up next to a black bicycle in the corner. Mike took a long, faltering breath. The idiocy of what he was doing began to dawn on him. Something had been hiding in the grass; the bites burned his ankles.

'I suppose we need some ground rules,' Stephen said.

Mike nodded. 'I sort of. I don't want it to show. If possible.'

'Okay. Just the core.'

'The what?'

'The trunk, the torso. No blows to the face or lower arms.'

'Right,' Mike said. 'Seems fair. Er. Should I stand, or kneel, or what?'

'I guess stand,' Stephen said. 'Look, are you sure about this?' He asked sternly, the way you read the small print to a customer, telling them with your tone that there's no backing out. But his voice wavered.

'Yeah. I'm sure,' said Mike. 'Are you?'

Stephen's punch, though not strong, contained enough force to wind him.

When the second one came, Mike caught it with his hands, squeezed the knuckles. Stephen winced.

'I'm sorry,' Mike said, letting go of Stephen's hand. 'It's instinct. Programmed in, you know. You got any rope or bloody . . . twine or anything?' Mike said.

Stephen unhooked a length of elasticated cord from the pannier rack of the bicycle.

'That should do it,' Mike said. Hesitantly, he turned around and presented his wrists, which Stephen bound together, leaving the hooks dangling.

'Okay?' Stephen said. They faced each other again. 'Ready?' And this time, Mike was.

Stephen's hitting was tentative and inaccurate, to begin with. If Mike tensed his stomach muscles, and leaned over, he could absorb the blows quite easily, though his skull and his joints jarred with each punch. Mike's senses were tuned in to the sounds in the shed: Stephen's quiet sighs of effort, Mike's own grunts, the muted clap of the fist on fabric. It took a while before Mike looked at Stephen's face. His bones were so fine, his features so small. The fading bruise looked like make-up. The man was close to tears. Mike was, too, as the blows squeezed the breath out of him.

Gradually, Mike's embarrassment and fear began to fade. In fact, his whole self seemed to fade. He felt like he was no longer a person, but just part of a situation. They had somehow managed to revert back to their roles in the street that day. Mike was just the driver, and Stephen the pedestrian.

After a few more minutes, they both began to tire. The pedestrian's punches deteriorated into short, underarm stabs. The driver could smell the dinner the pedestrian had eaten – something with chillies – and his own stale odour. Their bodies generated heat, which seemed to warm the slats of the shed, which in turn gave off their own mossy fug.

The pedestrian gasped with effort. He stepped forward, and steadied himself on the driver's shoulder. They forgot themselves, their faces close. The driver felt almost grateful. Then a punch caught him on the base of the ribcage, and he folded up in pain. 'Fuck,' he cried. 'Stop.'

'Jesus, are you all right?' Stephen said.

Mike turned away, and leaned, doubled over, against the shed wall. He coughed and retched, couldn't get enough air, but after a few moments, he got used to it. He overcame his panic. He wanted to laugh. 'Give me a minute.'

Stephen watched him carefully, frowning. Eventually, Mike straightened up. Stephen's nostrils flared. The tension drained away, and neither of them knew where to look.

'You okay?' Stephen said.

'Yeah. Well. I mean. All things considered,' Mike said. 'You?'

Stephen shrugged. 'Here,' he said, untying the elasticated cord. 'So, I suppose we're even now.'

'I guess,' Mike said, his nerves charged, his senses firing. 'Unless, you know . . .'

'Unless what?' Stephen said.

'Well, you said once wouldn't be enough.'

'I did say that, didn't I?'

Mike knew it would happen again. With time, he thought, and practice, they could get better.

After she saw the man reading to her dad, Linda tried to carry on as normal. You beat such disruptions with order and routine. You took the bus to the library, you wound on the date stamp, and you shelved books, bringing the spines to the front edge. At break-time, you drank tea from the black mug which used to say 'Mars' on it, though the lettering had rubbed off years before. You guided the homeless man from the Children's section to History. You kicked the drug users out of the toilets. At lunch, you ate a cheese sandwich, ready-salted crisps, and a satsuma.

But in the afternoon, as Linda reclassified a small section in the 300s, the label-maker started playing up. The first time she tried to print, the numbers ran off the edge. The second time, the digits came out ridiculously small, and she saw, in her mind, the man's black-rimmed spectacles blanked out by the light coming through the window in her dad's room.

Her pulse thumped behind her eyes. She took the label-maker out of the office, and into the alleyway. She threw it at the wall, and then she picked it up, lifted it above her head, and hurled it to the ground. Behind her, Suzanne stepped out, cigarette packet in hand, and froze.

'What happened?' Suzanne said.

'It wasn't working.'

'Neither is the work experience boy. Shall I bring *him* out here?'

Linda brushed a strand of hair from her face. They looked at the smashed machine, its ticker-tape unspooled, its hood cracked, a slash of ink on the wall.

'Linda, is there something you'd like to talk about?'

'I'll pay for a replacement.'

'You've worked here since there were three channels on telly, and you've barely uttered a cross word,' Suzanne said. 'I think we can say this is somewhat out of character. Now, I'm going to tell you something, and you don't have to respond: HRT has worked for me.'

'It's not—'

Suzanne raised her hands. 'That's all I'm saying.'

That afternoon, Linda stayed in the back office, did member-ship work on the new computers. She typed the man's name – Paul Landry – into the search bar, but she did not press return.

*

For a few weeks, she didn't visit her dad. Couldn't face him. But then, one Thursday, she found herself outside the pub across the road from Cedars, waiting for Paul Landry to leave.

She'd only seen him once, before the time in her dad's room, but the occasion was memorable. At fifteen, she'd skipped school to watch Julie Christie in an afternoon showing of *Darling*, at the Academy. Early in the film, she'd looked over her shoulder and seen her mum sitting in the adjacent block. Linda had kept very still: as much as her mum loved films, she'd have throttled Linda if she'd caught her playing truant. A few minutes later, a man ambled down the central steps, hands in the pockets of his trousers, and sat next to Daisy.

At first, Linda had thought the man was a stranger, but as she prepared to sneak out, he kissed her mum's cheek. Daisy said something to him, and he laughed quietly, his shoulders shaking. 'You may be right,' he said. The lenses of his glasses caught the light from the screen, as did the large round face of his watch.

Linda's throat had closed up. She'd remained in her seat for another few minutes, eyes stinging, and then she'd rushed down her almost empty row, and bolted for the exit.

Years later, Linda had found a letter tucked inside an old *Picturegoer* magazine amongst her mum's possessions. She'd read the letter, then torn it up.

So, that was it: she'd seen him once, in the dusk of a cinema, and read one old letter. But he wasn't someone she could forget. The glassy reflections from his spectacles and his watch face. The set of his shoulders, the foreign voice, the easy affection of his writing.

Now, he emerged from the care home in a brown coat and polished brogues, and limped towards the bus stop, carrying a blue canvas bag. Just an old man, really. His frosted breath rose into the beam of the street light. She crossed the road, and followed him, boarded the same coastal bus towards Newhaven.

When he sat at the front, she edged past him to the back. The schoolkids chewed their bus tickets until their lips went blue with ink.

Linda kept her head down, but he didn't notice her. He didn't read, or talk to the other travellers. He just looked out of the window. His fingers turned pale as he gripped the bag, his watch – that same watch – slipped down his wrist.

They rumbled up the coast, past the marina. White Regency squares gave way to drab normality. They passed the house where Linda had grown up, where her mother had died – the house which Mike had wanted demolished, but Linda, being practical, had had renovated, workmen tearing up the bloodied carpet and floorboards, stripping the paper and the plaster from the back wall, removing all signs of death, so the place could be sold. For a moment, the images of her parents' room came rushing in: the lace curtains, the porcelain figures of fox and hounds on the windowsill, that hideous stuffed owl her dad kept by the door, with its orange marble eyes. The only witness.

Rottingdean, Saltdean, Peacehaven – past the brightly lit Wimpey and Beefeater, the darkened pet shops. A woman whacked a thin rug outside her house with the back of a brush: a dusty drumbeat to end the day.

As Peacehaven faded, Paul Landry put his finger on the red button. Linda followed him off the bus, but gave him time to get ahead. He strolled into one of those mobile home parks that used to be known as caravan sites. The Outlook, it was called. Depressing coloured bulbs hung over the entrance, clinking in a coastal wind. Marble-look cherubs played their flutes in the tiny gardens. Linda took the tacky chalk path that wound through the skirted houses – shacks on jacks like cattle in the pasture, their gas extractors belching cold breath, their eyes lighting up in the blue night.

Up ahead, he climbed the steps of a neat house in forest green, orange moss on the roof. A moment later, television light filled the window.

Wasn't this where you lived if you were outcast, destitute, chaotic, ashamed? Linda considered knocking on his door, but she noticed a man in an ill-fitting grey suit watching her from the window of the site-office, so she pulled up the collar of her coat, turned, and made for home.

The meetings had a ritual nature. The two men always drank a cup of tea in the kitchen first. They sat at an oak table beneath a low-hanging light with a shade made from shards of coloured glass. Stephen kept a messy house, but the things in it looked good – the heavy blue stewing pot, the bright red bread bin.

Most of the tea Mike had drunk before lacked flavour, but Stephen's tea had a strong, woodsy taste. He used leaves instead of bags.

Mike didn't know anyone like Stephen – a man whose walls were hidden by books. He didn't know where a person might go to buy shoes with a cleaved toe, or transparent slivers of meat, and because their worlds seemed so far apart, it felt easy to speak plainly.

After the third meeting, the picture on the windowsill stood upright. It featured Stephen's wife and daughter. His wife was a good-looking woman with dark brown eyes and straight black hair. They were both pretending to be monsters, their teeth bared, their hands curled into claws.

'She was the only person I ever knew who still looked beautiful when she yawned,' he said.

'What happened?' Mike asked.

'Leukaemia.'

The only thing they didn't talk about was what went on in the shed. Probably, they both had their reasons for what they were doing, but those reasons seemed beyond words – certainly beyond any words that Mike knew. The kitchen section of the meeting would end when one or the other of them looked out of the window.

Over time, Mike found a way to transform himself as he walked across Stephen's garden. He became again the stranger who had emerged, enraged, from his car. Gratefully, he left his true self at the back door and became the driver, a man deserving of the punishment he was about to receive.

That said, it really hurt.

When he woke, the morning after the fourth meeting, Mike realised he'd been crying in his sleep. He wanted to call it off then. It hurt to lift his leg over the rim of the bath. The shower gel stung his skin. His abdominals were so sore that to get off his sofa he had to turn around and push himself up with his arms. Pissing was painful; getting into the car was painful. And breathing.

Eventually, as the weeks went by, his body began to turn a corner. He enjoyed the dull ache of recovery, the way the bruises lightened. His body worked its magic, and he was forgiven. Soon, he felt ready again.

In November, carved gourds filled Stephen's front window. Mike pondered the subtle expressions knifed into their faces. One of them looked confused, another exasperated, a third deeply depressed.

'Just admiring your pumpkins,' Mike said, when Stephen let him in.

A make-up compact lay open on a table by the hallway mirror.

'That's my daughter's stuff, in case you were wondering,' Stephen said.

'I wasn't.'

'My mother has already started talking about the eligible ladies round her way.'

'Eh?' said Mike.

'Rosa was ill for a long time, and Mother thinks that makes a difference. She wants us to move out to Cuckfield.'

'Nice place. Posh,' said Mike.

'I hate it. Mum says a neighbour of hers got divorced last year, and he's settled back down with a "nice young woman".'

'If she can't tell the difference between an ex-wife and a dead one . . .' Mike stopped, worried he'd said too much.

'Quite,' said Stephen, tidying away the make-up. 'What about yours?' Stephen asked.

'I'm not married. Twice divorced, I'm afraid.'

'I mean your parents. Are they nearby?'

'Dead.'

'I'm sorry.'

'Well. My dad's not . . . he's not actually dead.'

Stephen frowned.

'It was euthanasia, basically. Mercy killing, you know. My mum got cancer, and she was in a lot of pain. Dad couldn't handle it.'

'What happened?' Stephen said.

Mike leaned against the hallway wall. He hadn't often told the story. 'Dad shot her, and then turned the gun on himself. But he messed it up. She died, he didn't.'

'That's horrible.'

'This was, what, ten years ago. He's in a home. He's not really . . .' Mike tapped his head. 'His brain. There's nothing going on.'

'Right.'

'Coroner said it was a tragedy. An act of love, you know. They pretty much pardoned him, as much as the law allows. No point sending someone to jail in that state, anyway.'

'Who found them? The bodies, as it were.'

'My nephew.'

'Shit.'

'He was five or six years old. He doesn't remember, luckily. He's blocked the memory, or whatever.'

'Yes, but a trauma like that finds other ways of coming out, doesn't it?'

Mike shrugged.

'I never knew if Rosa wanted me to do that,' said Stephen. 'You know – end it for her. I don't think I'd have been able to.'

'Well,' Mike said. 'Best not to think about it.'

When she came back from work, Linda could hear the thumping of Lucas's music from outside the bungalow. He listened to rap and hip hop, for the big beats and basslines. When she went in, she flicked the lights, and waited a few moments for the flashing reply from his room.

Lucas had a manic energy about him recently. Last week, she'd found three cans of deodorant hidden inside his beanbag. Solvent-abusers sometimes hung around in the alleyway behind the library, and she knew the damage it could do.

She walked down the hall now, and opened the door to his room. The hi-fi speakers sat on his desk, and Lucas gripped the edge of the table, to feel the vibrations, while he studied the lyrics. He nodded his head on the offbeat.

Soon, he sensed her presence and spun quickly in his chair. 'What's up? Is it too loud?'

Linda wandered over to the stereo and turned up the volume. The green level-lights rippled and jumped. She began to dance. She two-stepped, with her hands up high, like she'd seen them doing on the Saturday morning chart show. Lucas tried to look horrified, but a smile broke through. The man on the stereo called out something about tearing the roof off the school.

Linda hadn't danced for a long time. The music stopped, and she straightened.

'Not bad for an old-timer,' Lucas said. He turned the music down.

'If you get bad reports from parents' evening, I will come in and do that dance during year eleven assembly.'

'Didn't know you liked Tupac, Mum.'

'They're great. But don't tear the roof off the school, okay?'

'What if it's got . . . asbestos?'

'Let the professionals deal with it.'

'What if the lessons are really boring, and I don't know what the hell is going on?'

Linda pretended to think. 'In that case, fine. Lucas?'

'What?'

'You do know that solvents can be incredibly dangerous, don't you?'

'Pardon?'

'Solvents. They can kill you.'

He looked at her blankly. 'Instantly, it says on the can.'

Linda's first year of motherhood had been hard. A single mum with no experience, she hadn't known what she was doing wrong. Initially, Lucas had seemed unusually calm – the only sleeping link in a chain of waking babies on the ward. But at home, at night, her voice couldn't soothe him. He only settled when she turned on the light. He wasn't diagnosed until he was eight months old.

It was her mum who suggested they learn sign language, on the bus back from the audiologist. 'You'll have to communicate with him, Lind.'

'But the man said that if he signs, he might never speak,' Linda said.

'Rubbish. If he'd've been born French, you'd have learned French, wouldn't you?' Daisy had said.

'*Born French*, Mum?'

'Bien sûr. Tell you what: we'll go to classes together.'

Daisy had soon realised that weekly sessions with a hearing teacher at the polytechnic were not going to be enough. So, she found a deaf woman, Gita, cooking in a café on the coast road, and employed her to come to the house four times a week, and teach them. Eventually, Lucas took part in the lessons. With hard work, the language took root in their home. Even Mike learned. By the time Lucas turned four, he had almost age appropriate language skills in sign, and had nearly outstripped Linda. His speech improved, too.

Linda recalled flashes of that brief period of happiness. She remembered seeing him do the sign for 'pig', his fat fist twisting in front of his nose. She remembered her mum whispering involuntarily, as she signed stories to him. It had seemed like everything would turn out well. Linda had recovered from the disastrous relationship with Lucas's father; there was talk of promotion at work; there was interest from men, which she didn't ignore.

But then her mum died.

One morning, during the autumn after her mum's death, Linda had found larch needles in the hall. Tiny, dry, coppery spines. She'd thought little of it. But later, as she changed the bed sheets, she shook more needles out of the linen. At lunchtime, she found them in the margarine. They were in the bottom of the cup that held the toothbrushes, and in her underwear drawer. When she coughed, she found a single larch needle on her tongue.

She hadn't believed her dead mother was trying to communicate with her through nature, but the needles had made her nervous. At dusk, she went out into the smoky air with her kitchen broom, and found the pavement two inches thick with larch needles. All together like that, they created a block of colour, rich and ginger.

Linda wanted them gone. She swept them into the brambles that grew around the base of the larches. Soon, her kitchen brush clogged, so she got a shovel, working until the street lights came on. Slits of yellow appeared in the curtains of her neighbours' houses, and she knew what she looked like to them, scraping sparks up off the tarmac.

Mike had turned up moments later, with little Lucas. Linda didn't even know where they'd been.

'Why don't you come inside, love?' Mike said.

Linda had shouted at him. She'd told him she ought to be able to sweep the pavement outside her own house without her brother trying to commit her to a mental institution. She spoke quickly, half-turned, so Lucas wouldn't understand. Mike steered Lucas into the house.

When she'd finished, Linda kicked off her shoes at the door. Mike had put some cartoons on for Lucas. He had his head in his hands. Seeing them there, through the open door of the living room – her two boys – Linda made a decision. For the sake of her son, and her brother, she had to find a way to go on. She would sweep away the feelings, the memories, the urges. There would be no new men, no work promotions, no bold home schooling, no frivolity. She only had Lucas now, and their lives would be simple, strictly controlled.

Over the following months, Linda had watched her boy for signs of distress. There was nothing much to see. During breakfast, he'd wait for his Coco Pops to bleed into the milk. He'd shake the carton of Five Alive. Just like always.

When he went back to school, he didn't do so well. The teacher for the deaf said he was no longer progressing with his speech, and they should stop signing at home. It was sign language, apparently – not grief, or trauma, or deafness – which held back his speech development. Linda didn't have the energy to argue. So, without her mum there, they'd stopped signing.

Lucas had hated it at first, begged her to sign, but the teachers told her to be firm, and she worked hard with him, every night, on his speech. She sat him on the kitchen counter while she did the washing up, and she talked and talked, while he swung his legs, bashing the cupboards with his heels.

Now, ten years later, Linda sat in the passenger seat of Mike's car, on the way to Lucas's final parents' evening. The interior smelled of the garages Mike visited: lubricants and steel.

'How's the flat?' she asked.

'A bit bare – Karen took most of the stuff. I'm thinking of framing a couple of takeaway menus. The Ying-Wah does a lovely one in red and green.'

He winced as he changed gear, pressed his soft paunch.

'You okay?' Linda asked.

'Yeah. Trapped wind.'

'Let's keep it trapped tonight, eh?'

At the school, they followed herds of parents along the corridors. 'Bet Lucas will be glad to see the back of this place,' Mike said.

'Yeah,' Linda said. 'But *then* what?'

As usual, the teachers remained perplexed, although Lucas had surpassed their extremely low academic expectations. 'He's doing *incredibly* well on his work,' they said. 'We should all be very proud – we've had other deaf children, in the past, who have left the school barely able to *read*.'

'That *is* something to be proud of, isn't it?' Mike muttered.

They spoke of an improvement in Lucas's social skills. The

maths teacher put this down to his new support worker. 'She's just lovely. And very good.'

At the end of the evening, they met his form tutor, 'Señor' Potts, a Spanish teacher from Essex who wore a suit he'd once bought for special occasions. 'Mr and Mrs Seacombe?' he said, hand extended, in the corridor.

'Sort of,' Linda said. 'This is my brother, Michael. Lucas's uncle.'

'Ah, buenas noches!' Potts said.

Mike frowned.

'It means: good evening,' said Potts.

He took them through to an untidy office and introduced them to an upright, fit young woman with fine blonde hair and a plain face. Linda didn't catch her name. They sat on plastic chairs, listening to Potts's hazy improvisations. 'Lucas is so enigmatic, isn't he? He has these flashes of insight. It's as though there's a little wizard in his head, who occasionally wakes, but otherwise lies dormant.'

Potts seemed pleased with that, but Mike had had his fill of feeble nonsense. 'A wizard?' he said.

'Not literally,' said Potts.

'I just don't get you blokes sometimes,' Mike said. 'You teachers. You're always talking about Lucas as if he's some character out of science fiction.'

'Mike . . .' Linda said.

'No, Lind. It's got to be said. If you could go to their house, if you could see him, of an evening. This is a kid who reads for two hours a night to catch up with the stuff he misses when you lot are facing the opposite way. He memorises the plots of TV shows in the *Radio Times*, just so he's got something to talk about at school. Him and his mother, here,' Mike pointed to

Linda, 'have spent probably ten years mouthing babble at each other, teaching him to speak. All those nights sat at the kitchen table in those bloody headphones.'

'Mr Seacombe, please.'

'Now if *he* can be arsed to get up in the morning and come to this dump, then you ought to be able to see him as a real person. He's not a puzzle, or a riddle, or some wizard or angel or bloody sprite or something. He's a real, *actual* kid.'

Linda looked away, because she felt like she might cry if she made eye contact with her brother. She saw, with surprise, that the support worker's eyes had also moistened.

'I'm very sorry,' said Potts, who'd clearly had a long night himself. 'I didn't mean anything by it.'

'It's all right, mate,' Mike said. 'It's all right. Just. No more wizards, eh?'

Potts lost his nerve after that exchange, and the support worker took over. 'I think Lucas has a lot of repressed rage,' she said. 'He's always saying everything is fine, but he's *angry.*'

'I'm not sure I agree,' Linda said.

'He's talking more now, but he's so used to bottling it all up,' said the support worker. 'That's Mario for you. Oh shit. I mean . . . Lucas. God, I'm so sorry.'

Linda knew about the nickname, although she'd never discussed it with Lucas. She'd seen it written on his exercise books, and not in his handwriting. She suspected it was meant unkindly. For a long moment, the room fell silent.

Finally, Mike smiled, his tension relieved after the rant. 'That's *Super* Mario to you, ha ha!'

Everyone laughed, except Linda.

*

As Mike's car flashed down the dual carriageway towards home, Linda remembered how, in the years after they stopped signing, she'd sometimes heard Lucas vocalising in the night. Making those little noises. She'd gone into his room (flowers on the wallpaper, back then, ThunderCats on the sheets), and seen him moving his fingers in his sleep. Sometimes he'd sign at the ceiling, sometimes at the wall. She couldn't understand him, in that light. She'd forgotten the language quickly.

He only did it in his sleep, and once, when he was about eight, Linda felt sure he was signing about his Nanna. He was impersonating her, reporting her signs: making himself narrow, shrugging his shoulders, just like Daisy. Linda considered trying to stop him. She might have taken hold of his wrists, and he wouldn't have woken. But in the end, she couldn't do it. She figured it would pass soon enough.

She was right. By the time he turned nine, she'd step into his bedroom and find that his arms had dropped by his sides, like he'd been knocked unconscious and was unable to break his fall.

Mike stopped his car outside the bungalow. 'Well, sis,' he said, with a sigh that deflated his big body. 'That was fun.'

'Yes, wonderful. Let's never, ever do it again,' Linda said. 'Listen, Mike. Did Mum ever mention a friend called Paul to you?'

'Don't think so. Why?'

'When I went to see Dad, the other week, there was this man in his room, reading to him.'

'And?'

'I thought I recognised him.'

'Where from?'

'I don't know,' she said.

Mike shook his head. 'Look, Linda. Do you really want to dig all that stuff up again?'

'No,' she said.

'Well, then.'

They both looked over at the bungalow, the muted light in Lucas's window. She punched Mike's arm, and he flinched. 'Hey, buenas noches, yeah?' she said.

'Same to you.'

'Your mum's a babe,' Cassie said.

'Whatever,' Lucas said, his hand chopping at his waist – one of the new signs he'd learned over the last few months.

' dad's also looking. shoulders.'

'That would be my Uncle Mike.'

Cassie showed Lucas the sign for *uncle*: two hooked fingers tapping the chin. They weren't supposed to sign, so Cassie drew the partition in the Basin, and wrote POINT OF VIEW in her notebook. *Very important for BSL*, she signed. *When you're telling a story, think of it like a film. You have the long shot . . .*

With her hands she created a thick forest. She made the sun plummet in the sky. Her fingers became the legs of an old man, walking between the trees.

'There he is,' she said. 'But now close-up.'

She made herself into the old man: hunched, heavy browed, fearful. She put an owl in the branches. Cassie described – and then became – the owl, looking down.

'You see,' she said, smoothing her skirt over her hips. 'Every deaf story is a first-person story. You become each character.   switch roles. It's very   .'

'Very what?'

She signed the word, but Lucas didn't understand, so she spelled it on her fingers. C-O-M-P-A-S-S-I-O-N-A-T-E. *My brother always said signing helps you think of others.*

What happened to him?

My brother?

The old man in the forest.

Don't know. What do you think?

Dead, Lucas signed.

For a few moments, their hands lay still. *I've forgotten. What's the sign for C-I-N-E-M-A?* Lucas asked.

She did it for him: the left arm horizontal, the right arm vertical behind it, fingers splayed, palm out, moving from side to side.

Is that the actor on the screen? Lucas asked.

Cassie shrugged. *Signs don't always look like the thing.*

It looked like a tree in a gale, or someone waving goodbye.

The language didn't come back easily, but Lucas didn't feel like he was learning it for the first time, either. It had taken a month of daily practice to get started. At first, he couldn't even do the alphabet. His fingers kept missing each other.

As winter deepened, he understood some of what Cassie signed. If he didn't try too hard, a blurry message appeared in his head. More like telepathy than language. He struggled to reply. Sentences ran towards his hands, but they got stuck somewhere around the elbow.

In early December, he signed the question *what did you do yesterday*, and as his finger flicked at his shoulder, he felt a surge through his body, as if his arm just remembered what to do. The thought flowed through his muscles, like the language had come from inside him. Like a door had opened to some dungeon.

At first, that feeling was rare, and he soon reverted to fumbling fingers and phrases in English sentence order.

Cassie told him that sign language had once been banned in France for being too sensual. *Too sensual for FRANCE!* she signed. (The sign for France was the twiddling of an imaginary moustache.) He could believe it. You constantly touch yourself when you sign. A thumb to the temple for *I know*, the fin of a hand slid down the face for *sad*. When she told him where she used to *live*, Cassie's middle finger pressed the top of her breast and circled, so that her white blouse dimpled and stretched, the lace of her bra showing through the cotton.

If Lucas had been a minister, he'd have banned it.

In the early days, he watched her fingers. *Look at ME*, she signed. *Not my hands.*

As a lip-reader, he'd stared endlessly at mouths. Teeth and tongues and chapped lips and beard hair. But now, he looked at Cassie's whole face. Amazing what a face could contain: anxiety in the jaw muscles, the moisture of cold weather on the lashes, his own silhouette in her pupils. He'd never looked at someone so deeply.

And then, eventually, another face returned. Lucas's first proper memory of his grandmother came in the moments after waking one Saturday morning. He saw her so clearly. Nanna, her grey and black hair pulled tight behind her head. She looked around a room (Lucas didn't recognise it), and made the sign for spectacles: two 'V's going up to her cheeks. Then she made the sign for 'where'. Lucas could see two pale dots on her skin, from where she'd applied the pressure for the first sign. He saw those marks fading back to colour.

He sat up slowly in his bed. It wasn't like a normal memory. He was shocked by its vividness. He could hardly believe that something so clear could have been inside him all this time, hiding.

He told Cassie about the memory. He told her about the skin changing colour on Nanna's face.

'What   it means?' she asked.

'Bad circulation,' he said.

You're very funny, she signed.

Is that why everyone's always laughing at me? he signed back.

She studied his face until he blushed. 'You shave quite high here,' she said, touching the joint of his jawbone. 'You should let them grow. Sideburns give shape to a haircut.'

Lucas tried to act like people touched him all the time, but his pulse quickened. 'Maybe I'll come to The Cut for a trim,' he said.

'You should,' she said. '   and reasonably priced.'

He liked to stride down the school corridor with Cassie, but here came Youds and co. Youds performed a jumble-fingered piss-take of sign language, culminating in a (quite impressive) mime of a blowjob, where the tongue pressed into the cheek to suggest the thrusting tip of a penis.

'What   mean, Mario?' Youds said. 'Because your mum says it means I owe her a fiver.'

Lucas laughed, as per the rules of Fitting In. But things had changed now. Firstly, Youds' taunts had become increasingly cruel over the last few months. A sliver of hatred replaced the old sense of pity. Also, Lucas could feel Cassie watching him. He didn't want to look like a doormat in front of her.

'Nice rhythm, Youds,' he said. 'You been practising?'

'Christh   ,' Youds said. 'When you talk, it makes me feel sick.'

'When *you* talk,' Lucas replied, 'it makes me glad I can't hear.'

He pushed past Youds, and strode on. It took him a while to realise Cassie had stopped. He turned to her. *Amazing*, she signed.

He couldn't stop smiling. Fitting In could go to hell.

That Saturday was the colour of a wet grey sock, but Lucas didn't care. When he reached the row of Ringdean shops, the front window of The Cut shone against dull bricks and sodden trees. From that distance, he could see the hard facts of Cassie: she was twenty-one, and – in an odd way – beautiful. She didn't look like the sort of person who might go out with a sixteen-year-old deaf boy, but who did?

People fell in love with film stars, but this was real. They had a language: a machine with which they could build another world. They had actual conversations. You couldn't deny that.

He crossed the street and stepped into The Cut. Cassie's mother greeted him. She wore a long denim shirt over leggings with foot-straps. She knew who he was. Her foot tapped – to music, probably – his aids didn't pick up much over the hair-driers. She made the sign for *sign*, but looked like she was dancing.

Lucas nodded.

Cassie's friend?

He finger-spelled his name.

She hung up his coat, and told him to sit in the waiting area, where he messed around on the mobile phone his uncle had bought him for Christmas ('The bloke in the shop said all the deaf people have them, for the SMS messages'). Soon, Cassie came over, and her eyes widened when she saw him. 'You're here!' she said, and held the black cape out before her.

'Wait,' he said. He removed his aids and put them in his coat pocket. *Don't want to get them wet*, he signed. He stood and put his arms through the cape, and Cassie slid behind to tie him up and manoeuvre him in front of a mirror. He felt her breath on his neck, smelled Juicy Fruit.

Good to see you, she signed into the mirror. *What would you like?*

I would like to get away from here. Into the wild. Some place hot.

I meant your hair, Cassie signed. *What style?*

Just a trim. Will you do it?

No. Mum does the cuts. I just wash.

Perfect, Lucas thought.

Don't ask for too much off, though, Cassie signed. *These sweet curls.*

Lucas rolled his eyes, but reddened.

She tucked the towel into the cape, and led him over to the sinks. She moved his body the way she sometimes moved his hands, pressing him into the thick leather seat, and positioning his neck in the cold cleft of the basin. His view tumbled up to the ceiling, the steam swirling there, and then focused on her face, upside down. The gummy smile.

The needles of water felt good against his scalp. Her hand reached round to ask him about the temperature. It was too hot, but in a good way. The water in his ear briefly reminded him of the caloric tests he underwent as a young boy, but soon all such thoughts left him. With her hand, she made a visor at his forehead. The scent of her wrist surprised him with its floral sweetness, but the cables beneath her skin reminded him of the perfect logic of her bicycle. She rubbed the calloused pads of her palm deep into his scalp, and scrunched the whipped-up weight of his hair. Where else could you go to experience such a thing, he thought, and what in the world could be better?

He felt his penis stretching out down his trouser leg, but he did not touch himself beneath the cape. He didn't want to cheapen it. He couldn't remember ever feeling happier.

He looked up at her. 'Done,' she mouthed. 'Okay?'

He smiled.

Take a seat over there, and Mum will be with you in a minute.

Thank you, he signed, standing up.

She looked at him for a moment, as if deciding something. *My brother runs a Deaf pub night. The next one's not until April, but you should come*, she signed.

I'm not sure.

I'm going, she signed.

Great. I'll be there.

They stood for a second. Later, he would think back to that moment, and feel certain that something passed between them. Surely, the feeling was too powerful for him to have experienced it alone.

Tiny white lights blinked in the palm tree outside Stephen's house: a tasteful nod to the season. When he opened the door to Mike, he looked shattered. He wore baggy clothes and his cleaved-toe boots, like a wood sprite from a fairy tale.

'Oh God,' he said. 'I completely forgot. I've had the day off.'

'You sick?' said Mike.

'Sort of. Sick in the head. Come in.'

They sat beneath the coloured glass of the kitchen lightshade, which sometimes appeared in Mike's dreams.

'You had one of them migraines?' Mike asked.

'I just feel a bit . . . well, broken. Angry, exhausted. You know. And there's this . . .' Stephen looked up at the ceiling. It took another moment for the rhythmic thumps to register with Mike.

'Are you having work done?' he asked.

'That's . . . my daughter and her boyfriend.'

Mike studied the ceiling further. 'What are they doing?'

'What do you *think*?'

'Surely not,' said Mike. 'She's, what? Sixteen?'

'She's just about to turn eighteen, actually. But, yes. A child.'

'What's the boyfriend like?'

'He's a cunt,' Stephen said.

Mike thought for a moment. 'Do you need me to . . . you know? Sort him out? Eject him from the premises or whatever?'

Stephen laughed into the steam from his tea. 'Jesus Christ. *No.* Look, I shouldn't have said he's a cunt. You're right, it could be worse.'

'I never said that.'

III

'I just mean. He's . . . melodramatic. A spotty teen. A kid, really, like her. Crying in the street at midnight, and then sending her mail-order stuffed toys that I have to collect from the neighbour.'

'But what are you going to *do* about it?' Mike said. 'About all *this*?' He pointed upwards.

'I try to imagine what Rosa would have done. She'd have said you can't stop her, and it's better she's doing it in the safety of her own home. She'd also have said I was up to much worse at that age. Which is all true, but that doesn't account for the moment, in about fifteen minutes, when I have to watch *him* come down the stairs, with a red fucking face.'

The ceiling creaked again. 'Also,' Stephen said, 'he's got no rhythm.'

Mike laughed. 'I'm not one to talk,' he said. 'I'm rubbish at all that.'

'What, *sex?*' Stephen said.

'It doesn't matter. Forget it. It's not like I'm getting any.'

Mike said things in that kitchen he'd never have said anywhere else. And now Stephen wouldn't let up. 'But what's the problem?' he said. 'You might as well tell me. It's usually one thing or the other, let's face it. Are you impotent?'

He was so straightforward, Stephen. Mike had never heard the word 'impotent' said outside of jokes.

'It's the other.'

'Premature ejac—'

'Yeah, yeah. That,' said Mike.

'Well, at least you can do something about it.'

'What, think of old hags? Try to remember all the FA Cup winners?'

'Give me a minute,' Stephen said, and left the room.

Mike sat there and thought of his two failed marriages. He hadn't blamed his first wife, Jacqui, for leaving him. They'd been childhood sweethearts, married too young, like just about everyone he knew. They'd tried to have a family, but couldn't conceive, and then Mike had totally lost the plot for a while after his mum died. He'd been intolerable. There were times when the only person who'd speak to him was his sister.

His second wife, Karen, had worked as a marketing executive for a Vauxhall dealership. At first she hadn't wanted kids, and then she did, but again no luck. So it seemed Mike had the problem: firing blanks, as his dad would have put it. He always told people he and Karen had divorced because they couldn't have children, but there was more to it. And his hair-trigger in the bedroom was just one of many neurotic symptoms he'd picked up, after the thing with his parents.

Stephen returned with a book. *Taoist Sexual Practice: What We Can Learn.* 'It's pronounced "Dowist",' Stephen said. 'Start with . . . well, start with chapter one, I suppose.'

Mike opened it at the first chapter, and read the title – *Self Cultivation*. He thought for a moment about what that might mean, and then slammed the book shut. Stephen laughed.

'You're feeling better, I see,' said Mike.

'A little, yes.'

The noises upstairs died down, and Stephen mumbled that he never should have let her have a TV in her room.

'So, with her being home, do you want me to just go, when I've finished my cuppa?' Mike said.

'No way!' said Stephen. 'They'll be off out in a bit.'

Mike flexed his core muscles in preparation.

Soon, they heard the teenagers coming downstairs. 'Wait here,' Stephen said, sidling out into the hallway. Through the half-open kitchen door, Mike could see the tall skinny boyfriend, who had an earring, and wore a white tracksuit with buttons up the side of the leg. He looked tired and sad and wistful (Mike remembered the aftermath of teen sex). The spots on his cheeks glowed from his exertions. 'Hello, Mr Bentham,' he said to Stephen.

'Hello, Matt.'

Stephen's daughter wore a tight, low-cut black top and baggy trousers with big thigh pockets. 'Who's here?' she said, trying to peer into the kitchen.

'Nobody,' Stephen said. 'A colleague from work. Have you eaten?'

'No. We're going out, okay?'

'Well,' Stephen said, 'have a wonderful evening.'

The girl swore under her breath. *Fucking weird*, or something to that effect.

'Bye, Matt,' said Stephen.

'Thanks for having me, Mr Bentham,' said Matt, and Mike almost gasped at the audacity.

The front door opened, and Matt jogged out into the frosty street, while the girl pulled on her coat. She sighed. 'Dad?' she called back.

'Yes?'

'I love you, Dad.'

The door slammed as Stephen reciprocated. The house rested, and Stephen came back to the kitchen. Mike nodded to the shed.

*

After the beating, they sat against the wall, drinking Bud Ice. 'Nice bike,' Mike said, nodding to the black racer, its drop handlebars like a ram's head.

'What? Oh, yes. Rosa rode it more than I did. We were almost the same height, but she had longer legs. I haven't ridden it since . . . well.'

'Is it the memories?' Mike asked quietly.

'No, no, it's not that,' said Stephen. 'It's my knee. It didn't heal properly, after . . . you know. After you and I *first met*.'

Mike winced with guilt. 'Can I buy it off you?' he said, without thinking. 'I mean, I'll give you market value. More, even.'

'Why not?' Stephen said. 'Better than letting it rust in here. It'll need a service, though. I don't want you flying off it.'

'Thanks for your concern,' Mike said, pressing the beer bottle against his ribs. 'Hey, I've done well from this visit. A book and a bike.'

'I still reckon I came out on top,' Stephen said.

The more of the language Lucas learned, the more memories returned. The next one came as he leaned out of his bedroom window, spraying bursts of Cassie's deodorant into the cold evening air. He looked out at the wispy spindles of the larches across the road. The street light came on, and the image just hit him, wallop.

In the memory, he stood at the window, just as he did now. It was early evening, and he was five years old. He opened the curtains and saw his Nanna coming out of the bungalow and crossing the road. He knocked on the window. Nanna froze, as though in a game. She turned and signed something that he couldn't see because of the falling dusk. He pointed to the street light, and she moved under the beam. Nanna was small at that distance, her long blue coat cinched at the waist. The smallness frightened him.

You didn't see me, she signed.

What? I don't understand.

I'm sneaking. Your mummy is asleep. Don't tell.

Lucas liked the idea of keeping a secret. *Where are you going?*

Cinema, she signed. She made another sign, too, that he didn't recognise: the index finger wagging and dropping, in a quick flash.

I won't tell, he signed. His hands were sealed.

Nanna blew him a kiss and signed *thank you* – the gestures almost the same. She looked left and right and then slipped out of the light. A moment later, a fox crept under the street light, looked at Lucas, and then dashed away.

Now, dazed at his window, Lucas tried to figure out the mysteries of the memory. Why had she sneaked away? And why did she seem so vulnerable to him? Perhaps it was just hindsight. Lucas knew what had happened to his Nanna. He did not remember, but he knew. There was a difference.

1961–2

At the divisional dance, held at the Corn Exchange, Daisy stood next to the chief constable's wife. She had a couple of inches on Mrs Clore, and could see the delicate skin of the older woman's scalp. Both wore black. Mrs Clore nodded across the vast hall towards Robert. 'Detective sergeant,' she said.

'I'm not even wearing my badge,' Daisy said.

Mrs Clore sneered. 'He's young for that.'

'He works double the hours of most men,' Daisy replied.

'Yes. Lucky you.'

Daisy's face had become sharp, and she could not suppress the thin fibres of muscle that shifted in her forearms. She looked up at the bright blur of the gigantic chandelier and wished it would fall.

'You're not dancing tonight, I see,' Mrs Clore slurred.

Daisy shook her head.

'I remember you were a good dancer,' Mrs Clore continued. 'I remember you dancing with *my husband*, at one of these events.'

'I don't recall,' Daisy lied.

'You needn't worry about hurting my feelings. You're too old for my Gerry.'

'It was ten years ago, I suppose.'

'You were too old for him even then. The girls Gerald prefers are barely older than your daughter.'

Daisy turned to Mrs Clore, alarmed. Linda had not yet turned twelve.

'I'm sorry,' Mrs Clore said. 'It's not Gerald's fault. He's frightened, I think. Confused. He can't sleep at night.'

'Really?' Daisy said. This, perhaps, was Mrs Clore's idea of a drunken heart-to-heart. Daisy thought of her own husband's night terrors, long gone now.

'He thinks there are . . . *persons* in the room,' Mrs Clore said.

'Persons other than you?'

'Other than me.'

'Victims, you mean? Ghosts?'

'No.'

'Murderers and villains, then.'

'No, Mrs Seacombe. When he wakes, he sees your husband.'

The Seacombes suddenly had some money. Robert had bought a bright black Standard Ten, second-hand, and a gas-powered refrigerator. They moved off the colony into a detached house in Saltdean, looking out over the Channel. In winter, up there, you could taste the sea before you saw it. The living room faced north, but even so, light streamed through the patio doors. The number of windows surprised Daisy, because her husband guarded his privacy. The street was pleasant, although Robert kept an eye on a family with three teenage boys. The Seacombes' house stood at the end of the row, so their garden blended into miles of fields. Robert built a fence the week they moved in.

One night, Daisy fell asleep in the living room armchair. Michael had a fever, and she'd stayed up late, looking after him. She woke to the front door opening, and watched Robert swaying in the hall, illuminated by the street light lapping in behind him. Green tie, grey suit. He rubbed his face with his hands, and kicked the door closed. After a moment, he began to undress, right there. Jacket off, shirt and tie off. His shoulders were wide, and his vest covered a hefty gut these days.

He dropped most of his clothes on the floor, but he loved his ties, and hung this one on the coat peg. As he did so, he lifted the cardigan that Daisy had knitted for Linda. Robert draped the plum-coloured wool over his hand. He put the garment to his face, and released a long, shaking breath. Daisy sat motionless in the shadows of the living room, observing the scene through the mesh of her eyelashes.

Eventually, Robert dropped the cardigan and bent down to untie his laces. He found something on the end of his shoe. He dabbed it with one finger, picked it up that way, and held it to his face. Daisy couldn't be sure from that range, but it looked like a whole fingernail.

Sometimes, Robert was gone for long stretches. When he came home, the changes in his appearance shocked Daisy. His hair had receded, or stubble grew on his chin, or a fading bruise left a green crescent beneath his eye.

One night, he sat at the oval dining table, and she almost forgot to serve him. He had brought home a bag of grey cod fillets, and she made parsley sauce from the packet. 'Looks very nice,' he said, when she placed the plate before him.

He wore a brand-new shirt, the weave thicker than the ones she usually washed. But it had been ironed. Daisy didn't know where to start with the questions.

Linda held her father's little finger. Michael seemed not to recognise him. The mashed potato, which Daisy had flattened down into furrows, made a dry tearing sound as Robert scooped up a forkful.

'How was work?' Daisy said, sitting.

Robert laughed so loudly and suddenly that Linda flinched with shock.

'Sorry,' he said. 'Sorry, Daisy. I can't really talk about it.'

'I think a man should be able to tell his wife about the day's events.'

Robert blinked and looked around the room. He stared at the deep blue corduroy of the curtains. 'I wouldn't know what language to use.'

Later that evening, after he'd bathed, she asked if he was all right.

'I'm just tired, girl, that's all.'

He sat on their bed, his back to her, his face half-turned, so she could see the sheen of aftershave on his neck. The sea wind droned outside the window.

'I worry about you,' she said. 'I read the news, and I worry.'

'The papers won't print it, darling.'

'Won't print *what*, Robert?'

He sighed. 'You're concerned I'll get hurt? Is that it?'

'There's that. And I worry that you'll hurt someone else.'

He lifted himself from the bed, and walked around to where she stood. He took her hand and kissed it gently. 'I'd never lay a finger on someone who didn't deserve it, Daisy.'

'But how can you tell?' Daisy asked.

He smiled and shook his head.

She liked *The Misfits* and *The Hustler*. Linda went with her to see *West Side Story* at the Regent, and they hummed the songs together all year. Alone, Daisy sat through two showings of *Last Year at Marienbad* and still couldn't fathom it. She liked the look of the film, liked what the black and white did to the cigarette smoke in the auditorium, but the other moviegoers looked so serious. It gave her the giggles.

Out on the street, still mirthful, she tried to imagine what Paul would have written about the film, and found she couldn't. And then she thought of Paul waiting for a reply to his confessional letter, and slowly giving up. A cold shock of guilt went through her. The voice of Paul's letters was slipping from her mind. Her own voice had eroded, too.

When she got home, she took two of the old letters she kept buried in the filing cabinet, and read them in the bathroom.

In spring, Robert bought a swing chair for the garden, with a pattern of orange and brown flowers, and a tasselled awning. He dug deep foundations for a shed, and he and Daisy carried the slabs for its floor, while Ray Harper watched, smoking, in his suit. Ray had a bad back, apparently. In the shed, Robert kept seeds, a sack of lime, and a padlocked gun cupboard, containing his sports rifle and an old revolver he'd found in an abandoned house.

A few weeks later, Daisy sat with the children in the living room, and listened to Ray and Robert talking through the patio doors. 'No,' said Robert. 'Their stories are fantastic. They've got nothing.'

'Not yet,' said Ray.

'Nothing they can use. It's going to be fine.'

Robert leaned back in the swing chair, rocking gently. Daisy studied her husband: his red and white polka-dot tie, his sleeves rolled up for gardening. She tried to know something of him, because she felt that should be possible, after so many years. But the shade of the awning covered his face. Ray Harper, standing beside the chair, watched her through the glass.

'Linda,' she said.

Her daughter glanced up from a game she was playing with some Union Jack darts she must have pilfered from the Fox and Hounds. 'Yes, Mum?'

'Let's go see a film.'

'Go *and* see, Mum. Go *and* see.'

Film came for Robert, too.

'Some spiv walks into HQ today, says he's making a picture about us,' he said, over dinner.

Daisy rested her hands in her lap. 'What are you talking about, Robert?'

'God's honest truth. Fellow with a bird's name. Vera, something . . . director.'

'Not . . . *Val Guest?* The Hammer horror man?'

'That's him. The chief's given him access, and he's been following detectives around. He wanted to come out with me and Ray.'

'What did you say?'

'I told him to bugger off back to Hollywood.'

The children looked up from their pork chops, and Robert

stared back at them. 'That'd be funny, wouldn't it? Old Daddy on the big screen, doing his job?'

'They'd use actors,' Daisy said.

'Dead right. And they'd have to make it all up. You couldn't show what I do, at the pictures,' Robert said, standing from the table and refastening his belt. He leaned down to Daisy on his way out of the room. '*It's not decent*,' he whispered.

Often, associates of Robert would call at the house: a moustachioed dandy in a three-piece suit, a harassed-looking man, balding in strange patches. 'I need the living room,' Robert would say, and Daisy thought how much it sounded like Michael's requests to go to the toilet.

Robert always made a show of larking with the children as they filed out into the hall. Cowboys and Indians. He always played the sheriff, sharp-shooting before tucking his pointed finger back into his pocket.

In the dying days of that summer, Robert took them out to the countryside. He drove quickly. His thick hands, grubby from the garden, gripped the wheel as if he was trying to snap it off. They parked on gravel, and walked out through the marshland towards Seven Sisters beach. Robert stormed ahead, in one of his strange moods. When the cliffs came into view, Michael stopped. 'Wow,' he said. 'Mummy, is that the end of the world?'

'It's not that bad,' Daisy muttered, eyes fixed on her husband.

Of course, Robert wanted to climb the steep grassy slope to the clifftop, and they all trailed after him, Linda chewing her hair, Michael silent and squinting. At the top, the green land rose and fell in waves, so that you never knew if the edge was over the next grassy crest. The clouds seemed close, rock-like in their definition.

Daisy turned to her daughter. 'Do you like it up here, love?'

'When you're on top of the cliffs,' Linda said, 'you can't see them.'

On the way home, the kids fell asleep in the car, and Daisy pretended to. Robert parked the Standard far down the road, because Ray Harper was due to visit and he always let Ray park outside the house. On getting out of the car, Michael stumbled, disoriented.

About six doors down from the Seacombes lived an older couple who owned a large black dog, a Chow. It barked as they passed, and Daisy heard Michael – too tired to control himself – take a fearful inhalation. It was all Robert needed. 'Right,' he said.

'Robert, leave it,' Daisy said.

But he took hold of Michael by the shoulders and dragged him back to the gate of their neighbour. 'You are the son of a policeman,' Robert said. 'The way you deal with any given situation reflects on me, and by extension, the Force. People *know*.'

Michael kept silent, swaying in his pumps. The couple who owned the Chow had reinforced their curlicued gate with chicken wire. The black-tongued dog, thick and overheated, did not appreciate the attention. It growled and pounced at the gate.

'This is nothing but a family pet,' Robert continued. 'And it is penned in. It cannot hurt you. The reason I joined the police is so that people do not have to live in fear on their own street. We're going to stand here until you get used to this barking, because that's all it is.'

'Robert, is this necessary?' Daisy said.

'It's fine!' Michael shouted, his voice cracking.

The dog sprang at the gate, and Robert's shoulders juddered as he held Michael in front of him. After a moment, Michael tried to escape, but Robert pushed him back towards the gate. He fell on the pavement.

'Enough!' Daisy shouted, going to them and pulling her son away. 'You leave him alone.'

She half carried Michael to the house, and when she turned to look back, Linda was scowling at her father who stood, arms folded, watching the dog lose its mind.

Daisy monitored her husband carefully that evening. She watched him while they ate their dinner of egg sandwiches and leftover pork pie. When she'd bathed the children and put them to bed, she watched him reading last week's local news-papers, one after the other. She went outside to tidy the garden, and found an old toy the kids used to play with: a short wooden staff with a heavy round base, and three coloured rings that slotted over it. She took off the rings, and inverted the staff, holding it like a hammer. She came in through the patio doors, and slammed the toy down onto Robert's wrist with all the force she could muster. He roared in pain and flung his news-paper across the room, but Daisy was already halfway to the door. 'That's for your son, who is too young to defend himself,' she called back.

She ran upstairs, and locked herself in the bathroom, hoping to give him time to calm down enough not to kill her. She heard a few pitiful curses, but Harper soon knocked on the door, distracting Robert from any thoughts of retaliation.

Later, when he came to bed, he apologised in the dark. 'There's a lot happening at work,' he said. 'It makes me jumpy.'

'You may bully people in your job, Robert, but I won't let it happen to my children.'

Robert was a puzzle she would never solve. Other women said they were bored by their husbands, but Daisy never knew what Robert would do next, or what he would say.

'I'm glad the kids have a mother like you,' he whispered. He took her hand carefully, and she rubbed his forearm, felt the jelly-like lump that had formed at his wrist, where she'd hit him. 'But they need me, too. And so do you, Daisy.'

The next day, Daisy finally wrote to Paul. She tried, several times, to address the subject of his last letter, but in the end she ignored it.

I am sorry not to have written for so long. There are too many loose ends in this serial! I need to know if you passed your engineering test, if the swelling went down on your mother's ankle. Did Marguerite's boyfriend propose? Hopefully I will find out in the next instalment. Same PO Box address. I will understand if you don't want to write.

She wandered into town to post the letter, passing the women's shelter – a former church, recently whitewashed. A woman of about forty, big, dressed like a tart, descended the front steps. She spoke through the window of a parked car, before turning, clearing her sinuses, and going back into the building. Daisy looked at the man in the car, and caught his eye before she realised it was Ray Harper. He winked at her, and drove away.

*

One morning that autumn, Mrs Harrison from number twenty-two paid a visit, with her limping Chow. Mrs Harrison was an amateur tennis player, always in white skirt and shoes. She dabbed at eyes reddened by tears. 'Someone's attacked my dog! Look at this,' she said. 'Will you just *look*!'

Daisy stared down at the dog, which kept its wounded left forepaw carefully off the ground. Mrs Harrison held two Union Jack darts, the points streaky with blood.

'Two of the things!' the owner cried.

'God help us,' Daisy muttered.

The fuss brought Robert to the door. 'What's going on?' he said.

'I just thought you might be able to do something,' Mrs Harrison said to him, 'you being in the police.'

'It'll be those boys down the road,' Robert said. 'The swines. Excuse my language.'

'That was what I thought,' said Mrs Harrison, reaching down – not very far – to stroke her injured pet.

'I'll have a word with them now,' Robert said. He stepped into the kitchen to get his coat, and Daisy followed him.

'Robert, wait—'

'Don't try and stop me, Daisy. They're a bunch of little sods, and I'm going to give them what for.'

'It wasn't them, Robert,' Daisy whispered.

'Of course it was.'

'It was Linda.'

'*Linda?*' Robert said, almost laughing. '*Our* Linda? Don't be ridiculous, woman.'

'She hates that dog. And those darts are hers.'

Robert's eyes widened. 'Where the bleeding hell is she?'

Daisy put a finger to her lips. 'She's taken Michael to the pictures. So, you need to calm down, and deal with this lady. I will talk to Linda when she comes home. If you so much as *touch* her, Robert, I swear . . .'

But Robert looked more bewildered than angry. He returned to the doorway. 'Mrs Harrison,' he said. 'I am going to speak to the local constable about this. He takes such incidents very seriously indeed. In the meantime, I suggest you take the dog to a vet.'

'But I thought you were going to—'

'Thank you, Mrs Harrison,' Robert said, already closing the door. 'It's a police matter now.'

Christmas came and went. Daisy's midnight blue coat had thinned at the elbows, so she made another, this time going for a double-breasted affair with two big lines of buttons.

In the new year, she wore it to the cinema. Val Guest's *Jigsaw* had come out, and Robert took Daisy to see it at the Academy, along with Ray Harper and his current squeeze. The film, a murder mystery, had a Hitchcock style to it, which Daisy enjoyed. But Robert and Ray laughed all the way through.

'It was pretty realistic apart from the ending,' Harper said, as they came out.

'What was wrong with the ending?' Daisy asked.

'Well, they solved it.'

She knew there was something wrong with the letter as soon as she saw it in the post office. She swiped the envelope quickly into her pocket, and left, shuffling through the brown water coating the lino.

When she got home, she could hear Robert and Ray in the dining room, so she went straight upstairs to the bathroom, where she found Michael on the floor with his father's shaving kit. 'God, Michael, you scared me to death. Watch out for the razors. What are you doing?'

'Just looking in the mirror,' he said, holding up a cream-spattered circle of glass.

'Well,' Daisy said. 'Did you see anything nice?'

Michael nodded, his black curls shuddering.

'You may take the mirror and play with it for a while,' Daisy said. 'But not in here.'

Michael bounded out, and Daisy closed the door. She loved the bathroom: windows scarred with flower designs, lots of light, wipe-clean tiles and a lock. She sat on the edge of the bath and took out the envelope. Alone, she quickly made sense of the mystery. It was the stamp which had looked wrong: Wilding issue – Queen Elizabeth half-turned, 3d. An *English* stamp. He was here.

She unfolded the letter. The return address read South London.

Dear Daisy,

Thank you for your note, which Marguerite forwarded to me. I hadn't given up hope that you would write, and reassured myself that you'd probably just lost your pencil in 1956. Glad you found it, Dee.

As you can see from the address, my circumstances have changed somewhat! A lot has changed.

His mother had died, just after he passed his engineering exams. He'd been in regular contact with Tony, a war buddy in London, who had told him of opportunities resulting from the expansion of Gatwick Airport. With his mother dead, he'd felt free to go. He left the house to Marguerite, and now rented a flat not far from Tony, in West Norwood. He'd been in England for three years.

Old Tony keeps saying I should take the 'Brighton Belle' down to the seaside with him and Janet (they say they go to a place called 'Rottingdean', but I think they're teasing). They say I should surprise you – turn up on your doorstep – but I told him that was about the worst idea I'd ever heard. I was pretty sure you wouldn't want to see me. Over the last few years I have felt more than sad to lose you as a pen friend. We are not twenty anymore, but you had been a significant person in my life for a long time. We had a good friendship, and I should have accepted that, but I had to screw it up by writing that dumb letter. I was so sorry Dee. Mainly for myself.

I am <u>somewhat</u> excited to receive post from you again, but I am not getting carried away. While it sure is hard to write and dance at the same time, I remain your calm, level-headed, patient, London friend,

Paul

Daisy composed herself before leaving the bathroom. She headed for the front door.

'Mummy?' Michael said, light flashing in the shaving mirror. 'One moment.'

'Leave her, she's in a mood,' said Linda.

Daisy left the house, crossed the road, and stood by the wire fence at the cliff edge. She looked out on the town. A train passed over the viaduct: London to Brighton.

When she re-entered the house, she heard Robert and Ray Harper's conversation stop, and then start again, in the dining room. She stooped into the storage space beneath the stairs, and crouched by the filing cabinet. She put the letter in amongst her old film magazines and remained in the dark for a moment. A phrase came to her, something to do with her mother's church. *Bodily presence.*

Their correspondence resumed. She wrote to say that she was sorry for the loss of his mother, and sorry for hurting him. He replied with his usual lightness, describing his attempts to adjust to life in London: the quirks of England, the particular difference between the cold here and the cold back home.

It's not so serious here, of course. It's not forty below. But it's deceitful! It lures you out with no overcoat, and then socks you with that wind! Like a bayonet!

He wrote about foxes and aeroplanes, the expat veterans' hockey team he'd joined, and trying to order a drink in a pub in Dulwich. She could easily imagine the exchange he'd had with the barmaid who – after several attempts to understand his order – began to mimic his accent. *I had to get a West Indian guy to translate for me.*

Dee, he wrote. *Do you still watch movies?*

Daisy felt unable to write her reply in the house. She went to the Lighthouse Café, on the seafront, at lunchtime while the children were at school, and ordered a bacon sandwich, a cup of tea. She worked quickly, having edited the sentences many times in her mind.

An afternoon in February: dusk closing in on the big window of the café, the sea blending into the sky, the lights coming on along the promenade; the smell of grease, vinegar. The paper stuck to the table. She made a decision.

It would be fine, I think, to see you. We could meet in this café, and pass letters across the table. Save money on stamps. She kept the letter brief and without flourish. A date, a time, a place. Her husband had told her never to sign anything she wouldn't be happy for the whole world to see, so she didn't sign it.

That first afternoon, in early March, she suddenly didn't know if she'd be able to go through with it. She waited across the broad stretch of Kings Road, her collar pulled up around her face, staking out the Lighthouse Café, where she'd sat to write the letter, where they were now due to meet. The cold waves hissed like hot fat on the pebbles behind her.

Would she recognise him, after all these years? Her clearest memory of Paul was in the light of the usher's torch at the Electric. In her dreams, he wore his uniform, but he'd outgrown it, comically. She thought he might be the type to sit by the window. A watcher. She didn't know why. Perhaps some elements of his personality had become known to her through the letters.

She was right. He arrived five minutes early, and she watched him enter the café, but she stayed where she was. From that distance she couldn't tell much about his features. The information came from posture, gesture. He was well-dressed, comfortable, straight-backed. He wore dark-rimmed spectacles, and his hair was flecked with grey. He sat down and engaged the waitress for a while, mostly listening.

Daisy realised she couldn't do it. She couldn't cross the road.

He sat for twenty minutes and did not once look at the huge clock on the wall. If he glanced at his watch, she didn't see. Time did not stand still. He sipped his tea, which he took black. Yellow clouds appeared in the glass front of the Lighthouse. Soon, the children would want their dinner. This was ridiculous, anyway.

Just as she considered moving, Paul stood and paid. Daisy held her ground. He stepped outside. She lowered her head and tried to blend into the scene. The road between them was mercifully wide. But Paul held up his hand to her in a brief, reassuring wave, and then he walked inland, through Regency Square, towards town. He did not look back.

Daisy turned to face the sea. Above the silky band of yellow, a strip of darkness had formed. That was the thing about seaside towns: you could see the weather coming, but you couldn't get out of the way.

When Robert arrived home that afternoon, earlier than usual, Daisy walked straight out of the living room and put a pan of water on the hob. Robert had a heavy step, for a detective. In leather-soled shoes, on a deep carpet, you could still hear him coming.

'Tea?' she said, as he blocked out the doorway.

When he didn't reply, she turned. He peeled notes from a roll and placed them on the kitchen counter. 'There's a dinner on Friday,' he said. 'We need to look nice.'

Linda stood by his side, holding what looked like a token. It was, in fact, dried mud. 'Dad, you didn't take your shoes off.' She held up the evidence, which crumbled slightly in her fingers.

Robert sighed. He slipped off the shoes, toe on heel, and left them in the kitchen doorway. He walked away in socks the colour of dishwater wrung from the rag.

Linda hesitated, studying the shard of mud. Then she bent down and placed it inside her father's left shoe.

A week later, a letter.

It sure was good to see you again. Thank you for recommending the Lighthouse, which was excellent. The tea was fine, but most of all I liked the view.

At the time, watching him walk away into Regency Square, she'd thought mostly of herself. Only later did she realise he'd had a limp. He had not limped when she'd first known him, but it seemed habitual, long-term. She thought back to a brief mention of a minor car accident in one of his early letters. The way he sat back in his chair in the café, the way he spoke to the waitress – he didn't conduct himself like someone with an injury. But in her memory, she saw him pressing down hard with both hands on the table as he rose to his feet.

She remembered a rare morning off for Robert, last summer, when they'd taken the children to the beach. 'It's an all right place to live, isn't it?' she'd said.

Robert, his eyes darkly ringed, had said, 'I suppose. Course, it's all mafia, the seafront.' He had aimed down the sight of his index finger at Michael and Linda. 'Rotten to the core.'

The Lighthouse Café. What had she been thinking? Robert probably had eyes all the way along the promenade. But what had she done wrong, really? She had walked to the seafront. Looked at a café. Walked away.

In her memory, she saw it like one of those modern paintings where nothing looked quite right. The sky and sea were made of the same glass as the Lighthouse's big windows. The mansion blocks in the square were the colour of buttermilk.

Paul Landry had waved to her, but she hadn't waved back.

I was surprised you chose somewhere so out in the open, Dee. I wonder if that stopped you from saying hello.

I once read a news article about a woman who cured her chronic fear of dogs little by little. She started off at Easter, standing half a mile away from a poodle, and ended up sleeping with a wolf on Christmas Eve. That's a rough sketch, of course.

I will be in the Bond Street tearooms, on Saturday at 2 p.m. If you want to watch me drink another beverage.

As she took the alleyway leading to Bond Street, she saw workmen demolishing the Europa cinema. They'd taken the face off it, and now wandered away for their lunch break. Daisy felt voyeuristic, looking in on the tiers exposed to the street. The Europa had once been a drama theatre, and brick dust now covered the balustrades. The seats had been ripped out, and a pile of joists lay like campfire kindling in the stalls. Daisy looked in from where the stage used to be. They'd torn up the floor, and she could see down into the basement.

A sad loss. The Europa showed banned and censored films every Sunday. *Had* shown.

When she saw Paul coming down the alleyway, she walked towards him, determined, this time, to speak. He had travelled to see her, and she didn't want to let him down again. Still, the nerves sparked. There he was, this man made out of words. Yards away, and closing. He wore a blue shirt, open at the collar, and a long grey coat. She dropped her handbag, and he stopped. He hesitated, and then laughed. 'I guess you dropped that for me to pick up. Like in the movies. A reason to talk.'

She felt herself blushing.

'It's a nice idea,' Paul said. 'The problem is, I have this injury . . . I'm very sorry, but I can't actually reach the bag.'

Daisy laughed at the absurdity of the situation. She bent down to retrieve the handbag. 'I'm sorry,' she said.

'Really, so am I,' said Paul. 'I'm usually very chivalrous, but the position I'd have to get into . . . I'd have to actually lie down!'

She laughed again. 'Stop it.'

'It would draw press photographers. We'd end up in the news.'

'I said *stop!*'

'It's nice to hear your voice again, Dee. The louder the better, I guess.'

He looked over her shoulder at the wreck of the cinema. He strolled towards the open front and leaned against one of the demolition vehicles. Daisy, remembering the tone of his letters, thought he might say, *I guess that's the way it crumbles, cinemawise*, or something similar. But he made no smart remarks.

Instead, he gave a solemn theatrical half-bow to the ghost of the audience.

'If you can bow, you could have picked up my handbag,' she said.

He smiled.

'I used to come here to watch all the highbrow stuff. Bergman and all that,' she said.

'Did you like those films?'

'They were all right. I would've liked to have known how to feel about them. I suppose you think that's silly. You can't learn how to feel about something, can you?'

'Sure you can. Why not? I'm a big believer in lifelong learning.'

They looked at each other, in the toothless mouth of the cinema. 'I don't know what I'm doing here,' she said.

'You live here. What am *I* doing here? – that's the big question.'

'I invited you.'

'You did.'

'I'm sorry I couldn't talk to you last month. You made the trip down, but I couldn't even manage to cross the road.'

'Lot of traffic.'

'Do you miss your home? Do you miss Canada?' she asked.

'I'll write it in a letter. We were going to get tea. You want to get tea?'

'I'm not sure. It seems too . . . open.'

'We're just two people taking refreshments. Just a couple of pen pals,' he said.

'Not everyone would see it that way.'

'No.'

'I feel a little strange about all of this.'

'Me too,' he said.

'But I'd like to see you again.'

'We have a lot in common, it turns out.'

Dear Dee,

I just saw Mutiny on the Bounty. *What a stinker! Sure, Brando is pretty enough, but even my British accent is better than his, and the whole film is really about cheese theft. Listen, would you like to spend a couple of hours in the same picturehouse as me? It seems obvious, really. I know those places are notorious, but I swear I wouldn't bother you. The auditorium lights flatter my complexion, especially when they turn them off. I know you are not scared of the dark, because you told me, last time we went to the Electric Theatre, about three hundred years ago. Shall we go to the Electric? Anything but* Lawrence of Arabia.

At home, she carefully cut out a square of newspaper and drew a circle around *The Loneliness of the Long Distance Runner*. She wrote a time in the margin. As she prepared to put the clipping into the envelope, she saw the listing for *A Very Private Affair*, the next day. She snipped it off. She could not stand the thought that he would joke about infidelity.

In the end, Robert came home late from work, so she couldn't go that first night. He was a little drunk, but not too bad. Tiny stars of liquid shone on his trousers: beer or splashback. He seemed edgy, restless. She stared deeply at her husband's face until it split into two overlapping images. Robert looked away first.

*

The Loneliness of the Long Distance Runner, the Electric, second attempt.

She watched Paul come in. He moved slowly down the aisle. At that pace, he could hide his limp. When he saw her, halfway down on the left, he stopped and sat on the right. He blinked behind his glasses, his eyes adjusting to the dark. He was working nights.

She had wondered all morning how it might feel to sit there with him. She had become anxious in cinemas before, for no obvious reason. But not this time. She looked across the aisle, and the words that came to mind surprised her. *For God's sake, Daisy, you've known him half your life.*

She stood and headed for the toilets. The cinema had hardly updated its pre-war interior. Thirty years of damp and gravity had taken a toll. The lobby looked like a sore throat now, with all that blotchy faded velvet. In the toilets, she stood before the mirror and acknowledged what time had done to her appearance. She waited for some ominous feeling to overtake her. Horror, or self-hatred, or mad passion. But she felt peaceful.

When she returned to the auditorium, she sat next to Paul. She didn't speak, or look at him. Wear had softened the seats. The lights dimmed further. *Wooooo.* He laced his fingers and placed them in his lap. She could feel him smiling. He slid down in his seat, and she remembered how he had done that, all those years before.

The film was good and bleak. She wondered if Paul would understand the accents, but he seemed just as engrossed. It was the prettiest, lightest feeling, being beside him. At the end, Daisy left before the national anthem. Paul didn't move.

And that was how it went, for a little while. They saw three films together over the next two weeks. They hardly spoke, and didn't touch.

Robert grew a moustache that year. He'd been suffering from cold sores, and wanted to hide the blemishes. Brylcreem had darkened his hair for so long that Daisy was surprised by the rusty orange colour of his moustache.

She opened the door to Harper, one Saturday morning. 'We need to talk,' he said, and she backed away.

'Why? What about?' she asked, too loud.

'Not you, him,' Harper said.

She turned to see her husband at the bottom of the stairs. When she looked back to Harper, he frowned.

That night, Daisy dreamed that the wall lights of the cinema lined the inside of her skull, like rivets.

On the Beat, Duke of York's, Preston Road.

During the two-reeler, she put her hand on the armrest (they never sat at the back) and watched the screen light on her own skin. The tendons and bones reminded her of the exposed structures of a building half-demolished. He put his hand over hers, slid his fingers into the gaps, and gripped. The delicate feeling moved up her arm, across her collarbone, down the other side.

They hadn't planned their visit, and when the main feature came on, Daisy soon realised that it was a police farce, and she didn't like it. 'I need some air,' she whispered, and walked out.

The rain fell gently. A train trundled over the viaduct,

only the bright window squares visible in the darkness, like little paintings in the sky. Paul soon emerged, blinking, and pulling up the collar on his coat. She waited for him to see her. She loved the way his face changed, when he did. The big beam.

'Too close to the bone, huh?' he said.

'Mm.'

'Apparently, it was a comedy. People falling about the aisles, in there. Maybe it's a British thing . . .'

'You don't find Norman Wisdom funny?'

Paul shook his head, his face serious. 'The guy is an idiot.'

Daisy laughed.

They walked around the block, an arm's length apart. Daisy imagined them as seen from above. A crane shot.

'The feeling of someone next to you in the dark . . .' Paul said. 'That's a real thing, you know.'

'Well, of course.'

'No, I mean it's scientific. I read about it. Humans know when someone's close by. It's an actual sense, like hearing.'

'It's so you can kill people before they kill you,' Daisy said.

'Remind me to sit away from your sword arm.'

'When Robert came home, the day after I saw you at the Lighthouse, I thought I might faint.'

'Not like you.'

'How would *you* know?' she said.

'You weren't afraid of anything when I first knew you. Remember when you broke the barricades?'

'No.'

'Remember *Casablanca*? Shouting at trained military personnel . . .'

'There wasn't so much to lose then,' she said.

She lay on the floor, amongst Michael's toy cars, exhausted on a Sunday afternoon. She half-thought, half-dreamed of Paul's wristwatch, its large white face. She liked the numerals, and felt like she knew how cold the glass would be against her skin. The smell of him would be deep-woven into the hide of the strap. Not that pleasant soap smell he had, but his real scent.

As she surfaced from these hazy thoughts, she heard Michael's concern. 'Mummy's not waking up,' he said.

Linda approached. 'Stand back, Michael.'

'I'll go and get something.'

'Good boy,' said Linda, crouching over her mother.

Daisy waited. She kept her eyes closed and tried to be absent. She wasn't playing dead. She didn't know what she was doing.

Linda put her head on Daisy's chest and listened. 'I can't hear a heartbeat.'

Daisy thought of all the actors she had seen playing dead, their chests sometimes fluttering, sometimes their eyelids. She wondered if lying there with her eyes closed was the only appropriate way to proceed with life.

Michael came back into the room. 'Is she all right?'

'I don't know!' Linda said. 'I don't know what to do. We should get someone.'

Daisy felt the pressure of Linda straddling her, sitting on her stomach, the girl's strong hands knitting together behind her neck. She felt her whole upper body being dragged forward and upwards. 'Wake up,' Linda grunted into her ear. 'Goddamn you, Mummy.'

Daisy opened her eyes and looked at her daughter, whose brown hair hung down over her face. 'Linda, I'm fine,' Daisy said.

Michael began to cry with relief, and dropped whatever he'd brought from the kitchen on the floor.

'We couldn't hear your heartbeat,' Linda said.

Daisy blinked. 'What did you fetch, Michael?' she asked.

'A packet of butter,' Michael said.

'The correct course,' said Daisy, 'if you think there's a serious problem, is to call for the emergency services.'

What a joke, Daisy thought. Imagine Ray Harper coming to her aid.

Linda trembled slightly, and Daisy got to her knees and embraced her daughter. 'Linda, love. Perhaps we should talk about your language. "*Goddamn you, Mummy*"?'

Linda looked away. Daisy couldn't tell if she was smirking or ashamed.

What Ever Happened to Baby Jane, the Curzon.

The cinema was full of too-old Teddy boys, a decade late for their own clothes, hurling food at each other. Paul asked them to stop.

'Sod off, Yank!'

Paul sat down, and whispered to Daisy, 'I didn't deserve *that*.'

'It's hard for them,' Daisy said. 'They bought tickets for an X-rated film. Probably expected something a bit racier than Bette, Joan and a dead parakeet.'

She glanced nervously towards the entrance.

'Are you worried about him walking in?' Paul asked.

'Of course. Irrational, I suppose. He hates films.'

'Do you think he's going to come and arrest these guys?' Paul nodded to the Teds.

'Not his scene,' Daisy said. 'I'm not sure he really arrests people, anyway.'

'It's difficult to know what you really think of him.'

Daisy shrugged. 'I don't know where he is.'

'Right now?'

'Ever.'

'It must be a hard job,' said Paul.

'The people he works with. The criminals, I mean. They're a new type. Sordid. The things they do are wicked, but not in an interesting way. Not like up there,' she said, gesturing to the screen. 'It's meaningless. I think it gives him this idea that people are disgusting. Why wouldn't he think that?'

Paul nodded slowly.

'And then,' Daisy continued, 'he does his calculations, and he realises that he's human, too, and therefore also disgusting.'

'And you? What does he think of you?'

Daisy shook her head, and then looked over her shoulder again.

'Do you want to go somewhere else?' he said.

'No.'

'We might have to, eventually,' said Paul, because the Palladium had closed down, along with the Kemptown Odeon – the first wave of closures, although they didn't know it then.

*

144

'Bring me the kettle out,' Robert called from the garden, one evening in August.

'What do you want, tea?' Daisy said.

'No.'

Daisy brought him boiling water. Robert took the kettle, and looked at her. His mouth hung open. He suffered from grass allergies, but he liked the garden. The swing chair creaked.

'What is it?' Daisy said. 'What's wrong?'

'Bindweed,' he said.

With his finger, he traced a vine with large, lush green leaves and bright white flowers, as it gushed over the fence from next door, spread all the way along the patio, and coiled around the drainpipe. The tail of the vine wove in and out of the slats of the shed, too. Robert bent down, and picked up a garden spade strangled by the weed. As he lifted the shaft, half of the garden seemed to rise up, and the fence groaned. He ripped the spade away.

The trumpet-shaped flowers glowed in the dusk, closing for the day. 'These are nice, at least,' Daisy said, stroking the underside of one of the flowers, thinking of poor Marilyn's dress from *The Seven Year Itch*.

Robert laughed bitterly and began to pour boiling water over the roots. 'You see it all over the banks when you're on the train to London. When we're all dead and gone, this stuff will take over the world.'

He reached down into the steaming undergrowth, wrapped the vine four times around his fist, and pulled. There was a deep tearing sound from the soil. 'Not yet, though,' Robert said.

The next morning, she smacked her hip against the table as she cleared away the breakfast things. Only she and Michael were in the kitchen. She closed her eyes and let the pain dig in, fade out. She hummed an old Dinah Shore song about how love makes you clumsy.

When she opened her eyes again, Michael frowned at her, a sharp angle of toast in his hand.

'Are you okay, Michael? What is it?'

'You don't sing, Mummy,' Michael said.

1998

The house lights lit the way across Stephen's overgrown lawn. Over time, they'd worn a path between the house and the shed, and Mike felt the give of the earth as he walked. Some months, this was the only grass he stepped on.

Stephen rooted for the key in his pocket. Mike took a few pulls of spring air. His senses sharpened here, and he took note of every eruption, every death. 'After you,' Stephen said, dragging the door open through the tangle of grass.

The driver nodded.

Over the months, they'd made changes – to themselves, and the shed. Stephen's punches had improved, and he now wore padded gloves. Mike had changed, too. During the early days, he'd moved with the blow, to lessen its impact, but that ignored the fundamental point of the meetings: he'd agreed to be hit. Why not get himself in shape, so he could absorb *more* punches? Soon enough, he'd found himself flicking through Linda's *Callanetics Countdown*, and doing some of the exercises on his kitchenette floor. He'd seen a documentary once, on boxing, where a young amateur had described the concept of a 'conditioned face'. Your skin gets used to being struck. It grows back stronger. It cuts less easily. That happened to Mike's body.

They'd gone halves on a halogen heater, and they brought with them a cool box of beers and ice packs. They kept a small tin of medical supplies in the corner: a styptic pencil, bandages, plasters, Sudocrem, Ralgex, Voltarol, Vaseline.

A few deep breaths now, and they began.

The driver no longer turned his back. It had taken a long time to get rid of the instinct. Standing against the wall helped. Now, the first blow thrilled him most. It made him want to laugh. Just giving up the power of self-defence. It was mad. That first strike seemed to re-enliven the old wounds and bruises. He felt the pattern of the pedestrian's hitting bloom on his body.

After a few minutes, though, the driver began to feel a more urgent pain in his ribs. The sensation radiated out, across his back, even his teeth. The heater glowed orange, and rotated, and the driver felt like he was being roasted alive. The pedestrian slowed, his blows becoming oblique, open-gloved slaps. Eventually, he rested his wrists on the driver's shoulder and hip. 'You okay?' he asked.

'Yep,' the driver said, but he knew something wasn't right.

Sometimes, when Mike picked Lucas up from school, they'd just sit in the car with the interior light on, talking. You couldn't have a conversation with Lucas while driving, because he couldn't see your lips. Mike unclicked his seatbelt and turned to face his nephew.

'Uncle Mike?' Lucas said. 'Can I ask you a question?'

'Yes, mate.'

'There's this girl at school.'

'Oh, shit. Okay. Right. Great. That's great.'

Lucas looked puzzled. 'It's not that great. Not yet.'

'No. Well, what have you done about it?'

'Pardon?'

'Have you asked her out?'

'Well we've sort of got a . . . it's not a date, but you know.'

'That's good!'

'It's not for a while. It's just that I feel like she won't take me seriously. As an option.'

Mike tried to think of what Stephen might have said in this situation, but his mind went blank. 'You've got to be assertive. She needs to know that you are calling the shots. You need to show her what you're made of.'

Lucas frowned at his uncle's catchphrase.

'You've got to dominate the situation,' Mike said.

'What?'

'Dom-in-ate.'

'No, I heard you. I just can't believe you said it.'

'Eh?'

'I just. I don't think that's very good advice, Uncle Mike.'

Mike opened his arms to protest, but then sighed. 'Yeah. You know, I'm not particularly successful with birds. Women,' he said. 'I don't have a great record.'

'That's starting to make sense,' Lucas said.

Mike shoved him lazily. 'Oi. You. Don't be cheeky.'

Lucas laughed, and his hearing aid squealed. Outside, the crowds leaving school thinned out to latch-key stragglers, blue and pink in the dusk and street light, shaking sips of Lilt out of cans they'd opened just a crack.

'Listen,' Mike said.

'I'll do my best,' Lucas said.

'I'm not the person to ask. Truth is, I'd rather be you than me.'

'Oh, come on. What, you'd rather be the deaf kid?'

'A smart, nice, funny young geezer.'

Mike looked away, but Lucas studied him. 'You have no idea, do you, Uncle Mike?'

'Nope. Not a clue, mate. Not. A. Clue.'

For Mike, overcoming premature ejaculation proved a long process. 'I suppose that's rather the point,' Stephen said. For one of the exercises in the Taoist book, Mike had to intermittently stop his flow of piss. He could feel the muscles behind his balls (he had muscles behind his balls, it turned out) trembling with the strain. If someone else came to the urinals at work, he stopped the exercise immediately.

One morning, Mike got to work early and read the Taoist book in his car. The whole philosophy was that, rather than trying to stop yourself enjoying the pleasure, you were supposed to get used to handling *more*. You were supposed to feel the rising orgasm in your shoulders and your hands. 'Weightlifters don't choose small dumbbells in the gymnasium, to prove they can *lift* something,' the book said. 'They choose the largest weights they can tolerate, and then they push that limit further each time. They become strong by confronting their weakness, over and again.'

The book had clearly been read many times, and this made Mike wonder about Stephen. One page had the corner turned down. Someone had underlined a phrase: 'Your goal, at this point, should be to have sex without ejaculating at all.' A pencil line led to a comment in the margin, the handwriting unmistakably feminine – slanted, with small, regular loops. It was, in all likelihood, the writing of Stephen's wife.

Yeah right!!! she'd written.

Mike dropped the book into the footwell, and rested his head on the steering wheel. When you fall in love with someone, you marry them. When you marry them, you are one certificate closer to death. Death is written into marriage, it's part of the contract. Just look at his parents. Talking to Stephen should have reinforced that morbid view, but for some reason it didn't. The scant traces of Stephen's wife – the photographs, their daughter's growing resemblance, the comment in the margin of the book – they were tender and fresh.

He took the bicycle out one Saturday morning. He had assumed that his exercise regime would give him some respiratory fitness, but cycling uphill, in a coastal headwind, proved brutal. He'd chosen the wrong footwear – too flat – and couldn't get used to the toe cage. Motorists insulted him.

He pulled over after fifteen minutes. He felt none of the freedom and flight he remembered from childhood cycling. The landscape around him was desolate, and his lungs felt scoured, acidic.

Discouraged, Mike walked his bicycle back to the flats, and lugged it up the stairs. That night, he woke a couple of times, imagining his head crushed by a car, the wheel of the bicycle spinning in the roadside grass. He imagined his face, recognisable, but flattened out, like a cardboard cut-out mask on the back of a cereal packet. He thought about going downstairs and taking the bike to the tip, but he didn't. Of the lessons he'd learned from Stephen, one thing stood out above all others: people could get better. He hadn't believed in change, very much, before meeting Stephen.

When the weather improved, he went out twice a week, cycling inland, to avoid the strong spring winds. He loved the feeling, when he got home, that his legs might just collapse, but it got harder and harder to achieve that level of exhaustion. He never thought he would buy cycle shorts, but he did because he needed the padding once his rides got longer. It felt like he had a nappy on. He wore them under his old football shorts, so as not to be on display. A cycle path beside the dual carriageway took him out onto the tilting Downland plains. Soon enough, he'd fall into a sort of trance-like state. He'd stop for a piss and not know where the hell he was.

When he looked in the mirror, these days, he could barely believe it. Before he met Stephen, he had sort of given up on his body – it had become like a toddler's: fatty shoulders, a pot belly, teardrop breasts. Now, his old physique began to re-emerge, only heavier and hairier. The thick wide arms, the plates of chest muscle, the swollen calves.

One Saturday, a cyclist in blue shot past him on one of the narrow roads above Ringdean. A woman. Mike flicked up to the big ring and dug in hard, got up out of his seat. She had a high cadence, a smooth power, and he found it tough to stay in touch, but she kept the headwind off him, and he fought for her back wheel. She remained unaware, for a while, that she was being drafted. She spat into the trees. Then she turned, and saw him. She wore those sports sunglasses – the wrap-around ones with mirrored lenses. She dropped him, pulled away as though truck-towed.

It took a huge amount of energy to catch up, and she shook her head when she saw him again. Up through the gears, and she was gone. He had to admire her technique, her *stillness*. It seemed like she only had to *think* about going faster, whereas Mike had to literally talk to his legs. 'Come on, you fuckers!' he said.

He leaned to grasp the downtube shifter. It snapped off in his hand, and he tumbled forward, skidding off the bike. 'Bastard!' he cried. He rolled into the weeds. His left leg was numb, and his right hand, unfortunately, was not. He put his head between his knees to stave off the nausea. 'Fuck, fuck, fuck,' he said.

Moments later, he heard the precise click of her freewheel, and the crunch of her cleats on the tarmac. 'Here's where you jump back on your bike and leave me for dead,' she said.

'Very funny,' he said.

'You know, it would have been easier just to ask me if I wanted to go for a drink.'

He peered up at her broad-shouldered silhouette. The sun and brittle trees looked small behind her.

'Do you want to go for a drink?' Mike said.

'No.' She laughed. 'Come on, let's have a look at you.'

He stood. His long-sleeved T-shirt was shredded from the elbow to the shoulder. Something bad had happened to his right hand. The fingers wouldn't move properly.

'So. How do I look?' he said.

She hesitated. 'You're very . . .'

'Bloody?'

'These clothes, this haircut. It's all *very* eighties.'

'Are you honestly trying to tell me that it's *not* the nineteen-eighties?' he said.

'Let me give you some advice,' she said, looking at his bike. 'Your brake pads are worn past the line. Your cables are rusted, and your seat is too low, which is probably because – looking at you – you are too short for this frame. Also, it's still wet, so get mudguards, for everyone's sake. If you don't know what you're doing, take it to Mountfield's Cycles.'

'Okay, whatever.'

'I'm not finished. Most importantly: don't get all pumped up when a woman overtakes you.'

He squinted at her. Her hair was longer on one side than the other. 'Have we met?'

'Jesus Christ Almighty!' she said. Her face became serious, and she really looked at him. In a quieter voice, she said, 'You'll have to do a lot better than that. Come on, there's a Little Chef up the road.'

'You'll have a cup of tea with me?'

'I'm going to make you order the most embarrassing thing on the menu.'

The view from the window of the Little Chef felt American. He'd never visited the States, but he'd seen *Northern Exposure*. Pylons, wide roads and distant pines. A group of stoned teenagers pushed the free hot drink refills to the limit, buzzing with Nescafé and shouting, 'Oi, garçon, coffee!' every five minutes.

She told him she favoured Audax cycling, a non-competitive endurance sport where you had a certain number of days to complete a set distance. 'You're basically left to your own devices. If you lose some time one day, you have to cycle through the night, sleep in a bus shelter or something. I rode sixteen straight hours, once.'

'Right. Could've done with knowing that before I tried to catch you.'

'I like the scenery. I discovered, when I was pretty young, that I could tolerate quite a lot of physical pain.'

Suddenly, it clicked for Mike – it was the way she used two fingers on each hand to trace the narrow winding roads. 'Shit,' he said. 'I *have* met you before. You work at the school.'

The parents' evening.

'I do. And you are . . .'

'Well, I'm . . . God, I'm . . .' There was no way out of it. 'I'm Lucas Seacombe's uncle.'

Her eyes widened.

'This is pretty embarrassing,' he said.

'I don't think there's anything to be embarrassed about,' she said.

'I've said a few things that I might not have said, had I known.'

She shrugged. 'Look,' she said. 'Everyone knows someone. How else do people meet? Anyway, Lucas is *amazing*.'

'Yeah,' said Mike sadly. 'Yeah, he is.'

The waitress came over.

'I'll have a bacon sandwich and a cup of tea, please,' said Mike. He nodded to Cassie but she raised her eyebrows and he sighed. 'She'll have the Intergalactic Super Space Station Breakfast.'

'Sorry, sir, could you say that again,' said the waitress.

Finally, the day of the Deaf pub night came round. A Wednesday. That morning, Lucas had biology with Cassie. In front of them, mung beans rested on a paper towel. Lucas didn't know why. Cassie studied the instructions. Since they'd met, the world looked sharper to Lucas. Details bloomed out of the blur.

He tapped her shoulder. *Did you know that Leonardo da Vinci invented the scissors*, he signed. Finger-spelling Leonardo da Vinci was a chore, but he'd been reading about hairdressing, to impress her.

Interesting, she signed. She seemed distracted. Perhaps she was nervous about the evening ahead, too.

And did you know that hairdressers . . . he opened her notebook, and wrote: HAVE THE LOWEST SUICIDE RATE OF ANY PROFESSION.

GOOD! she wrote. OF COURSE, IT WOULD BE 'BARBERCIDE'.

Lucas didn't get the joke.

Iona came over with a stack of homemade flyers. Lucas and Iona had hardly spoken since Cassie arrived. She'd fallen in with a crowd of older girls from the art college, and now had a severe undercut and dyed black hair. Most people listened to the Spice Girls, but Iona had written GOUGE AWAY on her art portfolio. She put a flyer on the desk. 'It's for my band, "Shovel". We have a gig, tonight.' She'd always been a clear speaker.

'Thanks, but I'm deaf,' Lucas said.

Iona frowned. 'You used to listen to music at my house. You and Nicky used to sit by the speaker.'

He shrugged. 'I can't tonight, anyway. Me and Cassie are going out.'

'Are we?' Cassie said.

Iona drifted off to leaflet the other desks.

It's the Deaf pub night, Lucas signed. *Remember? Which you're forcing me to go to!*

Tonight? Cassie signed. 'Shit.'

Lucas tried to swallow the hurt. *It's okay if you're busy. We can do it another time.*

No. It's fine. I'll come.

Before leaving the house that evening, Lucas did press-ups in his bedroom, showered for forty minutes, and put on a black roll-neck, which felt cool against his shaved skin. In the hallway, his mum considered him carefully. These days, she spent half the time in a dream world, the other half in a state of twitchy alertness. Before, Lucas would have monitored her behaviour, but since meeting Cassie, he couldn't really be bothered.

'Where are you going?' she said.

'Pardon?' he said.

'You heard.'

'Just out. A school thing. In town.'

'   wet hair?'

'Mum, Jesus.'

'   girl involved?'

'Maybe.'

She reached out to adjust the neck of his pullover, but he dodged her and grinned.

'Lucas,   anyth   you're not comfortable   press people.'

'Mum, girls aren't evil, you know.'

157

'I just don't want you   taken advantage of.'

'Chance'd be a fine thing,' he said.

'Lucas!'

But he ran for the door, before she could remind him of curfew times or force him to wear a coat.

He walked through town and waited for Cassie in a square near the seafront. The smell of fried fish wafted out of the Regency Restaurant. Street drinkers lounged on benches, sleeping bags pulled down to their ankles. In the grass, Lucas found a perfectly spherical stone – a beach pebble which had made its way up the promenade and across the road. It was so round he'd almost kicked it, mistaking it for a dog ball. A little miracle. He picked up the stone and weighed it in his hand. He took its uncanny roundness as a good omen for the evening ahead, and slipped it into his pocket.

For weeks, Lucas had imagined coolly embracing Cassie, perhaps kissing her on both cheeks, but now he flinched when she tapped his shoulder. 'Let's go,' she said. As they walked, Lucas glanced at their reflection in the dark shopfront windows. She wore pinstripe trousers and a red cowl-neck sweater, and carried a black leather shoulder bag. He was taller than her by a head. They looked good together.

Outside the pub, a chalkboard sign read: 'UNDER THE STREET LIGHT' – DEAF CABARET, OPEN STAGE.

He followed Cassie inside. Lucas had been in pubs before, but none like this. It was so *bright*, for a start. Chandeliers hung from the ceiling, and the bar was lit up like the star prize on a game show. Two golden cherubs burst out of the wall, holding a huge clock. A man at one end of the bar signed to a friend at the other. Everyone signed.

You okay? Cassie signed.

Bit nervous. He tapped his chest with a hooked finger.

Usually, Lucas found parties impossible – the chaos of music in his hearing aids, and rooms too dark to lip-read. But here, he saw snatches of signed conversation rise up with perfect clarity:

No, no, because she's seventy. She's much too old for

. . . everytime. Tuesdays are busy because of the kids

. . . an implant. Yes, actually the technology is really improving and

. . . injured, and they've still got to beat Derby. It won't be easy

. . . is that right? I never see him anymore. Last time was so painful and I drank too much, and I felt . . .

He'd never seen so much language in a place.

One tall man came clearly into view. He wore a blue shirt, the short sleeves of which clung tight to his shoulders. Elegant tattoos decorated his thick arms: a burning star, a labyrinth. He had long black hair. Cassie hugged him, and he pinched her cheek.

This is Dan, my brother, Cassie signed. She performed his sign name, but Lucas didn't catch it.

Welcome to our crazy town, Dan signed.

Thank you, Lucas signed. His fingers stiffened, and his mind emptied. *It's nice here.*

Are you hearing? Dan asked.

Fuck off, Cassie signed, and slapped her brother's arm.

The siblings began to sign so quickly that Lucas couldn't follow.

. . . not being cruel! Sometimes hearing teacher deaf with a small d, that's all, Dan signed.

Just remember how things were for you, before, Cassie replied.

Dan rolled his eyes. He turned to Lucas, and signed more slowly. *I'm really happy to see you here, tonight. Anything you need, just wave.*

Lucas waved spontaneously, and hated himself. Then, the most beautiful woman he had ever seen approached Dan and squeezed his bicep. She was about twenty-five, Asian, and wore a long white shirt, black jeans and bright yellow loafers. She was so gorgeous, Lucas didn't even fancy her. She made him want to *laugh*. She signed hello, and introduced herself, but Lucas couldn't keep his eyes on her hands.

Dan smiled broadly. He kissed the woman, and they took a step back from each other and began to sign.

Dan behaved as if it was perfectly normal for him to have a girlfriend, and for that girlfriend to be unbelievably fit. And Dan was *Deaf*. Just as Lucas began to calculate what that might mean for *him*, and his future, something even stranger happened. The woman bent down to take a mobile phone from her handbag, and she *answered* it. She put it to her ear, and spoke. She was *hearing*.

He had no time to dwell on such mysteries. Dan guided him to a semicircle in front of a small stage. Lucas sat near the back, grateful for a break from all the conversation. Cassie returned from the bar with a Coke for him, and a pint of Guinness for herself. She looked at her watch.

Lucas took the perfectly round stone from his pocket, and showed it to her.

What is it?

Just a stone.

It's very . . . round.

It's for you.

Cassie weighed the stone in her hand, and smiled. *Thanks. It's really nice.*

An old lady shuffled past to get to her seat, and she knocked Cassie's arm, spilling some of the Guinness. Cassie stood, and stared down in horror at the black stain spreading on her red jumper. Lucas got some paper towels from the toilet, but she looked miserable when he came back. He wondered if he was cramping her style.

Such thoughts vanished when the entertainment began. The first act was called 'Hearing Pete'. The title character, an obnoxious man in a suit, carried a number of caption boards and shouted things in English, using exaggerated lip patterns. Next to him, a woman gave sarcastic interpretations in BSL.

'EXACTLY HOW DEAF ARE YOU?' said Hearing Pete, holding up a board with the same words.

Are you worth bothering with? the interpreter signed.

'WHERE DO YOU WORK?'

Are you claiming benefits, funded by me, the taxpayer?

'IS SIGN LANGUAGE INTERNATIONAL?'

Like English.

'ARE YOU <u>SURE</u> YOU CAN'T HEAR?'

Didn't we solve the whole deaf problem?

Lucas roared with recognition.

At intervals, Hearing Pete said, 'CAN YOU LIP-READ?' and everyone shook their heads and said, 'No!' as if this was a well-known joke.

I should be taking notes, Lucas signed to Cassie. She smiled weakly.

Hearing Pete's act finished with the interpreter bashing him with his caption boards, and the audience clapped in BSL – their hands raised and waving.

The poets came next. At first, Lucas tried to translate the poems into English, but they used a lot of signs he didn't know, so he eventually just let the images slide over him. The last poet, a thin, grey-haired rocker, performed a poem about an argument he had had with a former lover. Initially, it seemed ridiculous when the man switched into the body of the young woman, but by the end of the poem, Lucas felt like he might cry. It finished with the man pondering his reflection in a toyshop window.

Lucas turned to Cassie, but she'd gone. The lights came up, and people drifted to the bar. He peered into the crowd, but couldn't see her. Thinking she'd probably gone to the toilet, he shuffled over to a table near the window, to wait.

After ten minutes, Dan sat down opposite, with two whiskies. He pushed one towards Lucas.

No thanks, I don't drink, Lucas signed. *Have you seen Cassie?*

Dan smiled.

She was here, Lucas signed, *watching the show, but . . .*

This is what happens. It's normal.

What?

They go, Dan signed. *They leave.*

I don't understand.

I know you don't. Come and meet some people.

Lucas sat still.

We're not monsters, Dan signed.

I know.

And neither are you.

Dan downed one of the whiskies, and stood. *You can sit here and wait if you want, but she's gone*, he signed. *It's what happens when you chase hearing girls.*

I'm not chasing her! Anyway, you have a hearing girlfriend.

Yes, but she pursued me. You're Deaf. When Deaf boys chase hearing girls, they fall into the big hole between. Dan opened the rift with his hands, and showed Lucas plummeting into the void. *You end up being neither.*

I'll be both! Lucas replied sharply. *Leave me alone. I'll be both.*

Dan smiled. *Your signing is much better when you're angry. More flow. You should come back here again. On your own.*

Maybe I will, Lucas signed, and then he looked away, ending the conversation.

He waited a little longer, and then made a circuit of the room. People treated him kindly. They knew exactly who he was looking for, but no, they hadn't seen her. When the cherub clock said ten, he slipped out, and caught the bus back to Ringdean.

The moon glared, as did the strip lights inside the bus. The top deck smelled of perfume and kebabs. He told himself Cassie probably had a good reason for abandoning him like that. It wasn't so much her leaving that upset him, as the fact she didn't say goodbye.

As she filled the reservations shelf at the library, Linda thought of Paul Landry's bloodless fingers around the handle of his blue bag. In her dreams, that bag was filled with viscera, staining the fabric black.

She'd begun to have intrusive memories, too. She remembered coming home from school one winter afternoon, and letting herself in to what she thought was an empty house. Half-past four, no lights, the living room a jumble of dark shapes.

'Linda,' her dad said, and she almost screamed. He sat on a dining chair, which he'd turned around to face the room. She could only make out his silhouette against the meagre light coming through the patio doors – she could see his arm across the chair back, the spread of his legs, the shining leather of his shoes.

'Why aren't the lights on? Has the power gone?' she said.

A derisory laugh. 'Not quite.'

'Is everything okay?'

'When were you going to tell me, Linda?' he said.

That was how he got you. He'd ask that bloody question, and then fall silent, waiting for you to confess every damned thing you'd ever done. Always the same show. Her brother had fallen apart many times in the face of that question.

'Tell you *what?*' she said.

'I think you know.'

'My conscience is clear,' she said. It wasn't. Not at fourteen years old. She thought of Owen Gregory from school, how she had pressed herself against his thigh when they kissed outside the Duke of York's. How she'd taken hold of him through his trousers. And now she heard the unsteadiness of her breath in the dark room. She could have switched the light on, but she didn't want to.

'Linda, you need to watch your mouth.'

'I haven't said anything.'

'You have. A boy at your school. You told him about me and Harper giving that kid from Minnie's a good hiding.'

'I didn't,' she said.

'Now you're lying. Don't lie to me.'

'I'm not.'

'My job is to know when people are lying. Whores and crooks. Don't make me think of you that way.'

Linda did not reply. She *had* told Owen about the beating, mouth against his ear.

'Privacy,' her dad said. 'Privacy is very important to us. What is said between these walls, stays here. It's all I ask of you, Linda. Do what you like, but do it with your mouth shut.'

The front door opened behind her. Her brother came in. 'S'dark!' Michael said, and he hit the light. Linda squinted, her tears exposed, but her dad simply closed his eyes, as if he'd been asleep the whole time.

It was a false memory. It had to be. Her dad had already left the police by the time she turned fourteen. The dates were all wrong. You couldn't trust memory.

Now, in the corner of the kitchen window, she saw a patch of red. Not blood, but a mass of ladybirds, crawling on top of each other, their legs slipping on the slick armour of the ones below, their wings sputtering.

Outside, beyond the ladybirds, Lucas trudged along Bramble Avenue towards home, his rucksack straps slipping to the crooks of his arms.

Linda rinsed out her vodka glass in the sink, and swilled some water around her mouth, spat. A ladybird in your garden was nice, but a hundred of them in your kitchen was not.

When she leaned in to study them, she detected their sour, putrid smell, like bins.

The light in the hall went on and off. Absently, Linda responded, and soon Lucas stood in the kitchen with her. She kissed his cheek, breathed in the cold metallic smell of the outdoors on his skin. 'Come and see this,' she said, and led him over to the window.

He flinched when he saw the ladybirds. 'Oh,' he said. 'Housemates.'

'What do you think it means?' Linda said.

Lucas looked at her.

'What does it mean?' she said again.

'Weather's up and down. They're cold, probably.'

'I think I've been bitten,' Linda said, scratching her arm.

'Cold and hungry,' he said, and made to leave the room.

'Lucas,' she said, grasping his wrist.

He turned to her.

'Have you thought about what you're going to do, once you've finished school?'

'Rock star,' he said.

'Seriously.'

'There's some jobs going at the school.'

'The *school*? Really? Why would you want to stay *there*?'

He shrugged.

'Anyway, what kind of jobs?'

'Caretaker-type jobs. Looking after the sports fields and that.'

'No. No way,' Linda said. 'You're a clever boy, Lucas. I'm not having you cleaning toilets in a school.'

'Well, I guess I'll just choose from the wealth of other fucking options, eh?'

'I beg your pardon!' she said. 'What's wrong with you, Lucas?'

'What's wrong with *you*, Mum?'

'Nothing.'

'Tell you what: find me some good jobs for a deaf boy, and I'll apply, okay?'

'There are plenty of opportunities out there, if you bothered to look.'

'Name one.'

Her mind went blank. Lots of the kids in his year would be getting these new call centre jobs with Amex, but he couldn't very well do that.

'Yeah,' he said, walking out. 'Do me a shortlist.'

He left, and she went through to the living room, got the Reader's Digest encyclopaedia and opened it at L.

Coccinella Septempunctata. The name 'ladybird' apparently came from the fact that the Virgin Mary wore a red cloak in early paintings. The seven spots symbolised the seven sorrows. In Polish, the ladybird was known as 'God's little cow'. But Lucas was right: they were insects, not omens.

Linda opened the window, but the creatures remained. The book said that their foul smell came from a fluid secreted by the joints to deter predators. To stay alive, ladybirds played dead. They pretended to rot. Wonder how long *that* works, thought Linda.

Lucas's dad was called Peter. He'd been parachuted into a strategic role with Library Services in 1978. Most of the members of the council's library management team were stuffy grey men in cheap suits, but Peter had a Springsteen look about him. He wore jeans which clung to a pert pair of buttocks, and spilled out over stack-heeled boots. He wore bomber jackets and check shirts, no tie. He had big ideas about libraries as centres for social change. He eagerly met the frontline staff, and when he came into Hove Library, he looked Linda right in the eye and said, 'I believe we can do something good'.

'So do I,' she said, holding his gaze.

He cracked first, smiled, whispered, 'You know, Linda, I'm making this up as I go along.'

He took her date stamp, and pressed it onto the back of his hand. A three-week loan.

Peter was solitary, self-sufficient. As a film fan, Linda had learned to love such men. The movies were full of obsessive, moody, gorgeous loners, and here was this bloke living out of a suitcase, lodging with an old lady in a house overlooking St Ann's Well Gardens. He was an amateur long-distance runner – a marathon man. 'I don't mind pain,' he said. 'I can take it. I don't care how badly you treat me.'

She'd laugh at those deep pronouncements, but he just gazed at her, straight-faced. The other girls at the library said he was the real thing, and that – at her age – this was probably her last chance.

She liked that Peter took over library story time, and read to the children on Saturday afternoons. She liked that he went out drinking with Michael, and that he had the guts to stroll into the library and announce, in front of her line manager, that he was taking her to dinner.

Linda had watched the wrong kind of films – the ones where, even if a relationship breaks down, the two characters have to spend eighty per cent of the screen time together. But Peter left before the first act climax, and by then Linda was pregnant. He had a wife and child in Tamworth, and another fiancée in Burton-on-Trent. Virtually a bigamist. He didn't even know anything about libraries, really; the council cancelled his contract and called it a failed experiment. It was all so obvious and trite. Had it really been a film, Linda would have walked out halfway through. Her colleagues consoled her, delighted.

Michael drove up the M1 and tracked Peter down, dropped him on his doorstep with a left uppercut, and took three pounds out of his wallet. He placed the money in front of Linda, on the kitchen table at their parents' house, his knuckles swollen, his eyes watering.

With help from her mum, Linda made the best of it. Over the years, she ensured that Lucas had a sense of family, first with Daisy, and then with Mike, but at the age of thirteen, the boy had wanted to know about his dad, and so she made some calls and found Peter living alone and bankrupt in a small town in Staffordshire, where he worked in a supermarket. She explained that Lucas wanted to meet him. 'The thing is, I can't afford it,' he said, so she paid his train fare to Brighton.

Peter and Lucas were to meet in a department store café which had a big plate glass window looking onto the street. 'Oh,' Linda said outside, tapping her boy's arm. 'That's him.'

She nodded at the man in a brown suit jacket, cheap jeans and white trainers, sitting at a corner table. He had a WHSmith carrier bag, and he chewed the rim of his paper Pepsi cup.

'That man there?' Lucas said.

'Yes. I'm fairly sure that's Peter.'

'But he's a dosser, Mum.'

Linda wondered, briefly, where her boy had learned such a term. 'Oh, Lucas,' she said. 'Do you still want to meet him? It's totally up to you.'

'I'll see you outside Marks and Spencer in an hour.'

Linda shuffled across the street and watched from a distance as they shook hands. Peter fidgeted as he failed to understand Lucas's speech. Eventually, Lucas took out a notepad and they wrote to each other, passing the pen and pad back and forth. The meeting lasted twenty minutes, and when he emerged from the department store, Lucas tore out the sheets of notepaper and binned them.

Later, at home, he was quiet. His dad had given him some cheap games for the Commodore Amiga. Four blue disks with no boxes, wrapped in a red elastic band, which Lucas twanged now, sitting on the living room carpet, his legs stretched in front of him.

Linda tapped him on the shoulder. 'Are you upset?'

'Just confused.'

'Peter had a lot of problems. It wasn't personal. If he'd have got to know you . . .'

'It's not that.'

'What is it then?'

'Why did you like him?'

'It was a long time ago.'

'Before carrier bags?'

'Lucas.'

'You're out of his league, Mum.'

If there was something wrong with Lucas now, it had nothing to do with his absent father. Best not to think about it.

In April, Mike arranged to meet Cassie in a small pub in town. He got there first, and didn't much like the place: city locals, transients, off-season tourists, students. Football on the big screen. Reds against whites. North versus South. A mouthy local bellowed at the television, and Mike couldn't tune him out.

Cassie walked in, wearing pinstriped trousers and a red cowl-neck top. She worried at a dark stain near the hem of the sweater. Mike felt his blood stir. The mouthy local stared at her.

'Sorry I'm late,' she said. 'I had to be somewhere. And then this . . .' She pointed to the stain.

'These things happen. Have a drink.'

It had been a long time since he'd got properly drunk with a woman. He liked it. She sank pints of Guinness and slagged off eighties music, but Mike put 'I Can't Go For That (No Can Do)' on the jukebox and they did a stupid dance at the bar. They talked about cycling. She wanted to go to France for some endurance event. 'You should come,' she said. 'Something to train for.'

'I think that's a bit unrealistic.'

Cassie looked scorched. 'Why not? You're a free man, aren't you?'

He felt himself go cold. Was she one of those mad women? A bunny-boiler?

'Yeeaaahhh! Suck on that, you provincial fuckers!' the mouthy local shouted at the television. 'Get back to eating out the fucking bins!'

'Might want to watch your language,' Mike said.

The bloke gave Cassie a long, leering look before turning to Mike. 'If you don't like it, don't bring your daughter down the pub.'

Mike clenched his fists, but Cassie held onto his arm, kissed him. 'There, there, caveman. These alpha shows are all very well, but there are better ways to deal with a conflict like this.'

An hour later, she had stolen the mouthy local's jacket off the coat stand, and they ran through the lanes towards the beach. To Mike it felt like a true shared experience: the sound of the wind quickening, the red blink of boats out on the dark denim horizon.

'Wish we had our bikes!' Cassie shouted, the man's army-green jacket flapping from her fist.

They stumbled over the stones to the path which led out onto the groyne, from where they could look down on the cream of the sea. It was like settling stout down there. Cassie took a tobacco pouch and a playing card out of the man's coat. 'I bet he writes his number on this, for schoolgirls,' Cassie said. She dug back into the pocket and pulled out a photograph of a woman from the seventies – a perm and tinted glasses. Cassie's face fell. 'Oh. Here's his mum. Deceased.'

Mike grabbed the coat from her, and tried to put it on. It didn't fit across the shoulders.

'You're a big hunk of junk, Michael,' Cassie said. She took the coat and threw it over the edge of the groyne. The wind blew it back, flat against the stone, where it stayed for a few miraculous moments, arms out, before floating down into the dark Channel to swell and blister.

1962–3

Daisy and Paul watched a thriller at the Academy. A stalker on the loose. Daisy rode the peaks and troughs of tension, and totally forgot that it was early afternoon on a Wednesday. In the corner of her mind, she was aware of Paul's body next to her. She felt the heat of him, the rise and fall of his breathing. The actors spoke in low, urgent voices, their options for escape diminishing. Daisy reached up and ran her left hand along the back of Paul's neck, into the short, freshly barbered hair, which prickled against her fingers. He put his hand on her knee, and slid it up and over her thigh. Her skirt crumpled. On the screen, a man moved around a room, lifting objects, putting them down carefully. Paul's hand reached the dark band of nylon at the top of her tights. She scratched the back of his head, slowly, feeling the flesh move under her nails. She put her lips against his neck. The scene changed, and the light on his skin turned blue. He gripped the hem of her skirt. She could almost hear the hum of her blood. 'Out,' she whispered to him.

Moments later, they walked the red carpet of the dimly lit corridors. Daisy opened a door marked 'Staff', and Paul followed. They went past a couple of small offices, and through another door, which led to some stone steps that took them down into a storage area. Daisy recalled that the Academy had once been a Turkish bath, and behind the stacks of orange juice cartons and boxes of sweets, she saw tiles in faded Moorish design. Together, they walked to the wall, and she wiped the dust from the tiles.

It was like nothing she'd seen in the movies: daylight came through the high frosted windows, weeds grew out of the cracks in the floor, and a mould stain on one of the pipes looked like God, with the cloudy hair and big beard. There was the tinny smell of water and rust, and someone had dropped a tub of rainbow sherbet, which spread on the cement floor in a powder bomb of colour. She tried to reach out for him, but he shifted her hands away. He turned her around and held her gently against the wall.

'I won't kiss you,' she said.

He used only his hands. She had known, she supposed, that what he did was possible.

That afternoon she returned to an empty house. She washed. She drank tea with bubbles on the surface. She cried. She cleaned. What they had done was wrong in almost every way.

There was a knock on the door. Outside stood her husband with two men in good suits. Robert gestured to the older one, a slim man with greying hair. 'Daisy, this is Inspector Lyle, and . . . what's your name, again?'

'Ford. Inspector Ford,' said a younger, broader man.

'I'm going to show them around the house,' Robert said. Daisy couldn't read his expression.

'Would you like tea?' she said.

Robert laughed.

'That won't be necessary, thank you,' said Inspector Lyle. 'We shouldn't be long, Mrs Seacombe. I'm very sorry to interrupt your day.'

'Robert . . .?' Daisy said.

'Later. I'll talk to you later.'

They went up to the master bedroom. Daisy waited a few moments and then gathered a pile of towels and quietly climbed the stairs. She stopped near the top and, through the slightly open door of the bedroom, observed an odd scene. Inspector Lyle carefully laid her husband's ties on the bed. He studied each label. 'Quadrant Arcade,' he said. 'Where is that?'

'You know where it is,' said Robert. 'Regent Street.'

'Did you buy this tie yourself?'

'Simpson bought it me. No harm in that, is there? It's only the one.'

'What about *this* one?'

'Well, yeah, he bought that, too.'

Daisy watched Lyle handling a tie she'd never seen before. Black. Red spots. 'Burlington Arcade. Simpson, again?'

'Must have been, I suppose. Wouldn't go there on my own.'

As he put the tie on the bed, Lyle turned and caught her eye. Daisy continued to climb the stairs, as if she hadn't stopped at all. She put the towels in the bathroom. The men fell silent, waiting for her to go, and so she descended to the kitchen and opened the window. Out on the street, she heard a boy commentating on his own game of football, his voice rising to a climax. *He slashes through the defence! He tears them open! Shoots . . .*

Soon enough, Lyle and Ford reappeared with her husband. 'Yeah well,' Robert said. 'I never said that. It was Harper said that.'

The young Inspector nodded to Daisy as he passed the kitchen and opened the front door.

'I imagine we will be in touch,' Lyle said to Robert.

'Can't wait,' Robert said, with a childish shrug of his shoulders.

'Good afternoon, Mrs Seacombe,' Lyle called.

They left. Robert stood looking at the closed door. The light through the coloured glass flickered on his shirt.

'What was that about?' she said.

'Sod all. I offered to show them around. The bloke's a pansy, and what he is implying is fantastic. They're trying to put together some sort of investigation. "Corruption." It's an internal thing. Won't happen.'

'What are they saying you've done?' asked Daisy.

He stared at her, and her breath came uneasily. 'Robert,' she said.

'It's all bollocks. Politics. They're working out of the Town Hall, trying to put the frighteners on us. But it will come to nothing.'

'Should I talk to the children?'

'They won't find anything. That's why I showed them around.'

'Who *are* they?'

'The Yard.'

'Jesus.'

He walked towards her, hands in pockets. She couldn't look at him.

'Daisy,' he said.

'Yes?'

'You don't talk to anyone.'

She didn't know whether that was an observation or a command.

Robert went over to Ray Harper's that evening, and Daisy cooked sausages for the children and tried to act normally until they went to bed.

Later, she stood alone in the dark kitchen, hating herself. Across the road, a car was parked near the bus stop. A Morris. It had sat there all afternoon. The young man inside turned towards the house as if posing for a portrait. Daisy made a cup of cocoa, and took it outside. The sea was calm, and goldcrests scattered from fence posts at the cliff top as she approached the car. The last days of summer.

Stupidly, the man in the Morris looked away when he saw Daisy coming. She knocked on the window, and he lowered it.

'I've brought you a drink,' Daisy said.

'Pardon me? I don't know what you mean,' he said.

Daisy laughed. 'You're not exactly KG bloody B, are you?'

The inside of the car smelled of average cologne. He was the new type of policeman: young, bland. She offered him the mug. 'Come on,' she said. 'Or it'll get a skin on it.'

'I can't take the drink, madam, sorry,' he muttered. 'Wouldn't be right.'

Daisy took a sip, herself. 'What time does your shift finish?' she said.

'Look, madam,' the man said. 'It's for your own safety, all this.'

Daisy walked back to the house, thinking about the letters.

Robert didn't come home that night, and in the clammy early hours, Daisy woke and went to the storage closet under the stairs. She opened the top drawer of the filing cabinet, and took out her stack of *Picturegoer* magazines. Corners of Paul's letters, and torn flaps of envelopes, protruded from the pile. Daisy realised she couldn't take them to the bin. Not now. She removed as many of the letters as she could find, and folded them into a small metal money tin. She locked the money tin, and took it up to the cold attic. She crawled across the floorboards, and pushed the tin to the back, against the pink insulation foam.

When she came down, she brushed the white dust from her skirt. She heard a noise, and glanced up, but it was only Linda, watching her through the gap in her bedroom door. Daisy blew her a kiss, but Linda backed off into the shadows.

Michael started to act strangely that autumn. He couldn't sleep, and developed a rash on his neck. He tried every old trick to stay off school.

'You're not hot, love. And you haven't been sick. Is there something else?' Daisy said, as Michael lingered in the hallway.

'I feel poorly.'

'You know, Dad is going to be fine. He hasn't done anything wrong.'

'It's not to do with that,' Michael snapped. 'I need to stay home.'

'Michael. We've been through this.'

He rubbed his face, exhausted. The gesture seemed so grown up.

'What is it? Come on, love. You can tell me.'

'I'm going to ruin everything,' Michael said.

'What do you mean?'

'I'm going to do something wrong, and the man is going to catch me,' he said, in a low voice.

'What man? I don't understand.'

'They're following me, Mum. They wait outside the school in their blasted car.'

'Who?'

'The men. The men who are after Dad. What if I do a bad thing, and it gets Dad into trouble? It will be my fault, and he'll kill me. I can't be good forever.'

Daisy opened the front door, and peered out. Everything seemed normal: the traffic hammering down the coast road, the groups of children walking inland through the network of streets which took them to school. She turned back to Michael. 'Was it the chap in the Morris? The dark-coloured car?'

'No. It's red. Look left. They're waiting at the corner.'

Daisy looked left. There they were.

'Michael,' she said. 'Take your books up to your room. I will bring you some toast.'

Michael's relief nearly brought him to tears, but he managed to gasp out a 'thank you'.

That afternoon, Daisy marched into the Town Hall, and took the wide curving staircase to the second-floor offices. A secretary stacked papers at a desk. 'Can I help?' she said.

Daisy ignored her. She had spotted the young Inspector, Ford. He leaned in the doorway of an inner office, holding a cup and saucer.

'You,' Daisy said.

'I beg your pardon,' said Ford. 'I don't believe we've met.'

'Oh, you're a top-class detective, aren't you? I'm Mrs Seacombe. You've been following my son.'

Ford had a short, thick frame, and a smug face – a type she'd seen enough of.

'Ah. Mrs Seacombe. Why don't you come through to our office?'

'No! Michael is a *child*. He has nothing to do with any of this.'

'Any of what, Mrs Seacombe?'

'Don't give me that rubbish. I've heard it all before. I know your bloody tricks.'

She expected Ford to back down and apologise, but instead he seemed affronted by her.

'With all due respect, we have no obligation to report our methods, or explain our reasons,' he said.

'Excuse me?' Daisy said.

'Do you know where your daughter goes, after school? Linda is it?'

Daisy lost her composure then. She strode past the desk of the secretary, who tried to reason with her, and she swiped the cup and saucer out of Ford's hand. It hit the wall and then the floor. Ford barely twitched.

'If I ever see you near either of my children again, or hear that you've been *loitering around their schools*, I will smash every window in your car, whether you're in it, or not!'

At that moment, Inspector Lyle emerged from the door behind Ford. 'What in the name of goodness is going on out here?' he said.

'And I'm holding you responsible, too!' Daisy shouted.

Lyle, in a navy blue suit and waistcoat, looked down at the shards of the broken cup.

Daisy shook with rage. 'This man seems to think he has the right to follow my son in his car.'

'Well,' said Ford. 'Mrs Seacombe seems to think I'm required to discuss our preliminary—'

'Ford,' said Lyle.

'Sir, I only—'

'*Ford!* Absent yourself. Now.'

Ford slouched out into the corridor, under the gaze of his superior. Lyle opened the door to a small, neat office, lit pleasantly by a desk lamp, and full of the sweet smell of pipe smoke. He guided Daisy inside, and offered her a seat. 'I am sorry about that, Mrs Seacombe. Ford is . . .'

'He's arrogant, and rude.'

Lyle considered this. 'His manner leaves a lot to be desired. Well. In any case. You mentioned your son. Michael, is it?'

'I want you to leave my children alone. Both of them. It's a disgrace,' Daisy said. 'Children have a right to their privacy, no matter how you feel about their parents.'

Lyle nodded. 'Fine,' he said.

'What?'

'You have my word. Neither of your children will be followed. I will see to it.'

Daisy blinked.

'I am glad,' said Lyle, 'that you came here, and we had a chance to meet.'

'I did not come here to meet you,' Daisy said. She stood.

'May I walk you down to the street?' said Lyle.

'I don't think so. No. Thank you.'

As she walked out of the office, Lyle called to her. 'Mrs Seacombe?'

'Yes.'

'What you said about children and the deeds of their parents. I agree.'

She thought about skipping her meeting with Paul, wondered whether it was too dangerous, but she couldn't stand the thought of missing him. To make sure she wasn't being followed, she walked into the Penny Farthing coffee bar, slipped through the kitchen, and out the back door into the alleyway. She looped back onto East Street, and ducked into the Electric.

The cinema echoed with coughing. She sat in the row behind Paul, and leaned forward. 'We have to be very careful,' she said.

'Oh. Hello,' Paul said.

'There's something going on with Robert at work.'

'What is it?'

'I don't know.'

On the screen, a woman emerged from the sea in a two-piece bathing costume.

'It's a cold day for that sort of behaviour,' Paul said. 'Hey, I've been thinking. A friend of Tony's has a flat going, here in the city. It's the same distance from work as London.'

'What?' Daisy said. 'You mean you're going to *move* here?'

'I guess you're a little cooler on the idea than I was.'

'It's not that. It's just not a good time.'

Paul nodded.

'Can we talk about it once this thing with Robert has blown over?' Daisy said.

'You mean your marriage?'

She said nothing.

'I'm sorry,' he said.

'I've got to go.'

'I shouldn't have said anything.'

'I just have to get home to Michael. He's upset.'

As she stood, the fire door banged open, but it was only the usher.

'I might have to . . . stay away for a little while,' she said.

'Is this because of what happened before? In the basement.'

'No. That's not it, at all,' she said, standing. 'Look. I just can't deal with this now. I'm sorry.'

Robert came home after the children had gone to bed.

'Is everything all right?' she asked him, standing from the armchair.

'Tell me you didn't go and speak to those bastards at the Town Hall,' he said.

'Robert.'

'What did I say to you, Daisy? What did I *tell* you?' he said. 'You don't say *anything*.'

'I'm sorry, Robert, but they were following Michael, and that's not fair, regardless of whatever you might have done.'

He smiled, briefly, then his face changed and he hit her in the mouth, so that she found herself sprawled across the armchair. She didn't look back, and it seemed to take a long time for him to leave. She tasted the iron and salt at the corner of her mouth, where her lips joined. Eating would be painful for a few days, but she thought she could probably cover the visible signs of the wound with lipstick. She'd hide it from the children, and anyone else who happened to see her.

In early December, Daisy took the children into town to replace the outdated Christmas decorations. Robert had said he'd come, but he didn't.

Daisy wore her blue coat, and a matching hat she'd made. She loved to see Linda and Michael walking before her, Linda so tall now, towering above her brother in the smoke and snow as the sky darkened to a royal blue. St Bartholomew's looked like a beached ark, looming over the houses. The Vietnam protesters wore Santa hats, their hands pink with cold. Michael pulled up the collar on his jacket like a little man.

At the top of North Road, Linda made them stop at the giant vending machine, and they bought lukewarm pasties. Coloured lights, strung out from the clock tower, clinked and pinged in the wind. While the kids ate, Daisy was approached by an old woman and her grown-up daughter, the resemblance unmistakable. Two generations of bad news. 'Yeah, that's her,' the old woman said.

'Here, Detective!' the red-haired daughter said. 'It's a shame they ditched the death penalty. Jail's too good for your bastard husband.'

Daisy straightened her back. 'You stay away from us,' she said.

'I wouldn't spit on you, darling. I hope it's true what they say about pigs in jail.'

'I am with my *children*,' Daisy said.

'Yeah, well, so was I,' said the younger woman, as they passed.

Daisy pulled her children close. Michael kicked the snow from his shoes, and the wind screamed up from the sea.

At home that evening, the kids insulted each other. Daisy burned the chops and the smoke stank out the house. At eleven o'clock, she finally sat, alone, by the Christmas tree, inhaling its rich northern tang, her throat burning from cheap sherry.

Headlights swung across the ceiling. The car smacked into the dustbin. Robert tried to enter the house quietly, and failed. Drunk. 'Jesus, it's freezing,' he said. 'Hey, Daze, wake the kids up, it's nearly Christmas.'

'Where have you been?' Daisy said.

'Ray's.'

'I thought you weren't allowed to see him?'

'Who gives a monkey's?'

'Don't you think you should be with *your* family at a time like this?'

'A time like what? Screw the Yard! Anyway, Ray hasn't *got* a family, has he? Sandra's buggered off because of all this nonsense. You women don't seem to have any notion.'

'What?' she said.

'Well, listen to you, as soon as I walk in the bloody door.'

He took off his jacket. No tie, she saw.

'Are you being investigated?'

'There's no way it'll go ahead. Forget it. They've gone in to talk to old Clore, but they won't get anything, because Clore owes me.'

'What does he owe you? All these people. What do we all owe you, Robert?'

Linda stumbled into the room, in pyjamas that were now too short and left her midriff bare. 'What's happening?' she said.

'Linda! Come here!' said Robert.

He sang 'White Christmas' and danced around the room with Linda, who was asleep on her feet. Soon after, Michael wandered in. He sat on the floor near the tree.

'It's late, Michael,' Daisy said. 'You should go back to bed.'

'I was having a nightmare.'

'What was it?'

'I dreamed I couldn't read, again.'

Snow covered the country for two months. On the wireless, they said the sea at Herne Bay had frozen for a mile out from shore. Up on the cliff, giant icicles hung from the Seacombes' guttering. The children pulled them down and used them as walking sticks and daggers. Steam rose from the shoulders of the workmen who gritted the roads. Steam and smoke rose from everything, as if the town was smouldering.

Inspector Lyle visited the house one morning, and left a crescent of unclean snow on the doormat.

'Robert's not here,' Daisy said.

'As it happens, I came to speak to you, Mrs Seacombe,' said Lyle.

Daisy looked over his shoulder, and saw Inspector Ford waiting in the car.

'Doesn't he want to come into the warm?' Daisy said.

Lyle hesitated. 'I thought it best if Ford remained outside, given your previous . . . disagreement.'

Daisy smiled ruefully, and they went through to the living room, where the gas fire glowed blue and orange. Lyle pinched the thighs of his trousers, and sat down on the sofa. Daisy took the armchair. 'Nobody will tell me what's going on,' she said.

Lyle took a piece of paper from a file, and passed it to Daisy. 'This is a list of household goods,' he said.

'Robert is not going to like that you came here,' Daisy said.

'But this is all very routine. Very normal. Would you look at the list, please?'

She scanned the inventory of her home. She felt exposed, and wondered how they had put together such a document. They knew the manufacturer of her cutlery. She stopped reading halfway down. 'Everything seems present,' she said.

Lyle took out a notebook. 'We believe the deposit for the car was raised by selling . . .' he consulted a page, 'a *gold necklace with leaf design* to a man called George Simpson, proprietor of the nightclub, Minnie's, on West Street. Was that necklace yours? Do you know anything about it?'

She shook her head.

'Also . . . we have been unable to trace any attendant papers of sale for the gas oven, or the . . . er . . . twin tub.'

'Is this what it's all about?' Daisy said. 'That my husband doesn't keep his receipts? What a lot of nonsense.'

Lyle simply continued down the list. Several of the items had a background of which Daisy was unaware. A butcher had 'donated' their television set. Half of Robert's wardrobe consisted of so-called 'gifts'.

'What do you want me to say?' Daisy said.

'Did you know the means by which these goods were procured?'

She felt heat rising to her face. 'How can I be expected to remember all that?'

'Mrs Seacombe, I appreciate this is not easy. Nobody likes to be told that their home is founded on—'

'You don't know what my home is founded on, Inspector Lyle.'

But he smiled, as if he did know.

February brought blizzards, and ten-foot drifts on the Downs, but when the thaw came, Daisy went walking as often as she could. She found it hard to stay in the house. One afternoon, she took the cliff-top path, and saw a kestrel's brick-coloured back beneath her, the only smear of colour on that misty, disintegrating day. She went to a café on the seafront – not the Lighthouse – and watched the fog creep towards the steamed-up windows. She had not seen Paul for months, and hadn't dared to send a letter. In her mind, she wrote to him. *It used to be good enough to carry on conversations with you in my head but since we met, I realise my imagination doesn't do you justice. I can't stand being away from you like this, but we must wait.*

When she stepped back out into the cold, she thought she saw him further up the street, as if she'd imagined him into being. Before she could stop herself, she called his name.

Several people turned, including the man she thought was Paul. He wore the same work clothes, had a trace of a limp, and the same afternoon stubble. It couldn't be him, she told herself. What would he be doing in Brighton?

Robert went to bed early that night, and when Daisy joined him, he shifted in his half-sleep. He'd bitten his fingernails down to the quick, so they looked painful and raw. 'It's okay, Daisy,' Robert muttered, through his slumber. 'You don't have to worry. I won't let anything bad happen to you or the kids.'

'Thank you, Robert.'

Hours later, she woke to Linda, standing silently by the bed. 'What is it, love?' Daisy whispered.

'Come with me.'

As Daisy stepped into the hallway, she heard a noise like a flailing electric cable. She followed Linda to the back bedroom, where the din became louder. Cats, fighting in the garden. Daisy parted the curtains and looked down on scores of cats darting and scratching at each other, their eyes flashing blank in the moonlight. It took a moment for her vision to adjust, but soon she saw the bloodied bodies of dead rats, scattered across the lawn.

'What's happening?' Linda said.

'Did you see the person who did this?' Daisy asked.

'Person? It's cats, Mum. They're cats.'

'Yes, of course.'

Linda breathed quietly. 'But . . . do you think someone might have put down the rats deliberately, to make the cats to come into the garden?' she asked.

'I don't know,' Daisy said.

'Dad doesn't like cats,' Linda said.

'No. Quite,' Daisy said.

'Should we tell him?' Linda said.

'Not now. Better let him rest.'

Whoever did it, Daisy thought, knows Robert well enough.

In the morning, she tried to keep Robert away from the back door until she could get out there with a shovel, but he opened the curtains in the living room, and wheezed for a moment.

'Robert, are you all right?'

'I will get them,' he said, striding past her, and shrugging on his coat. 'And if it's kids,' he shouted back, 'I'll get the parents, too.'

Daisy did not expect Lyle to return to her house. The Inspector came alone this time. The spring mist lingered behind him like a blank screen. 'May I come in, Mrs Seacombe?'

She took his hat and raincoat, hung them up, and put water on to boil. Lyle had haunted the city and the CID for only a few months, but he already looked like a changed man. He had a heavy cold, or possibly a hangover, and his skin was dull and dry. He had none of the cocksure attitude he'd displayed on his first visit.

'You've missed him, again, I'm afraid,' Daisy said.

'I know where he is,' said Lyle. 'To be quite honest, I'm glad to have a break from him.' He paused, shocked by his own words. 'I do apologise,' he said.

Lyle's legs were long, and when he sat down in the living room, his knees rose above the level of his waist. His trouser cuffs showed chalky stains. He looked outside at a seagull perched on the fence. 'I can't get used to it,' he said.

'What?'

'Those. The gulls. I'm quite unable to sleep from the noise.'

'I don't even hear them anymore.'

'I'm sure. Of course, my wife forced me to watch *The Birds*, and it had rather an impact. I don't know if you saw it . . .'

'I liked it,' Daisy said. 'Especially the opening, when she arrives at the bay.'

'Weren't you frightened?'

'Not by the birds. Some of the family scenes, perhaps. The mother-in-law, certainly.'

Lyle laughed. 'A film lover,' he said.

She ignored the comment. 'I'm not worried,' Daisy said sternly. 'Robert's not worried, so neither am I.'

'Can I be frank, Mrs Seacombe? I think you're intelligent. And I think it would be very difficult for you to remain unaware of your husband's various dealings, but it struck me—'

'You don't know what you're doing,' she said.

Lyle blinked, taken aback by her sharp tone. 'You sound angry. Do you want him to be investigated? To be convicted?'

'What kind of a question is that?'

'Given the nature of what we're talking about . . .'

'I don't *know* what we're talking about, Mr Lyle. I don't know anything. I wish to God I did.'

Lyle sniffed. 'Be careful what you wish for, as they say.'

'You're not formally investigating him,' she said. 'Should you even be here?'

'Mrs Seacombe, the irregularities we are looking into are wide-ranging and unpleasant. As a relatively minor example, has your husband ever spoken to you about abortions?'

She remembered an overheard conversation. Just a fragment of talk she didn't really understand. 'That's illegal,' she said quietly.

'Indeed.'

She couldn't imagine that her husband was liberating poor young girls who'd got into trouble. 'What's that got to do with Robert?'

'We know that for some time he's been visiting an elderly woman, Mrs Thorst, in Brunswick Square, who may or may not have performed illegal operations. It appears that this woman, who is quite frail – physically and otherwise – has been paying your husband sums of money.'

'You mean blackmail?'

'Mrs Thorst is not the sort of person who would last long in jail. And she has a daughter with a minor criminal record, whom she is trying to protect.'

'I don't believe Robert would do anything like that.'

'Ruin a family, you mean? That's a very small part of it . . . shall I talk about drugs? Or perhaps prostitution? Because that's where much of our preliminary work has focused.'

'Don't be ridiculous. My husband is not a pimp.'

'He's a racketeer. He and Ray Harper make money on every bad thing that happens in this city. They benefit from the very activities they are employed to stop.'

'Nonsense,' Daisy whispered.

'I'm telling the truth, and if you look hard enough, and deep enough, you know it.'

Daisy studied the carpet, unsure of how to reply. She was saved by the whistle of the kettle, and went through to the kitchen. She poured boiling water into the red teapot. When the traffic died down, she could hear the sea. She thought of Robert, in their old house, back in the countryside, and how he used to wake at night, crying out. She thought of the young girl who'd tried to kill herself in the bath, the fingernail lifted from the shoe. You make your choices without realising, she thought, but they are choices nonetheless.

When she returned, she placed the tray on the side table.

'I'd like you to take a look at some photographs,' Lyle said.

'I don't want to,' said Daisy.

'Pardon?'

'I don't want to look at your pictures, or read your lists about my house, or listen to what you've seen my children doing, or hear your vile lies.'

Lyle pressed his fingers to his temples. 'Mrs Seacombe. I thought, after what you've heard today . . . when you came into the Town Hall and confronted Ford, it seemed to me that you had a strong moral aspect to your character.'

'Excuse me?'

'I find that some people . . . especially women . . . have values which are higher than their own interests.'

'I don't believe that Robert did the things you say.'

'Oh, come on!' he shouted. The room whined with the following silence, but Daisy stayed calm. She'd lived with Robert her whole adult life, so she was not easily intimidated.

'Rumours and lies,' Daisy said. 'Not everyone likes you when you're in the police, Mr Lyle, as I'm sure you know.'

'It's *Inspector* Lyle.'

'Some people want to see you broken. Clearly, my husband has enemies, who are making these wild accusations. And you obviously don't have any evidence to prove them.'

'We certainly do.'

'You have nothing!' It was Daisy's turn to raise her voice. 'If you had any proof, you wouldn't be in *my* house, speaking to me *alone*, and telling me to "come on".'

'You're wrong.' Lyle said. 'You know Gerald Clore?'

Daisy shrugged.

'He's coming in,' Lyle said. 'He's going to talk.'

'I doubt it,' Daisy said.

'That's what your husband said. Detective Seacombe seemed to think his former chief inspector was under some kind of spell. But he's not. Clore is old. He's sick. These elderly ex-coppers. They go out on the golf course, they look at the pretty trees, and they start to think about getting right with God. Putting their accounts in order. They contemplate death, and it makes other people look less frightening. Old Clore's got nothing to lose. And I'll say this: he didn't weep at the thought of seeing Robert behind bars.'

'If you're so confident, why are you coming after me?'

'I need you both. And besides, Mrs Seacombe, I like you. When this case comes around, I want you to be on the right side of it. I'll admit that we've had some . . . problems during our enquiries. Apparently, people don't like talking about your husband. For some reason.'

'And you thought I'd be different.'

Lyle stood. 'Yes,' he said. 'I *do* think that. I still think it. The list of Ray Harper's female *friends* . . . we've spoken to them all. They despise the man. But they won't do the right thing. I believed you would.'

'You really think I'm going to cheat on my husband?'

'Cheat on him? Don't you think that's a very interesting way of putting it?'

'Not particularly.'

Lyle sighed. 'I didn't want to do this,' he said.

'I don't know what you mean.'

'I mean *Paul Landry*, Mrs Seacombe.'

It may have been the first time that anyone had ever spoken his full name to her.

'What . . .'

'Oh, don't,' said Lyle. 'Just don't.'

'Get out of my house.'

'No.'

'You come in here . . . you have men sitting outside in cars, following my son . . . my family . . .'

'You. Mainly we have followed you. We have a diary *full* of your meetings. We've spoken to Mr Landry, and—'

'You've spoken to him?'

She wanted to rage at Lyle, but she could feel the tears beginning. The image came to her of Paul turning away on the street, and now she knew why.

'What have you done?' she said.

'We talked to him, that's all.'

Daisy clenched her fists. 'Does Robert know?'

'I don't believe so. Incredibly. I do think he's probably a jealous man, given cause.'

Carefully, Daisy rose from her chair.

'It puts us all in quite a situation, though, doesn't it?' Lyle continued. 'Because what if he *did* find out? Having spent a little time with him, I can almost imagine what he'd do.'

'You shouldn't speak to me this way,' Daisy said.

'And I wonder how the employers of *Monsieur Landry* would feel about his having an affair with a married woman. I wonder, for that matter, how the lady in Canada, to whom Mr Landry sends half of his wages, would feel about it.'

Daisy glanced up at him.

'Oh,' Lyle said. 'Oh, you didn't know.'

'Don't you dare . . .' Daisy said.

'I am sorry. You see, men like that – it's very rarely ever one woman, in my experience.'

Daisy strode forward and slapped Lyle across the mouth. The surprise of the blow made him stumble backwards, and he knocked over the milk jug. In a moment, he straightened.

'You sicken me,' Daisy said. 'What business is it of yours? Paul has done nothing wrong. He's doesn't deserve to be dragged into this mess. He's done nothing, and you just trample him.'

Lyle pressed his lip, and then examined his fingertips.

'Mrs Seacombe,' Lyle said. 'On the one hand, I am sorry that your feelings have been hurt, but this case is bigger than your private concerns. The country can't be run by a mafia behind a badge.'

'You're the same!' Daisy said. 'Don't you see? You've done *exactly the same thing* as my husband has done all these years.'

'Pardon me?'

'You've picked the most vulnerable person, you've found their weakness and you've exploited it.'

'There is no comparison.'

'You've gone after Paul, and all he did was write me some letters. Fine, barge into the house of a woman on her own,' Daisy said. 'I married Robert. I stayed with him. I deserve it. But Paul is a good man.'

'A good man?'

'You don't know anything. Paul and I. We have a friendship, yes.'

'Oh, please.'

'These are normal things. Ordinary weaknesses. What's on *your* conscience, Mr Lyle? What are *you* hiding?'

'I'm afraid I'm quite incorruptible,' he said.

'No,' she said, her teeth gritted. 'No, you're not. From now on, you're just as bad as the others, and I don't want to talk to you anymore.'

Lyle bowed his head as he walked along the hallway to the front door. He retrieved his raincoat and his hat. He spoke softly. 'I want you to know that Mr Landry . . . he didn't betray any personal confidences.'

'Don't you *ever* speak to me about him again,' Daisy said.

'Look,' he said. 'It appears to me that you still have options.'

Daisy shook her head, and Lyle continued. 'You must have considered what will happen when Robert goes to jail.'

'He won't go to jail.'

'Just listen to me. Listen. What will become of you? And your children? You'll be penniless. This is not the sort of house that can be maintained on welfare payments. And God knows what will become of your lover. God knows what Robert will do to him. Or arrange to have done.'

'Stop it. Stop talking about it.'

'But there's another way. If you cooperate, the Force will support you. Robert needn't know a thing about Mr Landry. Your husband will be behind bars, and you'll be free to live how you choose. See whom you choose. Do you understand? Do you see what I'm offering?'

'Please just go.'

'Consider it. Consider making a good decision, while decisions can still be made.'

Daisy swung the door open. Lyle walked out into the mist. She closed the door, and returned to the living room. She poured the spilled milk from the tray back into the jug, and then she sat down and wept. After a while, she cast a glance around the room, and imagined the curtain pole ripped from the plaster, the radio tumbled, its works exposed, and the patio doors smashed. She imagined Robert, pale and drunk, or ruddy and drunk, garbling his accusations: *Who is he?* Or *I am going to jail because of you*, or *take the kids and get out of this house*, or *I will see to it that you are ruined*, or *he is as good as dead*.

Daisy made her decision. She took out a sheet of paper and her pen, and she wrote to Paul. She was sorry, she wrote, for the hurt she'd caused, for the position she'd put him in. *I do not know when this situation will be over, or how it will turn out, but for everyone's sake, I can't see you.*

She heard Linda and Michael on the path. She only caught part of their whispered conversation. 'She's crying,' Michael said.

'Let's walk around for a bit then,' Linda replied.

1998

A memory.

Lucas and Nanna wore fingerless gloves in the cold sunlight of the park, so they could sign. They noticed the leaves falling slowly from the trees on the high bank. Except, when they looked closer, they found that they weren't really leaves, but those helicopter seed-pods that spin in the air. In the strong wind, the seed-pods kept falling and rising.

Nanna suggested they play a game. You had to nominate a pod while it spun high in the air, and then you had to catch it.

Easy, Lucas signed. But the pods travelled great distances in the gales, and Lucas and Nanna sprinted over the boggy ground with their cupped hands outstretched. Sometimes, a seed-pod appeared to be dropping nicely into Lucas's grasp, but then the breeze whipped it away.

They became red-faced with the effort and laughter, and stopped to rest. *Okay*, Nanna signed, breathing hard. *Now, we pick the same seed. We must fight for it!*

Yes! Good idea!

You pick. Her fingers pinched the air.

A flock of seed-pods came sweeping high overhead. One broke from the pack, and floated over to his side. Lucas pointed to it, and ran. His grandmother chased him, pulling him gently back by the hood on his coat. He screamed with glee. Nanna got ahead, but then Lucas barged past her. The seed-pod came spinning down towards him, but he bumped into a tree.

Nanna overtook, pumping her arms. Lucas had no idea she could run so fast. The pod dipped again, and Nanna's hand came out, the fingers spread like star points. She dived forward to catch it, her arm extended, her body thumping into the muddy football pitch.

But a gentle breeze lifted the seed-pod one last time, and it spun down softly to land on the back of her head. Lucas crawled onto her, picked up the pod with two hands and raised it like a tiny trophy.

He was the winner, but when he looked down, Nanna clutched her stomach, eyes closed tight.

After the Deaf pub night, Cassie had taken the rest of the week off school, and Lucas had watched the class as if from a mile away. The other kids didn't really talk to him anymore. Iona gave him the odd weak smile, but Youds didn't even make the gurning faces, or shout into his hearing aid. Sometimes Lucas didn't even get his pencil case out of his bag.

On Monday, she came back, slumping into the seat beside him in the Basin. 'Every   kay?' she said.

Perfect, he signed. *How about you? You left the pub last week. I was worried.*

I was sick. A bug.

Simple as that. A new sort of contagious virus had emerged: twenty-four hours of vomiting, and then back to normal. Lucas hadn't caught the name of it. *Tomorrow virus*, or something like that.

But you're feeling better, now? he signed.

I'm fine.

The daffodils outside the open window smelled like animal piss. *I've been reading about* B-A-R-B-E-R-P-O-L-E-S, Lucas signed.

'Barber . . .? Oh, right, yeah,' Cassie said. She pulled the collar of her shirt away from her neck.

Lucas explained that the stripy poles referred to ancient days when barbers also performed blood-letting and minor surgery. They had the best tools, after all. On the hills of old England, they wrapped a blood-soaked cloth around a white pole, so that people knew where to go for help.

That's what they thought? Cassie signed. *They thought that cutting your veins open would help?*

She stared at the frayed ribbing of the rug, which made the Basin a homely place to learn.

Lucas took out his work. At the end of term, each pupil had to read their 'A Life in the Day' project in front of the class. 'I'm dreading this,' he said. 'Everyone watching me speak. I sound like a monster, and—'

Don't speak, then, Cassie signed.

What do you mean?

Sign it, instead. You sign it, I'll interpret for the class. Easy.

Is that allowed?

Cassie shrugged.

Lucas scanned the words on the page. 'So, I have to translate this?'

No. What you've written is boring.

Thanks.

It's very . . . stiff. How about we just chat, like this, and see what comes out.

Lucas lifted his hands, and then dropped them again. *I'm stuck.*

Okay, she signed. *I'll start. In the springtime, if I'm at home, I wake up early because I like to go on a bike ride before work.*

Slow down.

So. At 5 a.m., I'm awake. Bang. I stretch. She raised her arms above her head, linking the fingers together, and revealing the lines of her body. *I don't shower.*

Disgusting.

I shower after the ride.

Lucas didn't think he could take it if she was going to describe how she showered.

What do you have for breakfast? he asked, changing the subject.

Pasta.

No way!

With sugar.

You're joking.

For energy. Now your turn. Start anywhere. Doesn't have to be the morning. Start from when you come home from school.

Lucas thought for a moment. *It's hard to talk about home.*

Why?

I'm a . . . He wrote it down on his piece of paper: TEENAGER. *I want people to think I'm mysterious.*

Cassie smiled. *But you're not?*

No. I drink ... He finger-spelled K-I-A O-R-A. *Which my mum makes. Then I watch Neighbours. With my mum.*

Okay. Start at bedtime, then.

Even worse! What teenager is going to tell the class about his bedtime routine? He scribbled on the paper: AROUND 9 P.M. I SNEAK OFF TO BED WITH A HEADTORCH AND THE UNDERWEAR SECTION OF THE NEXT CATALOGUE, OR IF I'M LUCKY LA REDOUTE.

Cassie threw her head back and laughed. *That's going to look very funny when you sign it.*

They settled down, and sat still for a moment. Lucas took a deep breath. *You want to know what I really think about, at night?*

What?

You. I think about you. All the time.

Her smile dipped.

He began to sign again, but she reached out and took hold of his hands. 'Don't,' she said. She stroked his hands for a moment, and then let go. *I'm not going to be able to interpret that*, she signed.

It would be embarrassing for you.

I'm not embarrassed. But ...

I feel like there's a ... connection. Between us. Don't you?

Of course. I think you're amazing.

So, will you come to the cinema with me?

You're so sweet.

Lucas threw his hands up.

I don't know what to say, Cassie signed. *You've caught me by surprise.*

Doesn't have to be the cinema. Do you like K-I-A O-R-A? *I have two flavours.*

Stop.

I'm sorry. It's how I feel. I'm sorry. I'll stop. Forget I ever said anything.

I won't forget. But I have to be   about this.

Again?

She wrote it down for him. PROFESSIONAL.

He nodded.

'Okay,' Cassie said.

'Okay,' he said. 'Professional.' *It was nice to meet your brother,* he signed.

She nodded. *Dan can be difficult, sometimes, but it's good for you to meet other Deaf people. You'll see that it doesn't have to be like* <u>this</u> *for the rest of your life.*

She gestured to their surroundings, and Lucas followed her gaze. There was nobody else in the Basin. Her red lacquered nails glinted, and a shimmering heat haze rose from the fins of the radiator. Lucas had come to love the Basin. He *wanted* it to be like this for the rest of his life.

When Linda's mum got cancer, she'd missed the cinema most. The second operation and the chemotherapy left her too weak to go out. Linda remembered cranking the window open for the sea breeze, those fox-hunting figurines on the windowsill, the salt crust on the lace curtains. 'If it's going to be like this,' her mother had said. 'Then what's the point of going on?'

'Mum, that's not like you,' Linda had said. 'You'll be up and about soon.'

'I can't even get down the road to watch a damn movie.'

'We can bring the TV and video player up to your room.'

Daisy had a Betamax, but you could still get a few films.

'It's all right. I'm being grumpy. It's just . . . frustrating.'

Through the open window, Linda had heard her son kicking a ball around, and her dad working in the shed. She spent half her time looking after her dad, during Daisy's treatment. He'd never made a meal for himself. Every day, he walked to a food van on the beach and bought a cheese and onion roll. When he made Linda a cup of tea, she could taste the raw onion on the lip of the cup.

In the end, Lucas provided the link to the cinema. Young as he was, he'd forced Linda to take him to see a film every weekend, and then he'd sign the plots to his bedridden grandmother. Without access to the dialogue, Lucas had to make up the story from the pictures on the screen. The plots always differed from the version Linda had seen, but Daisy didn't seem to mind.

Labyrinth was a terrible choice of film for a deaf child – a puppet musical – but Lucas signed his enthusiastic interpretation to Daisy afterwards. It took Linda a while to realise that the 'rude but beautiful woman' he described was actually David Bowie.

Linda remembered her mum's fingers, trembling with weakness, rising to ask Lucas for clarification. She remembered Lucas stomping around the bed, his shoulders rounded in impersonation of the benevolent horned beast from the film, swinging his arms so wildly that he sent the porcelain fox crashing into the radiator, lost in a story which was better than the real thing.

Linda thought of Paul as one of those huge spiders that invade the house when the seasons change. You couldn't really do anything, but you had to keep an eye on them.

One Saturday morning, she looked out from the home park's site office – a double-unit mobile home, done out in red drapes and red carpet. Outside, mist fringed the park, so that the cabins and statues looked to be floating in a salty broth. Dale Robards, the site manager, sat on the edge of his desk, sucking McDonalds milk through the multicoloured straw. He was fiftyish, with hair growing out of a peroxide job. Linda thumbed a brochure for the park.

'We're in a development phase, Mrs Seacombe, to be honest. It's not just caravans, you know. We have people who live here practically all year round. I'm trying to raise the age restriction – not that you're . . . I just. I'd like a higher class of resident.'

Linda didn't know how to act around men like Dale – men who seemed to compliment and insult you in alternating sentences. 'Just because someone's old, doesn't mean they're a good person,' she said.

'Ha ha. You've got that right.'

'It doesn't mean they've never done anything wrong.'

Dale stopped smiling. Linda looked away. The place smelled of cigarettes and burning stand-up heaters.

'Do you do checks on your residents?' Linda asked.

'Financially?'

'Morally.'

Dale frowned.

'There's a foreign man, here. Older,' she said.

'We don't have many foreigners. Not in off-season.'

'Paul.'

'Oh, yeah, him. But Paul's American or whatever. He's all right.'

'What's he like?'

'Classic downsizer. Widower, probably. I think he volunteers for the handicapped. But mainly he stays home. Until Saturday night.'

'What does he do on Saturday night?'

Dale made a gesture: a glass repeatedly tipped towards the mouth.

'He's a drinker?'

'Not really. He nurses a couple, you know. It's looking out on the sea all week,' Dale said. 'Gives you a thirst. Happens to me, too. What about you, Mrs Seacombe? You like a drink?'

'Where does he go? What pub?'

'We can't really give out information to strangers,' Dale said. 'Although, I guess if you and I, say, went for dinner together, we wouldn't be strangers, would we? What do you think?'

'No, thank you.'

'What about the flicks?' Dale persisted. 'I clock off at four today, if you fancied seeing a movie.'

Linda shook her head. 'Definitely not.'

Cassie changed Mike. Nobody had ever described him before. *You could be handsome*, she told him. *You're funny. Your clothes*

are very eighties. Since his mum died, Mike had wondered who he was, and now someone was telling him.

'Sometimes you just have to ask yourself a serious question,' Cassie said, on the phone.

'Like what?'

'Do I own any garments from the Sweater Shop?'

She told him where to buy clothes. He resisted at first, but eventually emerged from these little boutiques, not with plastic sacks, but with stiff angular bags made from card. He held their rope-twine handles in his left hand, because his right hand still ached from where he'd come off the bike. The sleeves of his T-shirts now clung to his arms, while the cuffs of his jeans flared out over his boots. He went to a new hairdresser, who asked if he wanted his *eyebrows* done.

She was attractive. Sort of. Not in the usual way. They had sex in the dark, so he could hide his wounds. He slept in a T-shirt.

She called his mobile phone on lunch breaks, which he generally took in his car, in a lay-by or a pub car park.

'I'd like to see you, tonight,' she said.

'I can't make tonight. Got something on.'

'Look,' she said. 'Just be honest with me. Are you married?'

'No. It's not like that. I have to see a friend. It's difficult to explain.'

When Stephen came to the door, the inside of the house was dark blue behind him. Not one light on. 'Everything okay, pal?' Mike asked.

'What do you know about power?' Stephen asked.

'What d'you mean?'

'Well, it can't be a power cut because the neighbours are aglow.'

'Oh. I see. Okay. Make sure the appliances are off. Unplug the kettle and the toaster. That massive oven thing in the kitchen – what does that run on?'

'It's an Aga.'

'Yeah, switch that off. Is your fuse box in the downstairs bog?' Mike said, stepping beyond Stephen.

'I can't find the torch,' said Stephen.

'I've got one,' Mike said, holding up the mini Mag-lite on his key ring.

Mike had it all sorted in a couple of minutes. *The neighbours are aglow*, he thought to himself with a smile. *Silly twat.*

'Thank you,' Stephen said.

'Thank *you*,' Mike said, handing back the Taoist book. 'Looks well thumbed.'

'Yeah. You got the advanced level manual?'

Stephen laughed. 'Are you serious, though? The book really worked for you?'

'Yeah, actually. Yeah. You should give it to what's-his-face. Matt.'

'Fuck off,' Stephen said, with a smile. 'So you've had the opportunity to put your skills into practice . . .'

'You could say that.'

'Well, well. So, you've met someone?'

Mike shrugged. 'Don't know.'

'You don't know. But the sex went well, at least? In a technical sense?'

'Yeah. I actually . . . I pictured your garden. When I was on the job.'

'On the . . .'

'You know, I imagined the grass growing. To keep the wolf from the door.'

Stephen laughed. 'You're mixing your metaphors.'

'Eh?'

'Did you really do that? When you were making love?'

'Yeah.'

They both laughed now. *Making love.*

'God, that's hilarious!' said Stephen. 'If I'd've known, I would have mown the lawn.'

'It works, mate. You should try it.'

'Unlikely.'

The conversation stalled. Mike scratched his head. 'One day you'll get back out there,' he said. 'Meet someone.'

'You sound like my bloody mother.'

'My sister's single,' Mike said.

'That's a wonderful idea,' Stephen said.

Mike didn't know what to say next. He wanted to help his friend, and he really did think Linda would be a good match, but he felt embarrassed. So, he weighed a large pair of imaginary breasts in his hands.

'Oh, please!' Stephen said.

'No, no, seriously,' said Mike. 'She's a nice woman. Linda, she's called. She's clever. Doesn't watch much telly, and that.'

Stephen put his head in his hands. 'Oh, yeah,' he said. ' "Hey sis, there's this guy I know – beats me up in his garden shed. I think you'd really like him." '

Mike tried to protest, but then he started laughing at the absurdity of it. They both did. Tears in their eyes. They couldn't look at each other without starting again.

'"Aw, come on Linda, love",' said Stephen, doing a passable impression of Mike. '"He might be a fackin sadist, but at least he don't watch telly".'

The laughter died down and they fell silent. Stephen stared into space, bobbing slightly as though he could hardly support his own weight.

'You look knackered, mate,' Mike said.

'Yes, well. Thank you. I am,' Stephen said. 'I think I might be knackered forever. You know what it's like. You looked after someone who was dying.'

Mike frowned. 'Oh, you mean Mum. My sister did most of the caring, to be fair. Anyway, it wasn't the same with Mum. She was in pain, but I never thought she was going to die.'

'You were in denial?'

'The doctors always put a positive spin on it.'

'What do you mean?'

'You know – they said she had a good chance, and all that.'

'Wait. A good chance of *surviving*? They told you that?'

'Yeah. I mean, they might have been trying to make me feel better or whatever.'

'Did they tell your dad?' Stephen asked, a serious bite to his voice.

'I don't know. Why?'

'*Why?* Well, I think – given what happened, given what he did – that's a pretty important question, don't you? Whether or not he thought she was going to die.'

Mike shook his head. 'I don't know.'

And he didn't. The events and motives that mattered most in his family life remained murky, glossed over. You couldn't explain them to a stranger in a way that made sense. Life was a delicate balance of knowing and trying not to know. That was how you carried on. You didn't look too closely.

Mike and Cassie cycled out in a big loop, coming back along the coast, through Worthing, past the fairy tale castle of Lancing College, the Shoreham airport, the power station at Portslade, and Hove Lawns. They drank cold black tea from their bidons: Cassie's idea.

That night, he dreamed about Pop-up Pirate, the game he used to play with his nephew. In the dream, Mike was the pirate, but he didn't know who was sticking the swords into him. When he woke, the pain of the cutlass continued to throb. The ache seemed to go deeper than his ribs. It wrapped around his back, too. 'Jesus,' he gasped.

Cassie woke up next to him. 'Mikey? Are you okay?'

Mikey? How long had it been since someone had called him that? His first wife, maybe. 'It's just my back. It'll happen to you one day, when you're old.'

He hoisted himself out of bed, feeling the acids of the weekend's riding in his legs, along with the rib pain. It was just before dawn, and the bathroom of the flat looked as grey and grainy as the picture on a broken telly. Mike fell to his knees and gripped the little dreadlocks of the toilet lid cover. He yanked the seat up and vomited, barely had time to recover before the next wave came. When he'd finished he felt completely awake, but half-mad, and shivering. What he'd thrown-up looked like red clay. He tried to think what he'd eaten. Cassie had cooked carbonara when they'd got back to the flat. Nothing red. His rib still ached.

He talked himself calm. Some of the vomit had spilled onto his T-shirt, so he took it off, and put on an old dressing gown. It was the first time he'd worn it since splitting up with Karen. It smelled of the Ariel and Radox of his old life.

Cassie came in without knocking. 'Are you sick?' she said.

'I'm fine. Just a bug, probably.'

Cassie frowned. She parted the dressing gown and studied his body. '*Jesus*,' she said. 'Mike, what the fuck is all this?'

'What?' said Mike.

'These bruises. What happened to you?'

'Oh. I was carrying some boxes up the stairs at work and I tripped,' he said, wrapping himself in the dressing gown. Cassie tried to open it again, but he shrugged her off.

'Let me look,' she said.

'There's nothing to see. It was a little accident, that's all.'

Cassie shook her head. 'No,' she said. 'You're hiding something.'

'Don't be silly.'

'Mike. What's going on?'

He shrugged.

'Tell me,' she said.

'It's nothing,' he said. 'Just leave it, will you? Christ.'

She stared at him for a moment, her mouth open. 'Fine,' she said, and stormed out of the bathroom.

Mike cursed, and then brushed his teeth, waiting for her to calm down. He'd woken up spewing, and now *he* was in the doghouse. The gown sagged open again, and in the bathroom mirror, he saw the bruises as Cassie had seen them. Rotten rosettes.

For years, Mike had looked forward to the idea of

stupefaction and old age. The comfort of the same pub, the consolations of retirement. He hadn't minded, before, if the next twenty-five years went by quickly. Everyone always looked forward to Friday, after all. But now it was different. Now he had stuff to live for. What he felt, that morning, in the bathroom, was fear. Fear of being hit. Fear of the rib cracking and puncturing his lung, so that he fell down coughing blood onto the floor of that fucking shed. He re-fastened the cord of the dressing gown, and trudged back into the bedroom, where Cassie was packing her overnight bag.

'Look,' he said. 'You don't have to worry.'

'I'm leaving my job at the school,' she said.

'Eh? What happened?'

'Nothing, really. The other learning assistant is coming back from sick leave, and it seems like the right thing to do.'

'But you're going to keep in touch with Lucas?'

'Don't think it's a good idea. For now.'

'Why?'

'Because he thinks he's in love with me, Mike.'

'What? Oh. Oh, shit.'

'Yeah. I'm going to try to leave gradually.'

'Right,' Mike said. 'What a mess.'

'It's not a *mess*. It's life. And if this is going to work out, we need to be able to talk to each other, okay? I don't like secrets,' she said, gesturing to his body.

'Listen,' he said. 'It's all . . . there are a few things I have to sort out, but I have to do it on my own.'

'What things? What are you talking about?'

He shook his head. How could he possibly explain?

Cassie zipped her bag, and then took hold of his wrist. She

squeezed, and then released the pressure, tenderness overcoming her frustration. 'Call me when you're ready,' she said, and left the room.

'Okay,' he said. 'Okay.'

Lucas arrived at his next English class before Cassie. Mrs Finch welcomed everyone, and began talking at somewhere in the region of a hundred and twenty words per minute.

'   stress to you how important   in the exam,' she said.

Cassie came in late, carrying a small holdall. 'Sorry,' she mouthed. She unzipped the bag and took out her denim pencil case. The other pupils busied themselves with their green exercise books. 'What are you supposed to be doing?'

'I don't know,' Lucas said, nodding to Mrs Finch. 'I didn't see what she said.'

Cassie sighed. 'I'll talk to her.'

She strode up to the front of the class and spoke to Mrs Finch. The teacher rolled her eyes. Lucas cast a glance at the holdall beside Cassie's chair. The flap lay open, and within, her phone lay on top of a garment of dark blue silk. The dusty morning light made the fabric look like car metal. He forced himself to turn away.

Cassie sat down next to him, and said something he didn't understand.

'Pardon?' he said.

'You have to imagine you're a nineteenth-century farm labourer in the North of England,' she said.

'That's what the careers adviser said.'

Cassie didn't smile.

Were you out last night? he signed, nodding to the holdall.

She looked at him for a moment, but did not reply.

I thought maybe you had a boyfriend.

'No,' she said.

'Okay.'

'You have   even   stuff out, Lucas,' Cassie said, gesturing to his desk.

He felt a chill across his skin. To fend off the feeling, he dipped down and took his pen and exercise book from his rucksack. He began to write, trying to concentrate on the loops of ink. Cassie's phone glowed green in her bag. She reached down and turned it off.

What do you think they did with deaf farmers in the nineteenth century? Lucas signed.

' think   manage this on your own, Lucas, don't you?' Cassie said.

What's wrong? he signed.

'Nothing. Look. The   is quite busy at the moment.'

The what?

'The department,' she said. 'Pupil support.   funding.
    people like you who are doing fine.   new pupils.'

'Slow down,' he said, brushing his right hand along his left arm. He knew he'd spoken loudly, because he could feel people watching him. He fired a fierce glance of warning around the classroom, before addressing Cassie. 'What are you saying?'

'I've told them you don't need me in history and maths.'

'But the exams are coming up!'

'I won't be   forever, Lucas. You have   used to it.'

'What?'

'Also, there's a new boy in year seven.⠀⠀⠀⠀⠀⠀⠀into the area. He has⠀⠀⠀⠀.'

'I didn't get the last word.'

'Hydro. Ce-pha-lus. On Monday afternoons, he needs a *lot* of extra support.'

'So do I! On Monday afternoons, two of the teachers have facial hair! I can't see what they're saying!'

'Come on, Lucas.⠀⠀⠀⠀perfectly well alone⠀⠀⠀⠀even in the same league as this boy.'

'He should have to wait.'

'Do you know what hydrocephalus is?' she said.

'Yes,' he said. 'No.'

'It's water on the brain.'

'That's not my fault.'

'If he's lucky, he'll make it to twenty, okay?'

Lucas placed his pen next to his exercise book, in which he had written one and a half lines. He remained still until Mrs Finch called for a class discussion. In a classroom full of background noise, he turned his head just in time to see each speaker finish a sentence. He couldn't follow the conversation at all, but he didn't ask Cassie for help.

At the end of the lesson, she tapped his arm. 'I'll see you tomorrow, okay?'

That afternoon, his history teacher's thick moustache obscured much of a lecture on Native Americans. Lucas looked out of the window, and saw Cassie with the new kid. The boy stood about four feet tall. He had a very large head, and wore spectacles held in place with a black elastic band. Even from that distance, Lucas could see that he wore shoes from the infant section, although somebody had tried to hide the Disney characters with black polish.

Lucas covered his eyes with his hands. He regretted what he'd said about the boy, but he also had a familiar plunging feeling deep in his chest.

Mike cancelled a couple of meetings with Stephen, but he had to man-up eventually. His nervousness, when he arrived at the house, reminded him of their early meetings. He got there just after the morning school run, having called in sick to work. His core ached, so he parked unusually close to the house. He ran through the words he might use: *there have been some changes . . . I'm not sure I can go on . . .*

By the doorstep, Mike noticed the arm of an incipient tree with broad flat leaves, sprouting between two concrete slabs. The door opened.

'Hello, mate!' Mike said.

'Quiet,' said Stephen, ushering him in. 'My daughter's upstairs.'

'Not with Matt, is she?' Mike asked.

'God, no. She's revising. And Matt is no longer on the scene.'

'What happened?'

'He was putting it about.'

'I'm gonna kill him.'

'Oh, good idea.'

'Is she okay?'

'She's fine. The stuff she's been through, these last few years. *Matt* rather pales into insignificance.'

Mike glanced into the living room, which was a mess, even by Stephen's standards: piles of books, bowls of half-finished Golden Grahams, old coffee marbling in mugs. 'You do know that's a beech tree coming up by your front door, don't you?' Mike said.

'What? Oh, right.'

'If you let it grow, it'll split this house right down the middle.'

Stephen scratched his neck. 'Cuppa?'

'You got any of that gay tea?'

Stephen tutted and went into the kitchen. Mike followed, remembering a time when he used to goad Stephen, on purpose, so they could get the abuse over with. But he didn't want that today. He didn't want to be the driver anymore.

Stephen boiled the kettle and took three mugs from the cupboard. Mike tried to intuit something about his mood from the way he made the tea, but he couldn't. He didn't know anyone like him. Stephen was as shifting and opaque as a woman.

Soon the air smelled of vanilla and roses. Stephen passed Mike a mug, and held up another. 'I'm just going to take this up to Hannah,' he said. 'Then we can talk.'

Hannah. His daughter. Had he said her name to Mike before?

Stephen went upstairs, and Mike heard their muffled voices, the sound of gentle laughter. When he came back down, Stephen stepped outside. 'Back in a sec, Mike,' he called. 'I just remembered, it's bin day.'

Alone in the kitchen, Mike felt the breeze coming through the open front door. He tried to memorise the details of the house: the bright red bread bin, the key ring on top of the microwave with the faded photograph of Stephen's wife inside, the blue drawing pencils in a cup, that seemed to have been sharpened with a knife. He would miss this house. Without thinking too hard, Mike took one of the pencils and slipped it into his pocket. As he did so, he heard Stephen coming back through the front door. Mike realised, too late, that if they went out to the shed, the sharp pencil would be a hazard to both of them.

'Okay, all done,' said Stephen, washing his hands.

'Yeah, so if we could have a chat.'

'You'd like to do it before we, er . . .?'

'Yes,' Mike said, his ribs thrumming with pain. 'Actually. I mean, I thought, with your daughter being here, we probably shouldn't . . .'

'Forget it,' said Stephen. 'What did you want to say?'

Mike cleared his throat. 'There have been a lot of changes, recently,' he said.

'Oh, for fuck's sake,' said Stephen.

'What?'

'*Changes?* Come on. This is about your new girlfriend, isn't it? I'm assuming it's a girl, despite your choice of tea.'

'Steady on.'

'You've met someone, and so you no longer have the time or the inclination to come here and see me. Suddenly, you need to account for where you go of an evening, and explain to her why you've got bruises all over your body. That's it, right?'

Mike let his shoulders drop. 'Look. It's not just about what I need,' he said quietly. 'It's not like I've forgotten why we started doing this. If you want to carry on, we could.'

'No, you're right. It's time.' Stephen rubbed his eyes, and then yawned. 'I feel like your dad,' he said.

'You can have him,' said Mike automatically.

They drank their tea quietly.

'So,' Stephen said, after a while. 'Another victory for Taoism.'

'Sod off, you!' Mike said, laughing.

'Is she young?'

'Yes, but it's not what you think.'

'I suspect it probably is.'

'She works with my nephew, at the school. Or. She used to.'

'Bra-fucking-vo.'

Mike tried to think of promises he could make, but found none he could realistically keep. 'Stephen,' he said eventually. 'I'm sorry.'

'I forgive you,' Stephen replied.

They walked to the door. Mike winced with pain when he stepped down onto the path, but he was nearly free.

'I need you to do something for me,' Stephen said.

Mike's stomach dropped. 'Of course. Whatever you need.'

'This girl, and everything. Just be careful, will you?'

Mike smiled. 'That's rich, coming from someone who can't even cross the fucking road.'

Driving home, along the coast road, Mike noticed a smudge on the front of his bonnet, and when he pulled over and got out, high above the town, he saw that the badge from his car – a silver 'H' – had been removed. Vandals, he thought.

On Saturdays, Paul Landry drank at the Bear.

There were pubs, these days, with soft lamplight and leather-style sofas, and wine glasses like big bowls. Pubs where you could order Bolognese in a large dish, with powdered parmesan. The Bear was not such a pub. As Linda walked slowly past the windows, 10.30 p.m., she saw smoke in the strip light and red patches of carpet the texture of very old tennis balls. The drink prices were written on orange, star-shaped pieces of card stuck to the optics and pump handles. Outside, the chalkboard advertised yesterday's 'Kenny-oke' with Ken Randell.

Paul Landry sat at the bar, on a stool, like a drunk in a film. The bar towel wrinkled beneath his forearm. He drank two slow pints of Caffrey's, and a Drambuie.

Linda took a position across the road, outside a row of dark-ened shops, and peered through the windows of the pub. She had dressed up, relatively speaking. A lime-green sweater, a pencil skirt, an old long coat dragged from the back of the wardrobe. More make-up than usual, God knows why.

The young locals had worked out that they could get served in the Bear, and fifteen-year-old boys in bright shirts, with wispy goatees, went up for Stellas and Smirnoff Ices for their girlfriends. Paul nodded to them. A lonely, guilty drinker who needed company.

She waited a long time. People – men, mainly – walked past and made their comments. About the way she dressed, what she was doing out there on her own. You couldn't even stalk your dead mother's lover in peace.

Standing there outside the pub, she had a flash of memory. Another pub, with a garden, when they were young, Linda sipping shandy, and supervising Michael on the slide, and their parents arguing at a wooden table in the distance. She saw her dad walking around the table, picking up each almost-finished glass, and hurling the dregs over their mum. She saw her brother watching too, trembling. She could almost smell the yeasty odour that came from her mother's blouse on the drive home. Did that really happen? How had she forgotten it? All these pieces of memory, but what did they add up to?

The youngsters burst out of the pub at 11.30, the girls talking about Brighton, the boys arguing for Newhaven, and chips. Last orders came and went, but Paul Landry remained at the bar.

Linda shivered now, despite the coat. Her eyes watered, and her mascara swelled.

He came out shortly afterwards. He zipped his coat, hunched up against the breeze, and began to walk home slowly, along the main road. Linda stepped out of the shadows and followed.

At the point where he had to cross the road to the park entrance, he turned, and saw her. Linda continued to walk towards him. It was as though the white beam of the street light had him frozen. The suffering in his face reminded her of old paintings – the 'O' of his mouth, the pitiful set of his brow, his crippled stoop.

The taxis and the boy-racers flashed past, and Linda felt fuelled by their speed. She stopped a few metres from him.

'Please,' he said. 'This has got to stop.'

Linda did not speak.

'I'm tired,' he said. 'I'm dog-tired. And you come around, talking to the site-manager, following me onto the bus. What's wrong with you?'

'I think you know.'

He looked at her, disbelieving. 'She speaks,' he said. 'It's Linda, right? Can we at least do names? I'm Paul.'

He held out his hand, but she kept her distance.

'I know who you are,' she said.

'Listen. What do you *want* from me?' he asked.

'I want you to leave my family alone,' she said. 'Leave my dad alone.'

He shook his head. 'He's all I've got.'

'When you stop, I'll stop,' she said.

'Can we talk? Can we just *talk* about all this?'

'No,' she said. She didn't want to be rational. 'I have worked my whole life to try and keep things . . . *normal*, for my family, and now you come along . . .'

'I've been here the whole time,' he said.

'And you think that's okay, do you? You think that's acceptable?'

He put his hands to his head, dug the fingers into his scalp. 'It was all my fault, anyway,' he muttered.

'What?' she said. 'What was your fault?'

He took off his glasses, put them in the pocket of his coat, closed his eyes, and stepped out into the road.

Spontaneously, Linda reached for him, though she was too far away. A red Golf hurtled round the bend, and swerved to miss him. No cars came from the left, and he limped across to the other side – something oddly animal in his gait. Without looking back, he shuffled through the park entrance, and down into the valley of squat houses. Linda, still in shock, did not follow.

The next day, she called St Raphael's Readers. She could have done it months ago, perhaps, but now that she'd spoken to him, it felt easier. 'I don't want him reading to my dad,' she said to the woman from the charity.

'You sound upset. Has he done anything wrong, specifically?'

Linda thought about that for a long time. 'Just make him stop,' she said.

1963

Daisy stood in the hallway, and checked her watch. She forced herself to think about Mo Williams' funeral until the tears started. When she'd got a decent flow, she opened the door, ran across the road in her slippers, and startled the young man from the Yard, who was sitting in his Morris.

'Oh, God, please! Can you help?' she said.

The young officer had been half asleep, and the appearance of a crying woman disturbed him. He wound down his window. 'What is it?'

'It's my Robert: he's got himself into some bloody stupid fight ... he's ... someone's hit him, and I'm worried about what he'll do.'

'Where?'

'You have to help.'

'Where is he?'

'The Eagle, I think.'

'In town?'

'It's your fault!' Daisy cried.

'Pardon me?'

'You people. You've driven him to this!'

'How did you find out about the fight? Who told you?'

'I'm holding you responsible if anything happens to him. Oh, God, he's going to *kill* someone.'

'Look, just . . . calm down, will you, for goodness' sake. I'll go over there and take a look.'

'No! Please don't! What if he comes back here?'

'When does he ever do that?' the officer said, starting the engine.

'Be careful,' Daisy said. 'He gets so angry when he's had a drink. Please don't tell him I told you.'

The young officer drove away without another word. Daisy waited until the car was out of sight. She dabbed her eyes, walked back to the house, changed into her flat shoes, picked up her handbag, and caught the bus to the golf club.

As she strode towards the clubhouse, she found something soothing about the bare green spaces of the golf course: everything trimmed and under control, the rake marks in the cold white sand of the bunkers. The sky above the eighteenth hole was dark grey, and very occasionally, a ball came from nowhere, like a lost hailstone.

Gerald Clore sat in the clubhouse bar, which was filled with smoke and smarmy laughter. Daisy liked golf courses, but golfers she could take or leave. A few of the men glanced at her when she walked in, but it was Clore, on his bar stool, who spoke, barely looking up from his brandy. 'Sorry, madam. It's no ladies in the bar,' he said.

'Well you'd better talk to me outside, then, Gerald, hadn't you?'

Now everybody turned to watch. Clore was tall and broad, with a big shining dome of a bald head, and a white moustache. He wore an argyle tank top and matching socks. To

Daisy's surprise, he stood from his stool with a resigned sigh. Did he recognise her? Perhaps this was a familiar clubhouse scene – a man called out by some female he'd wronged. 'You can walk me to my car,' he said.

'You can drive me home,' she replied, making sure everyone heard. She followed him out of the bar.

'Listen,' he said, as they stepped into the gravel car park. 'I don't know who you are, but I'm retired now. I assume you have some squabble with the police?'

'You could put it like that.'

'Well, I suggest you take it up at HQ. Even if you feel that I may have been involved *at the time*, it's really no longer my problem.'

'I want to talk about Robert Seacombe,' Daisy said.

Clore tried to maintain the same dismissive attitude, but she saw him flinch at the name. 'Whatever that man did to you, it's nothing to do with me.'

'He's my husband.'

'Well, then, I don't see how I can help you.' He cast his gaze across the car park, both ways. 'And it's really out of order for you to be speaking to me at this point.'

'Because of the investigation, you mean? Because of what you're planning to say about Robert.'

The skin on Clore's face hung loose and smooth. His blood-shot eyes watered in the fresh air. 'I have been told to cut all contact with Seacombe and Harper.'

'I'm sure you didn't need to be told,' Daisy said. 'If I were you I'd be in hiding.'

'He may think sending you here will intimidate me, but he's wrong. This silly stunt is exactly the kind of thing that will get

228

him into trouble. It's always been Robert's problem: he can't just leave people alone.'

'He doesn't know I'm here,' Daisy said.

'Oh, nonsense,' Clore said. He walked over to an awning by the clubhouse, and retrieved his golf bag. Daisy followed him.

'He doesn't know you're cooperating, either,' she said. 'He doesn't know you're a rat. Yet.'

Clore took out an iron, and turned to her. 'Who do you think you are? I've a good mind to call the Yard and tell them what you're up to. Besides which, marching into a gents' bar like this, dragging me out, and then ranting and raving, name-calling – it's completely undignified. Especially for a woman of your age.'

'How old would you like me to be?'

'What?'

Daisy reached into her handbag, and produced an envelope. 'Fourteen? Twelve?'

'I don't know what you're talking about.'

She held the envelope out to him. His grip on the golf club tightened.

'What is this?' he said.

'Would twelve be young enough?' She nodded to the envelope. 'It's difficult to age some of these girls. The way they dress. That thing they do with their eyes. They look so much older on camera.'

Clore went for the envelope, and she pulled it away. He took a step towards her, and she backed up.

'I'll break your neck, woman,' he said.

'Not a clever move,' Daisy said.

In the fading light, Clore looked over his shoulder at the big clubhouse window. Daisy put the envelope back in her handbag, and tried to hide her shaking hands.

Clore smiled. 'It's all a bit ridiculous, this, isn't it? Why don't we take a little ride, talk it over? I can drop you at the bus stop. It's a long walk back to civilisation from here, and it's getting dark. What do you say? We could have a chat, sort this mess out.'

'How's your wife?' Daisy said.

Clore shrugged.

'She used to talk about this little place you had in Wales. The Gower. A bolt-hole, she called it.'

He put the golf club back into the bag, and turned.

'It always sounded so ideal,' Daisy said. 'So peaceful. You could go there, forget about everything.'

But Clore strode off, across the car park. Daisy took a few steps towards the clubhouse, and made sure she was in view of the large window. Clore got into his kidney-coloured Jaguar Mark 2, and just sat there. *Go on, go on*, Daisy muttered to herself. *Just go.* Clore was right: the golf club was miles from the nearest village. If she began to walk first, he would pass her in his car. She didn't like the idea of that, and didn't fancy a walk through the woods, either. She shuffled into the small porch of the clubhouse, which stank of mud and chalk and sweaty shoes. The men in the bar watched her, but she ignored them, and waited until – finally – the headlamps of Clore's Jag swept across her body, and the noise of the engine receded.

'Has that rotter left you here without a ride home?' one of the men called from the bar. 'Bloody coppers! Why don't I give you a lift, love?'

'I'll walk,' Daisy said.

When she got off the bus, an hour later, she vomited into the long grass by the coastal path. Relief. They never showed this scene in the movies, she thought. She tidied herself up, and went home. Robert wasn't there, and the children huddled together before the fire. Linda stroked her brother's head. 'He's asleep,' she whispered.

Daisy nodded to her daughter, and went up to the attic, where she opened the envelope, and replaced her old scrapbook photos of Ginger Rogers, Deanna Durbin and Barbara Stanwyck.

Two weeks later, Daisy stood at the kitchen window, looking out at the sea. A huge ship lay on the horizon line, the bent arm of some giant crane rising from its body. Upstairs, she heard Robert turning over in the bath, his loud, startled cough. He and Ray Harper were to travel up to London that day, to hear of their fate.

Through the window, Daisy saw a car slow down and pull in to the kerb across the road. The driver peered at the house. It was Inspector Lyle. For a moment, she didn't know if Lyle could see her, but eventually he nodded, slowly, before driving away.

Robert pulled the plug, and his bathwater gushed through the pipes. Daisy could not bear to speak to him that morning, so she slipped out of the house and took a brief walk, mentally rehearsing her schedule for the day.

Her original idea – more instinct than plan – had been to destroy everything. She had stooped into Robert's garden shed, with its gun cabinet, its lime sack, its spiders and shears, and had settled on the mallet he used to knock cricket stumps into the ground. She'd hauled the mallet into the kitchen, and after a couple of unsteady practice swings, had brought it down on the Moffat cooking range, one of the first items on Lyle's inventory. The blow was relatively ineffective – a minor dent in the corner of the stove top. She took off the metal frames above the hobs, and placed them on the worktop. She swung again. This time, she felt a massive jolting pain in her shoulder, and heard the hissing of gas. She panicked for a moment, but she'd simply knocked one of the knobs, which she turned off gratefully. Daisy had put the mallet down, massaged her shoulder, and looked around the kitchen at the sturdy fridge, the oak table and the stainless steel sink. She had decided to change her tactics.

Her revised strategy had taken some planning, but Daisy could plan better than she could swing a mallet. As soon as she'd known the date of Robert's trip to London, she'd set everything in motion. She promised the car to a garage in Kemptown, with the understanding that they should strip it for parts, and she'd called a removal firm from Petersfield – far enough out of the city so that Robert wouldn't know them. She donated clothes, jewellery and smaller furnishings to places even Robert wouldn't hassle: the Sisters of Bethany, the synagogue, the women's shelter.

The removal van turned up at eleven that morning, by which time Daisy had dragged most of their lighter belongings into the living room.

When Robert arrived home, she was sitting on one of the wooden chairs from the old county-beat police house. It still smelled damp. The carpet showed angular patches of fresh colour where the sofas had been. The television set and the radio had gone. The big mirror remained on the wall, because they'd bought that before he became CID.

She stood when she heard the front door open.

'Daisy? Get dressed, we're going out for dinner,' he called.

'Probably a good idea,' she said to herself. They didn't really have much crockery anymore.

He looked young when he stepped into the living room, his eyes filled with a kind of wonder. He wore his best blue suit, and a pale green tie. She could smell his sour aftershave, and talcum powder, beer, cigar smoke. The stink of celebration. He put his hands deep into his pockets, and squinted. 'What's this?'

'Retirement present.'

'You what? Where's the car?' He pointed back out towards the road.

'Gone.'

'What are you doing? Are you trying to . . . leave me?'

'No. The opposite.'

He smiled, as if he'd found the answer. He strode across the living room and put his hand on her arm. 'Oh, darling, listen: it went *well*. Really well. Everything's going to be fine. You don't have to do this. Whatever you're doing. They're dropping the case. They thought Gerry Clore was going to testify, but he's bottled it. Gone AWOL. We're in the clear. We're all right.'

'We are not all right. And you're handing in your resignation.'

'You're not listening, Daisy. They've got nothing, love.'

'They've got *me*.'

He winced. 'What are you talking about, woman? What's happening? Where's the bloody settee?'

'It's all gone.'

'You sold it?'

'After a fashion.'

'For cash?'

'I gave it away. This house was rotten, Robert. The things we had – they were bought with dirty money. I won't have that in my home anymore. You're going to hand in your resignation from all police work by the end of the week. If you don't, Lyle gets everything I know, and everything Gerald Clore knows. And I'll leave, and take the kids.'

Robert almost laughed, but then he cast another glance around the room, as though looking for some kind of weapon. '*Seriously?*'

She nodded.

'You've gone mad. This is *ridiculous*. We come through all of their shit. On the day we finally come through their shit, you go and do this. It's unbelievable. Anyway, what do *you* know? What could *you* tell anyone?'

'I know enough. You resign, or they get it all.'

Robert sighed. 'Obviously, Daisy, I can't let that happen.'

'You'll stop me, will you?'

'If I have to.'

'You lay one hand on me, and Lyle gets documents from Clore's solicitor. It's been arranged. You're done. You jack it in. Friday at the latest.'

'Then what?'

'We start again, Robert. We have our house, we have our

children. I still have some money put away, from when Mum and Dad passed. We'll start again.'

Robert looked at his watch. Daisy knew every little phase of his temper, and this was the critical point. He'd either snap, now, or crumble.

He walked away from her and slammed his fist into the wall. Then he sat down on the carpet and put his hands over his face. Daisy approached him carefully.

'Isn't it better, Robert, to know that all that poisonous stuff is out of our house?'

'I earned all that. I bought it for my family.'

'Robert, that's not fair. Your family don't want you to be a criminal.'

'Don't you dare call me that,' he said.

'You don't have to do those wretched things anymore, Robert. Don't you feel better?'

'Not really,' he said.

'You will,' she said.

'Why are you doing this?'

'Because I chose you.'

'I don't believe it. When they told me Gerry Clore wasn't going to talk, this morning, I thought it was all done with. We were home and happy.'

'People can change, Robert.'

'No, Gerry's finished. He's had a breakdown or something.'

'I was talking about you.'

Daisy had predicted that Linda, as a teenager, would take it hardest, and initially that seemed to be the case. 'It's just one humiliation after another,' she had cried, before storming out of the house. Daisy had not touched Linda's belongings, but she understood her daughter's anguish. She could only hope for forgiveness.

Michael's silence surprised her. On that first evening, she and Michael ate beans on toast, alone at a picnic table in the kitchen. He wouldn't meet her eye.

'You know, it won't be long before we have a TV again. Certainly a radio. And you have your comics, of course,' she said, her voice echoing. 'And your cars.'

'But they're not . . . *after* us, anymore?'

'They were never after you, Michael.'

'I meant Dad. It's all over, is it?'

'Yes. It's finished.'

'So he's not going to jail?'

'No, love, it's going to be fine,' Daisy said. 'Nobody's going to jail.'

Michael finally looked up from his dinner, and she saw that he wasn't relieved, but troubled.

She had left Robert one good suit and two ties, for job interviews. They had the same argument about his resigning several times over the next few days, but Robert heard rumours of high-level changes in the squad, and so he gave in. The CID men presented him with a garish, beady-eyed stuffed owl, similar to the one he'd killed on the hunting trip, years before. 'I suppose you want me to give this to charity, do you?' he said.

'Nobody would take it,' Daisy said.

Robert insisted on placing the huge owl by the door in their bedroom. At dawn, Daisy could see the fake eyes glowering.

For the first few months after Robert's resignation, Daisy wondered if she'd made a mistake. He would wake just after noon, and drink steadily until the early hours of the next morning. His weight dropped, and he sometimes went days without bathing, his greasy hair staining the pillow.

'Why don't you go out for a walk?' she said, returning from a frugal trip to the high street to find him eating dry slabs of bread at the kitchen worktop. 'Go to the pub or the bookie's or something?'

'Don't you see?' he said. 'I can't go to those places now. Not anymore.'

'Have you thought about work, Robert?'

'Where? Where can I work? I used to run this town, and now you want me to ask some spiv if I can work the door of a nightclub? I'd be a laughing stock. I've lost everything.'

'No you haven't, Robert,' she said.

Daisy found employment first, at the White Dove coffee bar in town. The clientele were young people with earnest faces and odd clothes. Revolutionaries with good manners. Linda had taken a part-time job shelving books at the local library, so she could have some 'independence', and she came to the Dove to spend her money. At first, she treated Daisy with disdain, but the older kids ordered their coffee politely, and Linda eventually heeded their example.

The coffee bar was right next to the Regent cinema, but Daisy couldn't go in. She blamed the rise in admission prices, but there were other reasons.

One afternoon, she returned from work to find Ray Harper in the kitchen, drinking tea with Robert. 'Hello again, Daisy,' Harper said, baring his small teeth. 'How was your shift?'

'Fine,' Daisy said, aware of the coffee grounds staining her fingers. 'How was yours?'

'Raymond is a man of leisure these days,' Robert said. For the first time in a while, Robert wore a clean shirt, and he'd slicked his hair back, revealing small red spots at his temple.

'Really?' Daisy said.

'Yes,' said Harper. 'I'm afraid I met the same fate as Robert, although – in my case – it was a new chief inspector who gave me the final push, rather than a family member.'

Daisy shot him a stern glance.

'Me and Ray are talking about ventures,' Robert said.

'What do you mean?'

'We're going into business.'

'Bus boys?' Daisy said.

'Private security,' Harper said.

Daisy took a step towards the table. 'You better be straight,' she said. 'I won't have Robert involved in any nonsense.'

'Relax, woman,' Robert said.

'Don't talk to me like that,' Daisy said. 'I mean it. If there's even the hint that you two are up to your old tricks . . .'

'We couldn't get away with it,' Harper said, and Daisy heard a new weariness in his voice. 'They'll be watching us. Besides. I don't have the stomach for it anymore.'

Harper stood, put his teacup in the sink, and nodded his goodbyes. A few moments later, the front door slammed shut.

'Robert, I'm telling you now: I don't like this idea,' Daisy said.

'There won't be any funny business,' Robert said.

'Can't you find someone else to work with?'

'You have to be realistic, Daisy. Working together is the only solution for me and Ray. Nobody else will have us.'

One evening in July, a newspaper landed on the mat and unfurled as Daisy passed through the hallway. Daisy only stopped because she was already carrying that day's edition in her hand. She saw a blurred figure at the coloured glass in the door. As she went back for the paper, the figure slipped away. It was no paper-boy.

'What was that, Daisy?' Robert called from upstairs.

'Nothing. The newspaper.'

She knew where to look. The cinema listings. A film, underlined.

Daisy could not justify going to see Paul, although she tried. She told herself that she'd sacrificed enough, that she was looking after her children, that she'd emptied her house of ill-gotten gains, that she'd saved her husband from his crooked ways, and refused the opportunity to leave him. But none of her arguments sounded convincing. And yet she went to the cinema anyway.

In the plush red dark of the Astoria, Paul kissed her cheek. 'When you wrote to say you couldn't see me,' he said, 'I didn't know what had happened at first. *You've blown it*, I thought. *She thinks you're a freak.*'

'You *are* a freak. You always have been – writing letters to girls in different countries.'

'Just the one girl.'

'What did they say to you? The inspectors?'

'Everything you'd imagine. I was pretty sure I'd ruined your life.'

'Paul, it's none of my business, but they said something about you sending money to a woman back home.'

'A woman?' he said. Then he laughed, so that people in the cinema turned around. 'I'm paying off the last of the house, for Marguerite, my half-sister. Listen, there have been stranger marriages in the prairie lands of the Canadian west, but Marguerite's not my type.'

'Stop it.'

'The age gap is too big, and quite frankly she is stone cold crazy.'

'Paul.'

The auditorium darkened, and there was a rustling, and then a hush.

'What happened in the basement of the Academy . . .' Daisy said.

'Yes.'

'It can't happen again. I'm married, Paul. I made my choice. It was a long time ago, but I made it, and now I have to live with it.'

'And so do I, apparently,' he said. 'Why would you punish yourself like this? Is it fear?'

'No. And it's not a punishment, Paul. He's my husband. They're my family.'

'So, you don't want to see me anymore.'

'I do. But does it have to be some ruinous affair, like in the thirties? Could we not just be friends?'

Paul looked away. She'd thought he'd be angry, but it seemed he'd come to the same conclusion, though it was clearly harder for him to accept.

'If we're just friends,' he said, 'then why are we sneaking around like criminals?'

'Robert wouldn't understand this. He wouldn't understand what we have.'

'But we *do* have something.'

Someone in the row behind told them to hush up.

She'd have understood if he never wanted to see her again, and it was two weeks before they next saw a film together. Afterwards, he asked her to take a bus ride.

'Where to?'

'It's sort of difficult to explain.'

Mid-afternoon. The bus struggled up the city's steepest hill, past the yeasty stink of the brewery and beyond the school, and the tight terraced streets packed with bright-coloured houses and pubs on every corner. They alighted at the top of the hill, in the area known as Hanover. Daisy's grandparents had once lived around there, amongst the railway workers and herring curers and the Italian street vendors.

'What are we doing here?' Daisy said.

'This is where I live now,' Paul said.

'Excuse me?'

'I moved to town. Are you angry?'

'How long?'

'A few months ago. That's my flat.'

He pointed at the top floor of a terraced house. The hot, sweet smell of chemicals came from the launderette next door.

'Oh God, Paul.'

'Are you furious?'

'I'm so sorry.'

'I'm not. You want to see inside?'

She nodded.

Cats roamed the communal hallway. They went upstairs. 'It's a lot of climbing, all told,' she said.

'Yeah, but you should see me getting to the station in the mornings. I roll down that hill like a cheese wheel.'

Daisy was still laughing when they got into the flat. She had expected the place to be spare, plain and fastidious, but it was full and warm. A bright striped rug covered much of the floor. Over by the sash window, junk cluttered his writing desk — cigarette cards of old ice-hockey players, and a tourist image of the famous giant smoking pipe from his hometown. On the walls hung photographs of his family, along with film posters, some of them in French.

'This must be your mother,' Daisy said, touching a black and white picture of a smiling, dark-haired woman with a baby on her hip in front of a towering wheat field.

'Yes. And this is me as a kid,' Paul said, pointing to the chimp in a poster for *Bedtime for Bonzo*.

'You're funny,' she said.

'Inspector Ford said I was an unnatural man,' Paul said.

Daisy took a long breath. 'I have seen a lot of things these past few months, Paul. Honestly. There is nothing wrong with *you*.'

He made tea, and they both tried not to cry. It seemed that another life was pushing against their reality, but the pain of that would fade. Daisy felt a tentative sort of freedom in the privacy of his flat. She could hear kids out on the street, and the whir of machines from the launderette, and barrels being rolled into the cellar of the Bricklayer's Arms, but all such noise seemed mercifully distant.

1998

During the first few days of Cassie's absence, Lucas asked the teachers for information. He simply wanted to *talk* about her, but the staff didn't know anything. The only reason they noticed she'd gone was because they had to deal with *him* now. He sent her a text: I HOPE ALL IS OKAY. When she failed to reply, he wrote GET WELL SOON. X

Later that week, his old learning assistant returned. As he came into the classroom, Terry waved and mouthed 'hello' in a huge, exaggerated way, sticking out his turtle-like tongue. He sat next to Lucas. '   miss me?' he asked.

Lucas tried to smile.

Terry pointed to a small white plaster on his cheek. '   a chunk out   much better   .'

Lucas raised his hands to sign, and then dropped them. 'Good to see you,' he said, but Terry was like a monster to him now. He'd read about the word monster, and where it came from. It meant 'omen'. Terry meant that Cassie wasn't coming back.

The next week, he told Terry he didn't need any help. There was a year seven boy, he said, with hydrocephalus, who could do with some extra support. Terry clapped him on the back. '   you'd be fine.   anyway.   me, just call. I'll come runnin'!'

Soon enough, Lucas really began to suffer – not in the dramatic way they did at the end of Shakespeare plays, but in that mundane everyday sense he'd suffered before her arrival. Only worse.

'Hey, Mario!   slut gone?' said Duncan Youds.

Youds' friends insinuated that Lucas had raped her, and dumped her dead body in the sea. He watched them bellow at him. For the past few months, he'd stood up to those boys. He had smashed his rules for Fitting In, because she'd told him to. But now she was gone.

His fingers twitched.

On Thursday of the second week, Lucas visited The Cut before school. At seven in the morning, the barber's pole stood still. Cassie's mum was setting up the shop: flicking switches, and dragging huge leather chairs to the sinks. Lucas knocked on the door. She looked at him through the plate glass of the shopfront.

Closed, she signed.

Lucas pointed to himself. *L-U-C.*

I know. I remember. I know who you are.

He realised she would not open the door for him. She wore a faded, sleeveless Guns N' Roses T-shirt; her hair was tied back, streaked blonde, and Lucas saw for the first time her resemblance to Cassie.

Is Cassie here? he asked.

No.

Where is she?

She straightened up and took a long breath. *Don't know. She's an adult.*

Do you know when she is coming back to school?

She made a pitying face. He certainly recognised that expression. *It's not my business, really. You'll have to talk to her.*

But I don't know where she is! You must know. She lives here!

Not really, these days.

What do you mean?

I'm sorry, she signed, her fist circling on her chest. She looked away, down the street, disengaging. He tried to catch her eye again, but she'd reached the limits of her patience. Lucas gave up. As he turned to go, he noticed the name of the blue-green liquid that disinfected the scissors: BARBERCIDE.

Sometimes, he didn't get the joke until it was too late.

Even after three weeks, a part of him absolutely believed she would return for their joint performance of 'A Life in the Day', which they had practised together. Even when she failed to appear at the start of the lesson, he thought she might arrive, just in time for his turn.

Mrs Finch called his name, and he strode to the front and stood before his peers, who sat in curved rows. He had brought with him a typed version of his original 'A Life in the Day', written in English. Just in case. He glanced at the door one last time, and then at his watch. Mrs Finch waved at him, told him to begin. She kept plants in the room, and Lucas could smell the warm soil in the pots. He looked at his paper, and then turned it face down. Cassie wasn't coming, but he decided to sign, anyway:

I usually wake up with the sun. My curtains are red, and on a summer morning, they glow like a heart! I go downstairs and have breakfast with my mum. My mum is beautiful, and she tells jokes that are a little bit funny and a little bit sad. For example . . .

Lucas paused, because Cassie was supposed to tell the joke here. It didn't make sense in sign language. He glanced up. Some of the kids grimaced, others smirked. He continued to sign.

I like school. I wish the teachers would look at me when they're talking, but I just read to catch up. Cassie helps me, of course. School has been so much better since she came.

Cassie hadn't known about that bit. He'd put it in secretly.

I've never known my dad, and that might sound sad, but it isn't really.

In his peripheral vision, he saw that Iona had stood up. She began to speak, and for a moment Lucas thought she was talking to him. But then he realised she was trying to interpret for the class. All the other kids stared at her. Lucas frowned, but then went on, more slowly.

I don't know my dad, but it isn't sad, really. I have a cool uncle who takes me swimming after school. He thinks he looks like Ryan Giggs.

Iona signed to him. *What? Over my head. Again. Again spell.*

He finger-spelled: R-Y-A-N G-I

Okay. Understand. Man football. Iona signed.

Lucas smiled, and ploughed on. *I love to swim, and I'm pretty good. I like to just let loose in the water, really smash it. You can get all your emotions out.*

At lunchtime, my favourite is spaghetti Bolognese. I often go back for a second plate. The dinner ladies say, 'You can't have two! You have to pay again!' But I tap my hearing aid, and pretend I don't understand, and they just give it to me.

He waited for Iona, who struggled to keep up. Pink blotches had broken out on her neck. She looked at him.

Again, she signed. *Dinner, what? Understand no.*

It's okay, Lucas signed. *You don't have to do this.*

Just slow slow sign, she replied.

But Mrs Finch intervened, tapping him on the arm. 'Luca. You mus' speak, plea. Otherwi we can't understan. Iona, sit down.   not group work.'

Iona took her seat. She signed *sorry* to him, and he signed *thank you* back. Mrs Finch spent a minute or so calming the rest of the class. She turned back to Lucas. 'Please begin, Lucas. Speakin, plea.'

He turned over the piece of paper on which his original 'A Life in the Day' was printed. 'Okay,' he said aloud, in his distorted voice. 'Okay. I wake up at 7 a.m. My bedroom has a red colour scheme. I brush my teeth, and take a shower. Sometimes I read. At 7.30, I have breakfast. I have a high-fibre cereal, such as Weetabix, or Shredded Wheat. I have semi-skimmed milk. My favourite subject at school is PE . . .'

He read as quickly as he could, and soon finished. He did not look at the door again.

At 3.30 p.m., he walked home. He couldn't face the bus. Lorries rolled past on the B-road, their wake almost dragging him off the pavement. He took the alleyway behind the back-yards of Ringdean. The alley smelled of strimmed nettles, dog shit and Diamond White.

When you signed, Cassie had taught him, you could rebuild a space. You couldn't do that in speech. Words slipped off the surface of things. Her brother, she'd said, could reconstruct, in perfect detail, the flat in London where they'd lived as kids. He'd assemble it, item by item, in the air around him.

Can you do it? she'd once asked Lucas, in the Basin. *Describe a room from your house.*

When she signed *describe*, it was as if she was pulling something out of her chest, hand over hand.

He'd told her about his bedroom, leaving out details he'd thought childish, such as his Michael Jordan beanbag, his old posters of Prince and John Barnes, the cupboards full of ancient toy figures. But now, in the alleyway, another room abruptly came to him, and the memory was so vivid, he stopped walking. He focused on the image. He delved into the memory and looked around it. He saw a brown, corduroy, button-backed sofa, and a leather strap of horse bells on the wall. A shelf of videos stood on the right, next to a television with a wood-look side and metal teeth for the channels. He saw himself in the room, but younger, sat before the television. Summer light came over his shoulder, making reflections in the TV screen, so he couldn't see the programme.

The older Lucas rotated the image, and saw a set of patio doors. Outside the doors, in the garden, a man stood by the shed. It was Lucas's grandfather. He stared up at the house – at the roof or the top windows. In one hand he held a garden tool, in the other hand a folded piece of paper.

Now, in the alleyway, Lucas didn't know why the memory disturbed him. It was something about the blankness of his grandfather's gaze. Lucas felt sick. He put his hands against the flint wall of the alley and spat.

Maybe she'll be back tomorrow, he thought.

Throughout spring and early summer, Cassie's appetite for bicycle-related physical agony just seemed to grow. More often than not, she would sleep over at Mike's the night before a ride, so they could get an early start. She never moved in, officially, but in late May Mike had noticed that she'd left the big black plug that charged her mobile phone in his bedroom socket.

They bathed together, his bruises fading now. She shaved his legs for aerodynamism. Didn't even nick him.

'There are these times,' she said, 'when you get right out on the Downs, and you haven't seen a house for an hour, and the sun is dropping and everything's gone, like, violet in your shades. It's not that you forget where you are . . . it's like you forget *when* you are. There was this one ride, and I thought it was the sixties. No kidding! This fit woman drove past in a Mini with a really sixties haircut, a little bob, and I was like, whoa, I've sliced through time!'

'You didn't know the sixties. The food was shit,' said Mike.

'We should camp, Michael. We should do a tour together! Don't you want to get out into the wilderness, with the beasts?'

Mike examined his legs again. They felt cold and open, but not unpleasant. The tap dripped. 'I like hotels,' he said. 'I haven't worked my arse off for two decades to get laid in a tent.'

'You will *not* have the energy to get laid, mister.'

'Well, I'd rather not have the energy to get laid in a hotel.'

That June, they set out on another big ride. On the way out of town, they stopped at a supermarket, and Cassie went in, while Mike waited outside with the bikes. When he glanced over at the car park, Mike saw Stephen and his daughter get out of a silver Mondeo and walk towards the supermarket entrance, deep in conversation.

'Hey. Erm. Stephen,' Mike called, before he could stop himself.

Stephen looked up. 'Hi. Oh, Jesus, hi!' he said. 'I didn't recognise you in your . . . you look very *bright*.'

Mike glanced down at his Lycra. 'Yeah. It's so people don't knock me off my bike.'

'Perhaps it just makes you a more visible target,' said Stephen, before turning to the girl. 'Hannah, this is my friend Mike. Mike, this is Hannah, my daughter'

'Oh, hey,' Hannah said.

'Hello, love,' Mike said. He smiled at Hannah, and noticed that the missing 'H' from the front of his Honda shone at the end of a chunky silver chain hung around her neck.

Hannah spoke to her dad. 'I'll nip in and get the stuff, yeah?'

'Okay, sweetie. Thanks.'

Mike and Stephen stood in silence for a moment, until Stephen nodded to the bicycle. 'She's still going strong, then.'

'Who? Oh yeah. A couple of adjustments,' Mike said. 'So, did I just see you get out of a *car*?'

'Mm,' Stephen said.

'I thought you hated cars.'

'Just yours,' said Stephen. 'It's a hire car. We're driving up to Manchester for a look round. Oh. I didn't tell you: Hannah got an unconditional offer from the university there.'

'Wow. That's amazing.' Mike found himself moved, and then embarrassed. 'What subject?'

'Anthropology.'

'What's that, dinosaurs?'

'No.'

'Are you going to move up there, too?'

'While I'm sure she'd love that,' Stephen said, 'I'm going to stay here. You have to let them make their own way.'

'You always know the right thing to do,' Mike said.

Stephen laughed with surprise. 'Not quite.'

'Hey, listen, when she hauls her gear up there – I could get a van from work. I could help.'

'That's kind, Mike, but I will never, ever, get in a motor vehicle with you.'

Mike snorted. 'You're a daft twat, you are.'

'Yeah, well,' said Stephen. He looked down at the two bicycles. 'So are you.'

They smiled at each other. 'Right,' Stephen said, nodding to where Hannah was coming back out of the supermarket with a shopping bag. 'Here she comes. Take care, eh?'

'You too, mate. And listen. If you need anything – you and Hannah . . .'

'Thanks. Thanks, Mike.'

Stephen patted the seat of the bicycle and walked off towards the car. Behind Hannah, Cassie emerged from the supermarket, arms loaded with satsumas and packets of crisps. Both women were in his eye line. What was the difference between their ages? Five years? Three?

'You all right?' Cassie said. 'You look pale.'

'Yeah, no. I'm okay.'

She crouched to study his bike.

'Is your wheel true?' Cassie asked.

'Yes.'

She pretended to sniff with tears. 'And is your heart, sir?'

Riding out into the countryside, Mike thought of Hannah as he'd first seen her, walking to school with her injured father, recently bereaved. And now she was going to university. He worried about Stephen, though. His wife and daughter both gone within a year. Did he have friends? Mike didn't know.

Eventually, the ride brought quiet to his mind. Mike and Cassie passed vast fields of high crops that made them feel like they were swimming, somehow, or parting the waves.

Fifty miles later, as the day cooled, the route took them along an unpaved path, and Cassie's slicks skidded on the gravel. She toppled, and came down badly on her hip, yelping and laughing with the pain.

Mike dismounted and ran over. 'Cassie? You okay?'

'I'm fine, I'm fine. Bit of a stinger, that's all.'

She turned her hip, to reveal a rip in her shorts, blood from the graze soaking into the dark Lycra.

'I've got some Savlon in my saddle bag,' he said.

'*Really?*' she said. 'What are you, a granny?'

'You never know when you might need it.'

He retrieved the tube of antiseptic, while Cassie stood. He knelt at her feet, and squeezed the white cream onto his dirty fingers. It smelled like Stephen's shed. 'This might hurt,' he said.

When he rubbed the cream into the wound, she walloped him across the head. 'Shit, sorry,' she said.

Mike stared up at her, shocked, his vision rocking.

They rolled down to a pub, the inside of which smelled of fag smoke and toilet cleaner. Farming implements on the walls, Stevie Wonder and Oasis on the jukebox. Cassie danced in the middle of the empty carpet, bent over, swishing her arse in the air. They drank limeade and ate prawn cocktail crisps, then switched to lager tops and microwaved barbecue chicken wings, clawing back the calories.

The pink and blue sunset came through the window like neon. Like disco lights.

Cassie received a text message, and she swore and deleted it. Perhaps she wanted him to think it was another man. The high from the ride had faded, and she looked miserable now.

'Everything okay?' Mike asked.

'Let's go,' she said.

On the train back to Ringdean, Cassie began to talk about her family. Her father had deserted them, and when she was twelve, she'd cycled all the way across London to confront him. She'd wheeled her bike into every bookie's and every pub in Streatham, and eventually chased a guy down the high street, screaming abuse at him, even when it turned out not to be her father.

'Sometimes,' she said, 'it's whoever happens to be there.'

She moved her hands while she spoke, almost signing. The memories of those movements, and that language, upset Mike, but he resisted the urge to tell her to stop.

At the station, before they parted ways, she asked him to promise to take her camping. He told her okay. He held her, one hand steadying their bikes. He felt her need and the inevitable way he would manipulate it.

Having shouldered the bicycle up the stairs into his flat, Mike noticed that the black handlebar tape hung loose on the right-hand side. He unwound it to reveal worn white tape underneath, covered in oily fingerprints – Stephen's, perhaps, or those of his wife or his daughter. Mike sat on the laminate flooring, and thought again of Hannah and Stephen on the M1 North. He felt an odd flaring of hope, but not for himself.

From her seat at the enquiry desk, Linda saw Paul come in through the library doors. He glanced around. Maybe he didn't know she worked here. Their eyes met. He knew.

He approached the desk, not bothering to hide his limp. He had undergone a transformation since she'd last seen him. Behind his glasses, his eyes were swollen and dark. Splinters of white stubble glinted on his cheeks. 'I need to talk to you,' he said.

'Not interested. I told you, very specifically, to stay away from me.'

'Yet you hang around outside *my* house, and you call my employers, get me fired.'

'Are you drunk?' she asked.

'I'm an old man. I'm not going to be around forever.'

Linda shrugged. 'I can call security, have you removed.'

'I'm really past caring,' he said. 'Daisy was a part of my life – by *choice* – for a long time, and whatever you may think of that, I want it to be understood.'

Linda looked at the OAPs stirring in the soft seats. Her

colleague, Suzanne, craned her neck to see what was happening.

'Not here,' Linda said. She stood, and marched towards the back exit. Paul followed. Out in the alleyway, the sun glared so that she had to squint. She started in before he had a chance. 'Listen,' she said. 'What happened between you and my mum – I can't do anything about it, and I don't want to know. But what the hell did you think you were doing, sitting in that room reading to my dad?'

'Penance,' he said.

'What?'

'It was *my fault*. What happened to your parents was my fault.'

'What are you talking about?'

'Your father found some letters I wrote to your mum.' He stared at the ground. 'Daisy had given most of them to me, for safekeeping, but she must have kept a couple.'

Linda thought of the letter she'd found tucked into the old copy of *Picturegoer*.

'I wrote to her a lot,' Paul said. 'Mainly when I lived in Winnipeg, but there was the odd note, after I moved here, too. It's what people did.'

'How do you know my dad found them?'

'She called me, the day she died. Asked me to go see a movie with her. I said, *When?* She said, *Right now*. What with the treatment and all, I hadn't seen her for months, and wasn't expecting to. I told her she sounded terrible.'

'What did she say to that?'

'She said, Let's hear your singing voice after three rounds of radioactive therapy.'

Yes, thought Linda. That's exactly what her mum would have said.

'But I knew something was wrong,' Paul continued. 'I pushed until she came clean. She said, Robert has found the letters, and he's got your address, and he's mad as hell. She told me to get out of the flat – I was in Hanover then – I haven't always lived in a trailer.'

'Did you? Leave your flat?'

'No. I said I was going to wait for him, that we were finally going to talk, like grown-ups. We were nearly sixty, for God's sake. Too old to have secret friends.'

'*Friends?*'

'Yeah, friends. I told Daisy it was about time. I said me and him were going to work it out.'

'You didn't know him.'

'That's what Daisy said.'

Linda wanted out. She didn't want to listen to this. But Paul carried on talking, steadying himself with a hand on the brickwork of the alley.

'I waited for him. I just sat there, thinking about what I was going to say to him.'

'And what *did* you say?'

Paul frowned. 'He never came. Don't know if he ever meant to. He went back to the house. To Daisy. I'm sorry.' He removed his glasses, and wiped his face with his hand. 'I've never told this story before. Not out loud. Can you believe that?'

'Yes.'

'I was in the flat, waiting, and time ticked on. Finally, I figured out he wasn't coming. I called the house – first time ever – but nobody picked up, so I did what I should have done straightaway. I went over there. But it was too late. Place was taped off. Police everywhere.'

Linda could hear herself breathing. 'How did you find out what had happened?'

'I went to the hospital.'

He'd been there, this man. Linda might have passed him in the corridor.

'Had to hear it from some damn nurse,' he said.

'You never called the police? Afterwards.'

'He *was* the police.'

'He'd quit by then.'

'I was sure they'd come for me, because of the phone records and the letters. I was sure they'd have questions. And when they didn't come, and I saw what the newspapers said, well . . . They said it was a mercy killing. So, what good would it have done to come forward with my version of things? I wasn't going to make a murderer out of him, and make something else of your mother. It would have wrecked your family.'

'So, why are you telling me now?'

'Because you came after me. You came to my home. I think you wanted to know.'

'I don't believe you,' Linda said.

He spread his arms. 'Not much I can do about that.'

'I do not believe you. You're lying to make him look bad. He did it because she was in pain. She was dying.'

'She wasn't,' he said. 'Christ, you know she wasn't dying. She was going to make it.'

Linda clenched her fists, and backed slowly away from him. 'What the hell are you doing here?'

'I had to come . . .'

Her voice was cracking now, her breath ragged. 'How could you sit in that room, reading to him, after what he did?'

'It was my punishment. His too.'

'It wasn't enough. It is not enough.'

'I shouldn't have said anything. I should have left things as they were.'

'There are a lot of things you should have done differently.'

'You think I don't know that?'

'You need to leave now. Don't you ever come back here again.'

He stared at her for a moment, and something in her features made him buckle. He stepped towards her, but she turned, went back into the library, and slammed the door behind her. She could still hear him out there. She kept her hands on the door until she heard the dry drag of his limp, getting quieter, as he made his way down the alley towards town.

Lucas worried that he would forget his conversations with Cassie. At school, he hid in the pines surrounding the swimming pool. He inhaled the warm chemical mist, and recreated their exchanges, trying to stamp their gestures on his memory. He made subtle improvements, came up with answers that made it impossible for her to leave.

Despite his best efforts, he soon felt his sign vocabulary fading. He was no longer sure of the hand shape in 'stressful', and forgot the whole sign for 'busy'. He thought of Marty McFly's fingers disintegrating in *Back to the Future*.

*

In maths on Thursday, Youds came over and tapped the table. He smiled at Lucas, but without the usual cruelty. Lucas noticed, for the first time, that Youds had eczema. The skin flaked in the webs of his hands.

'Good to see   itch   back in town,' he said.

'What?' said Lucas.

'Cassie. Your   port worker. I just saw her outside the staffroom.'

'Really?'

'Yeah. She said to tell you   see you in biology.'

Lucas stood, and the faces in the room turned towards him.

'She's got   nice   , man. I'd probably do her,' said Youds.

'Whatever,' Lucas said, his hand instinctively chopping at his hip. He walked towards the door, but his teacher ordered him back to his seat. Lucas obeyed, partly because his heart was thumping so hard he could barely see.

The biology lab reeked of burned metal. Lucas waited fifteen minutes, perfecting an expression of sadness, which he intended to brighten into relief when she arrived. But she did not arrive. He walked up to Mr Solomon's desk, and made his inquiry. Mr Solomon had a Beckham haircut, and rolled up his sleeves during the summer term. The girls adored him. He scanned the register, trying to answer Lucas's question. 'Cassie? Do we have a Cassie?'

'My learning assistant.'

Solomon blinked. 'Oh yes.   left, though, hasn't she? I thought Terry   .'

Lucas returned to his desk. He tried to remember his old,

pre-Cassie, self. That boy would have advised self-control. So, he sat down before a diagram of the human lung, and he tried to breathe.

At form period, after lunch, he approached Youds. 'You were lying, weren't you?' he said.

Youds nudged his friends, and they all laughed.

'What's up, Mario?' said Youds. '   gone and left you?'

'Please,' said Lucas. 'Please don't call me Mario. You didn't really see her, did you?' Lucas said.

'   hard to see someone, Mario, really, when they're suck-ing   .'

Lucas grabbed Youds' neck with one hand, and squeezed. Youds' eyes bulged, and he tried to take hold of Lucas's wrist, but he had no grip. One of the other boys pushed Lucas, but Lucas kicked him. He walked with Youds, pressing harder into the thick flesh. He felt like he could kill him.

Señor Potts stumbled across the room to break it up. Lucas knew that Potts was probably shouting in Spanish. He let go, and Youds fell backwards, his eyes red. He kept repeating a word, over and over. Lucas had to look beyond Señor Potts to see. Youds was saying, 'Soon. Soon. Soon.'

That afternoon, they had PE. Lucas's kitbag went missing. He searched the onion-stinking changing rooms, but nobody would make eye contact with him.

Eventually, he found his dark blue polo shirt soaked and swelling in one of the toilets. All pretty standard schoolboy stuff. He used a cricket stump to fish it out, and transferred it straight to the bin. The PE teachers told him he had to find something to wear from the lost property box, and the only thing that fitted him was a pink Global Hypercolor T-shirt from about 1990. He wore it with white shorts, black socks and his school shoes.

Mercifully, the afternoon's activity was cross-country running, and Lucas pounded the chalk trails of the nearby woods alone. The sky turned white, and then graphite grey. With his body-heat, the borrowed T-shirt changed colour, too: from pink to purple.

Back in the changing rooms, Youds and his crew were waiting.

'What now?' Lucas said, bored.

They all repeated his words, contorting their mouths. Lucas sidled past to get his clothes. He checked his trousers for wet patches, and his shirt tail for shit. Everything seemed normal, but he stuffed his uniform into his bag, anyway. He needed to get out of there, quickly.

Youds put a hand on his shoulder. 'We're not   anything to you, now, Mario,' Youds said. '   better to wait   last day. Then, we're going to fuck you up.'

'Like you did today, you mean?'

'You'll see.'

Lucas waited for his uncle outside the school gates in his improvised sportswear. The other kids left on buses and bicycles. They clambered into cars, or marched off in big walking groups, licking Twisters or supping Tango. Soon enough, the street emptied, and Lucas stood alone, looking back at the school buildings. In the high window of the dance studio, girls pretended to be ponies.

It rained, of course. The big cold drops threw up puffs of dust from the pavement. Lucas's hair cream ran down his face, smelling of oranges and almonds, and his Hypercolor T-shirt turned pink again. It would be typical, he thought, if Cassie appeared now, and saw him like this. He wished it, in spite of himself, but she didn't come, and neither did his uncle. Drenched, he stared at a yellow traffic sign, which read: DEAD SLOW CHILDREN.

Walking home, he saw flags of St George in the windows of the houses he passed, ready for the World Cup. They drooped, sodden, around lamp posts, red and white and twisted like the barber's pole of old. Come here to get your flesh slit, they seemed to say. Come here for help.

Back home, Lucas slipped off his shoes in the hallway. He switched the light on and off, but no reply came from the depths of the bungalow.

In the living room, he found his mum staring at the blank screen of the television, her eyes raw.

'I didn't know you were here. You didn't do the thing with the lights,' he said.

'I'm sorry,' she said.

'What's up, Mum?'

'Nothing. It's okay.   okay.'

He felt angry with her suddenly. There was obviously something wrong, but he didn't have the energy to coax it out of her, and he didn't have the strength to cheer her up anymore. He had his own problems.

'Uncle Mike called,' she said. '   sorry   picking you up   .'

'Fine.'

'   was school, today?'

'Like an acid bath.'

She nodded, but then looked up at him. 'Pardon?' she said.

'It was fine,' he said.

'Oh well,' she said. 'Not long until it's all done.'

Maybe this was how life would go for him, without Cassie. The best he could hope for, from anything, was that it would soon be over.

'Yeah,' he said. 'Not long.'

1965–87

Of all the melodramatic endings she'd rehearsed, Daisy had never imagined that it would all work out.

After two years, the jobs were coming in steadily for H&S Security. They signed big contracts in the smaller coastal towns, doing surveillance at dockyards, factories and offices. Soon, they gave the nightshifts to younger men, and worked purely on the administrative side. The ordinariness of the work changed Robert for the better. When Linda put on her records, he lay on his side and walked around the carpet in circles. Even Michael smiled.

One Sunday morning, Robert watched her making breakfast. He'd had a lot to drink the previous night, and sat hunched over at the kitchen table. When Daisy brought him scrambled eggs – a little crisp, as he liked them – he looked at her carefully. 'You seem happy,' he said.

The smile dropped from her face. For a moment, he wore the expression of a detective again: bullying, relentless. But he was too hung over to sustain it. He looked down at his food. Daisy took the pan to the sink, and it hissed when it hit the water.

They bought the corduroy sofa, a cheaper car, hung a strap of horse bells on the wall. As he grew, Michael covered his bedroom with pictures of motorcars: the Lamborghini Miura, the Ford Mustang, the Pontiac Firebird. Robert derided his obsession as 'Polari American nonsense'. For a while, in his teens, Michael dressed almost like a Modern, with a thin tie and tight shirt, but his body broadened and coarsened. By the age of sixteen, he had a five o'clock shadow, and the only clothes that seemed to fit were overalls. He spent his spare time either with Jacqui, his silent sweetheart, or in the workshop of a garage on the outskirts of town. He'd come back filthy with grease, his eyelashes thickened and dark.

Linda's moods fluctuated. One day she screamed at Daisy when she suggested they watch *Fahrenheit 451*, starring her hero, Julie Christie. Maybe she'd read the reviews. But her teenage fires cooled. She had a talent for drawing and painting, but the comprehensive school laid out her options in binary: nurse or secretary. She was scared of blood, but her boss at the library saved her from the typing pool with an offer of full-time employment, and after a few years she moved into a flat in Portslade.

Robert's longer, more regular working hours gave Daisy a certain freedom, and she and Paul continued their cinema-going. Sometimes they went frequently, sometimes less so, as their lives allowed. Paul had a succession of relationships, and even lived with a woman for a while – an Irish nurse called Edna, who enjoyed Downland walks and wanted to get a dog.

In the end, the biggest barrier to Paul and Daisy's meetings was the closing of the cinemas. The West Street Odeon shut in 1973, along with the Regent. Daisy told Paul that one of her first memories was the sight of a German fighter plane positioned as if crashing into the Regent's canopy, as part of the promotion for a Jean Harlow film. She told him about the budgerigars in the foyer and the shining steel teapots, how she'd danced on the sprung floor of the ball-room upstairs.

The next year, they stood on that same street, an arm's length between them, and watched the Academy pulled apart, layer by layer. The crumbling art deco interior was stripped away, revealing the Moorish tiles of the old bathhouse.

'Eventually,' Paul said, 'we're going to have to find some-thing else to do with our time.'

'Not until they pull the last one down,' Daisy said. 'They'll have to drag me out of my seat.'

Michael married Jacqui in '77, and people worried that Linda would be left on the shelf. But in their quiet conversations, during the theatrical trailers, Daisy spoke up in favour of the single life. 'It's better to be alone than unhappy.'

'Mum, please,' Linda said.

'I'm just saying that independence has its benefits. Spinsterism has an unfair reputation.'

'I'm not a spinster, I'm a woman.'

'That's right. That's what I mean.'

But along came Peter, who ruined it, and then left. Daisy mourned for her daughter's lost future until she saw the baby in the cold light of the County Hospital. She persuaded Robert to re-mortgage the house, and they helped Linda to buy the tiny bungalow in Ringdean. That was 1981, by which time the

Astoria had been turned into a bingo hall. The Curzon was already a Waitrose, and later Daisy and Paul went there to run their hands across the dessert freezers, where they had once sat, shoulder to shoulder in the dark.

The decade rolled on. Daisy got small, round reading glasses. The Seacombes bought an iron table and chairs for the garden, where – a glass of bitter in his hand – Robert asked Jacqui when they could expect another grandchild, and Jacqui ran off crying.

When Linda returned to work, Daisy happily took her grandson to the Electric. On the way, they would stop on Kings Road, watching the crane reaching up into the cavity in the Grand Hotel. In the cinema, Lucas sat with the straw of the juice carton resting on his lip, while his eyes marbled in the light of the screen. He fidgeted less than Linda had, and only sometimes did he pull her face towards him to ask, in his language, for clarification. Many of the children's films on offer were musicals, or animations, or both. Nobody could read the lips of a singing cartoon cat. So she took the boy to see grown-up features. He sat, rapt, for two and a half hours of *Out of Africa*. She tried to cover his eyes during the scenes with the lions, but he shrugged her off, calling out with excitement.

She told Paul about her diagnosis in the cinema, so she wouldn't have to look at him in daylight. He nodded slowly. It was 1986, and they'd come to watch *Mona Lisa*.

'I've got a decent chance of a full recovery, they say.'

'Will they start the treatment straight away?' Paul asked.

'Yes. At least one operation, and then the chemotherapy and all that.'

'It takes time . . .'

'I won't be going out much for a while afterwards. They say I'll be very weak, but I feel all right now, apart from the pain, which is pretty much constant to be honest.'

They sat quietly. She searched her handbag for a handkerchief, took out a smaller plastic bag containing the ceramic fox from her bedroom, in four pieces.

'What happened to that?' Paul said.

'Little Lucas dropped it, and it hit the edge of the radiator. I was going to see if I could get it fixed in town.'

'I know a guy on London Road, does that stuff. Here.'

He took the fox, and turned to look at her. Despite the semi-darkness, she could see him just fine, his lips turned down at the corners, his nostrils flared.

'I'm sorry,' she said.

'Daisy. I want to help you. I want to be there.'

'You can't,' she said.

He leaned over the arm of the seat, and they put their foreheads together. He kept his hair unfashionably short in those days, and she felt the soft bristling of it against her skin. From the cinema speakers, the advertisements roared.

He sat back, and she listened to his breathing. Over the years, she had learned to read the signals from his body. 'Dee,' he said. 'If there's anything you need. You want organs, I've got organs. You want blood, I've got blood. Anything at all . . .'

She smiled. 'From you, I will need patience.'

'Anything but that,' he said.

*

A hard year passed, of cutting and probing, of poison in the veins.

Through her sleep, Daisy thought she heard footsteps on the ceiling above. Accustomed to surreal nightmares now, after all the treatment, she thought nothing of it.

The next time she woke, the noises were very real. Lucas had turned on the television downstairs. The sound rose alarmingly, so Daisy could hear the theme music from a children's show as if the band were at her bedside. Lucas must have accidentally twisted the volume knob to maximum. Daisy waited for her husband to go into the living room and turn the TV down, but Robert must have been in the garden. He took Friday afternoons off, and brought Lucas back to their house after school to wait for Linda to finish work. Daisy smiled to herself, and signed pointlessly. *Loud!*

The sign – a finger rotating by the side of the head – was the same as the one hearing people used for madness.

The sound of studio applause made the walls shake, and Daisy knew she had to intervene. She reached for her glasses, but couldn't find them on the bedside table. No matter. She rose slowly from the bed and made her way past the garish owl, onto the landing. She felt a draught and looked up, saw a slight gap in the attic hatch. She would get Michael to sort it out later. Each stair took several seconds to negotiate. She felt like she was moving at the pace of a lengthening shadow.

In the living room, sunlight came through the patio doors behind Lucas, his skinny little body and mass of black hair like the boy Maradona, whom her husband was always cursing. Lucas's hearing aid lay on top of his satchel, switched off but ready to be refitted should his mother walk in.

Lucas waved.

The TV is a tiny bit loud, she signed, and turned down the volume.

He said sorry, a fist rubbing his chest. He looked at her carefully. *Are you okay?* he signed.

Yes, thank you.

When is Mummy coming?

Now. Soon, Daisy signed, squinting at the clock. *Where are my glasses?*

A hammering sound came from the shed outside. Daisy looked up. Blurrily, she saw the swing chair, the pinkish patio slabs, the snapdragons, their colours muted in the shade like lamps turned off. She felt her grandson's gaze follow her own.

Grandpa? he signed.

Yes. Working in the shed.

Lucas rolled his eyes.

The phone rang, and Daisy moved towards it, startling her grandson. *Phone*, she signed. She picked up the receiver and leaned against the back of the sofa. It was Linda, calling to say she had to attend a meeting. She'd be twenty minutes late.

'Don't rush, Lind,' she said. 'Yes, he's helping me. He's fine. Yes, so am I.'

She passed the message on to Lucas, who took it well.

You should go back to bed. Don't worry about me and Grandpa. I'll play with him, if he gets bored! You have to rest.

Will you carry me upstairs? she asked.

You're too heavy.

She laughed. Her doctor would have told her to take it as a compliment.

Outside, Robert emerged from the shed, and peered up at the house. He seemed to be holding a piece of paper in one hand. Daisy couldn't make out his expression. She waved, but maybe he couldn't see her through the patio doors. Then she saw the metal money tin, cracked open on the lawn.

'Oh Christ,' she muttered. 'Lucas.' *Let's go upstairs. Come on.*

I'll walk with you, he signed to Daisy, standing with elastic ease.

He held her elbow, dragging it a little, and they slowly climbed the stairs, pausing at the top. Lucas tapped her hand. *I'm going to play in Uncle Mike's old room*, he signed, pointing down the hallway to the last door on the left.

Ah, yes. Lovely. Stay in there until Mummy comes, okay?

The lure of vintage toys, and the wonder of finding out that your uncle was once a boy too, with his own basket of Matchbox cars. Lucas skittered off, and the door banged shut behind him.

'Stay in there,' she said quietly.

The effort of climbing the stairs again left Daisy exhausted, and she sat down on the edge of the bed, trying to catch her breath. Through the open window came the shush of the Channel, and a breeze which lifted the net curtains and made her husband's suits and shirts and ties tremble in the open wardrobe.

Daisy shuffled back on the bed, and propped herself up with pillows. The air in her nostrils sounded like the bellows she'd used to get the fire going in the old police house. In truth, she couldn't wait to get out of this room, couldn't wait to go to the cinema again with Paul. They had found their unlikely peace, a way of existing, and she did not want to miss a moment of it.

Eyes closed, she remembered how Paul had stood up at the end of the front row during the *Double Indemnity* re-release, and pretended to be felled by the giant cigarette Barbara Stanwyck flicked off-screen, Daisy laughing so hard she missed the gunshot. She remembered *The Exorcist*, the way the tension built and released so that – during one calm, expositional scene – a woman in the audience started screaming, unable to bear the pressure any longer. She remembered how she and Paul had burst out of a rain-drenched black and white thriller, into the hot colour of a summer afternoon.

Eyes open, she watched the hound figurines on the window-sill, locked into their endless chase of the missing fox.

'We'll always have the Electric,' Paul had joked, when they closed practically all the other cinemas in town. Daisy recalled one summer evening in the late sixties. She'd gone to the toilets before the film and saw a girl rinsing out her bathing suit in the sink. The lights in the theatre had malfunctioned, and it was like the old blackout days, an usher's milky beam in the smoke of the aisle. You could smell the dirt and brine of the sea, sharp and pungent on the bodies of the audience. The usher pointed his torch at the beach pebbles on the floor. 'Watch yourself,' he said. 'Just watch yourself.'

Downstairs, she heard her husband enter through the kitchen, the laboured slap of his steps across the lino. Moments later, he was slowly climbing the stairs, scraping something against the banister.

That day in the Electric, she had found Paul slouched in the dark, but only when the film lit up. She felt so at ease with him, it was like she wasn't there. Strange what she remembered. It was like the films she walked into, halfway through: when you see the ending the first time round, it makes no impression, but then, somewhere in the middle of the next showing, you begin to understand.

1998

Linda spent several days in bed, although she hardly slept. Sometimes, she drifted down the hallway, and took shallow baths. She lay there until the water turned cold as her body.

She remembered washing Lucas on the day her mum died, seeing the blood coming off his hands, diluted in the sink. She had tried not to cry, for her son's sake. She didn't want to leave him with a babysitter, but knew she couldn't take him to the hospital either. Eventually, Mike came, and took over.

'How could he do that, with Lucas in the house?' Linda had said to her brother.

Mike was pale, red-eyed. 'Probably didn't know the kid was there,' he said. 'He thought you'd already picked him up. You were late, weren't you?'

At the hospital, the stories of euthanasia and broken hearts had begun to surface. People kept saying that her mum's suffering was over, but Linda demanded to speak to the oncologist. Her dad's old partner, Ray Harper, stopped her from asking questions. She tried to pass him in the hospital corridor, but he spread his arms, stood firm.

'I need to speak to the doctor,' she said.

'You need to leave it, darling,' Harper said.

'For God's sake.'

'For everyone's sake.'

She tried to pass again, and again he blocked her path. She pushed him, and tried to hit him, but he did what men do: he wrapped her in his arms, as though consoling her.

The incident made the front page of the local newspaper: EX-DETECTIVE SHOOTS DYING WIFE AND SELF IN MERCY KILLING.

Such a stupid sentence, Linda had always thought. The newspapermen sniffed out the quirks of the story. She begged them not to mention Lucas, not to print that he had found his grandparents. *What can we do?* they said. *We have a responsibility to the truth.* Linda knew they wanted to work an angle on Lucas's deafness. They saw that as the unique selling point. As if Lucas could have prevented the shootings, hearing or otherwise. He was just a little boy.

Linda had blamed herself. Mike was right: had she not been late, had she arrived at her parents' house twenty minutes earlier, Lucas would never have walked into that room and found the bodies. She wouldn't have had to scrub the blood off his hands and arms. Had she arrived on time, it never would have happened.

And now, all these years later, Linda and Lucas haunted each other in the bungalow. If she felt able, she cooked him dinner, and left it under tin foil on the kitchen counter. Sometimes, she found his big wet footprints in the grey carpet of the bathroom, or heard the gate rattling as he went to school or came back late at night. When they switched the lights on and off, to say that they were home, it was as if they existed only in the circuit boards of the house.

One night, they met each other in the hallway, as he came in after eleven. 'Where have you been?' she asked.

'On the bus,' he said.

'Where to?'

'Here, of course.'

Fortunately, back in 1987, the local journalists had discovered other twists beyond Lucas's inability to hear. They found extra clauses for their headlines: EX-DETECTIVE SHOOTS DYING WIFE AND SELF IN MERCY KILLING. WAKES.

Robert Seacombe – who apparently could not live without his wife – didn't die. His first shot killed Daisy instantly, but when he put the gun against his head, he must have underestimated the awkwardness of the angle, or the force of the recoil, or his sheer, stupid fortune.

When Linda first went to visit her dad in hospital, she hardly recognised him. She found a man with swelling and blackness around the eyes, his head heavily bandaged, and a left cheekbone which had dropped like a coin through a pocket.

She thought, that day, about his old insistence on privacy. *As children of mine, you represent the Force. Your conduct is on show at all times. What goes on between these four walls stays here.* That philosophy had bound and gagged her family for years. And now, here he was, daubed all over the papers he had fought and controlled for much of his career.

He woke once while she sat by his side. She'd stayed beyond visiting hours, dozing in a wipe-clean chair near the bed. His voice roused her. He looked frightened. 'Where is she?' he said, one eye open.

Linda sat forward. 'You know where she is,' she said.

At the time, she had felt guilty for saying that, but the next morning she couldn't be sure the conversation had even happened. Three weeks later he came out of the coma with what the doctors called 'limited cerebral function'. The nurses, the journalists, the coroner – they all said he had never regained the power of speech.

She returned to her parents' house then, and found the police dismantling the bedroom. She would later discover that the crime scene had been mismanaged, half of the evidence spoiled or lost. Nobody could confirm when the police had first arrived on the day her mum died, or who had called them. Former detective Harper had got to the scene before the ambulance. He'd been paying an impromptu visit to his business partner, he claimed, and couldn't remember his precise movements on reaching the house, because he'd been 'overcome with emotion'.

Linda couldn't go all the way into the bedroom. Instead, she looked through the half-open door. She had not expected death to be so colourful. Her dad had fallen backwards and taken down the dressing table. Compact powder and eyeshadow and perfume soaked into the carpet. Yellowing pillow feathers trembled on the surfaces.

The miracle, she'd thought back then, was that something could happen between two people in a room, and nobody would ever know the truth of it. Nobody would ever know what they'd said to each other.

*

Now, she forced herself out of bed, into the muggy grey warmth of a mid-week afternoon. She took the bus to Cedars, walked halfway across the car park and stopped by the huge tree, leaned against it. The low building, with its red bricks and double glazing, and hanging baskets full of primary colours, seemed like a child's toy. Linda watched the people go in and out of the doors – the workers, the relatives. They clocked her, as they got into their cars, and quickly broke eye contact.

She imagined herself walking in through the entrance, and down the corridor. She imagined slipping into his room. But what would she say to him now? He couldn't answer her questions. His last great victory: silence.

Linda took her hand from the cracked grey bark of the cedar, and examined the marks on her palm. She turned and walked back to the bus stop.

The lamp came on, and Linda woke.

'Mum?' Lucas said, perched on the arm of the sofa.

She must have fallen asleep. Through the gap in the curtains, she saw the pink and grey clouds of early morning. 'Lucas?'

'I was just wondering,' he said.

'Yes?'

'If you were looking for someone, where would you start?'

Linda sat up, her mouth sour, her face scarred by the grid pattern of the cushion. 'Well, it depends who you're looking for. Who's missing?'

'I don't really know what I'm doing wrong, but people keep . . . *leaving*.'

'What are you talking about? What's going on?'

He shook his head. 'It doesn't matter,' he said.

'It's okay. You can tell me. You can talk to me.'

'It's fine. Everything is fine.'

'Is this about your dad?' she said.

'No.'

Linda sighed. 'I'm sorry, Lucas. I realise it's been a tough few weeks.'

'Pardon?'

He leaned over to study her lips. His face loomed above her.

'It's been a difficult few weeks,' she repeated.

His body shook with laughter, almost silently, apart from a long, high wheeze.

'Lucas?'

'*A difficult few weeks*,' he said, standing. 'Jesus.'

'I'm worried about you,' she said. 'You're acting strangely. Tell me who you're looking for. Who's missing? What's wrong?'

But Lucas just trudged out of the room, out of the house. After a while, Linda rubbed her face and stood. She went to the kitchen and poured herself a glass of water.

Out of the window she saw the larches in full green blush. The gate clanged, and the postman struggled down the path, a large, lidded box in his hands. He coughed, and knocked on the door. Linda sank back, away from the window. She crept into the hallway, and flinched when he knocked again. His footsteps receded slowly. She waited a few minutes before opening the door, and looking along the street. He'd left the box on the path. She ripped off the tape and lifted the lid. The envelopes, of various colours, their tops torn away, were stacked neatly in the box, the letters folded within. Linda put the lid back on, and left it there. She closed the door, and only returned to haul the box inside an hour later, when the clouds broke.

It took her two days to read them. Paul had sent the full correspondence – her mum's letters as well as his own. The handwriting – Paul's particularly – proved difficult to read; damp and time had damaged the paper. There was Linda's reluctance, too.

She read them in no particular order, simply taking them out of the box one at a time. This one from 1954, this from 1978. She transcribed the more faded letters, slowly copying the words onto an A4 pad at her kitchen table. She found the process strangely absorbing. She didn't know what a sentence was going to say until she'd written it, and then there it was: the thoughts of these people on the bright white page, in her own hand.

Her mother's replies read formally at first, but soon loosened, expanded. They wrote plainly about their days: the coffee they drank, the songs they heard, the films they watched. The later notes were simply arrangements to meet.

At the kitchen table, Linda got to know Paul Landry as he had been. She wanted to hate him, but couldn't. She came to understand his sense of humour. She found herself laughing, the noise echoing through the bungalow. How long had it been since she had got to know someone? By the second day, a bright swelling had risen on Linda's middle finger from where the barrel of her Parker pen dug into the knuckle.

Linda realised, as she read and transcribed, that this man had influenced their family life in all sorts of small ways. The music he wrote about – Linda Scott, The Flamingos, Connie Stevens,

Chuck Berry, The Chantels – had ended up on their record player. He crossed his sevens, and so did Daisy, so did Linda.

She got to know her mother again, too – her resourcefulness, her warmth, her humour in the face of adversity. Through their correspondence, she saw the relationship change – Paul's hopes for it, Daisy's caution, the compromise they reached. For a decade, Linda had told herself lies to numb the pain of her mother's death, but at least Daisy had *lived*, first. She had found a way to live.

When Linda finished transcribing the last letter, the kitchen was all indigo shadows, and the clock on the cooker showed 01:23. She stood and walked down the hallway to her son's room. He lay across his bed, his right arm dangling over the side. She watched him sleep for a moment and then retrieved his discarded shirt for the washing machine. He would be done with school in a matter of days. For his sake, she had to pull herself together, one last time.

When he got home from work, Mike took off the leather jacket Cassie had suggested he buy, and threw it on the sofa. It wasn't an old-style biker jacket, but more like a soft blazer, with lapels and a burgundy lining. It cost a bomb, and gave Mike a deeply savoury smell only partially covered by the freshness of CK One. He sat down and sent a text message to Cassie: CAN YOU COME OVER TOMORROW FOR A CHAT?

The harsh entryphone sounded, and he stood again, felt the old twinge in his ribs. He had the absurd thought that it could be Cassie, here already. But his sister's voice came through the receiver. He buzzed her in, and waited for her at the door to the flat. She climbed the stairs – a dark shape against the sunlight in the window behind her. It could have been his mum, the outline.

'I was going to call you,' he said.

She smiled, her hair wet and fragrant from the shower. She put her arms around him, and rubbed his back. 'Hello,' she said. 'I need to talk to you about something.'

They entered the flat and sat down at opposite ends of the sofa. 'How's Lucas?' he said.

'Up and down.'

'Listen, Linda. I'm sorry I didn't pick him up the other week, and I'm sorry generally. I've not been acting right, lately.'

'Is she young?'

'*What?*' Linda had used the exact same words as Stephen. 'Yeah,' he said, with a sigh. 'Quite young.'

'Is it serious?' Linda asked.

'It's over, is what it is. From tomorrow.'

Linda sniffed. 'Are you cooking steak?'

'No. It's my jacket.'

She laughed.

Mike's mobile phone beeped: a text from Cassie: A CHAT?!!!

Mike turned the phone over, and then covered his face with his hands.

'You all right?' Linda asked.

'I'm a fucking idiot.'

'Oh, love.'

'Anyway,' he said. 'You came here. What can I do for you?'

Linda stared at him. She opened her mouth and shut it again.

'Spit it out,' Mike said.

'Well. You know on the last day of school, they do this thing where all the kids sign each other's shirts with marker pens, right?'

'Oh, yeah.'

'I've just bought Lucas a couple of new shirts, in case he needs them for interviews and stuff.'

'Right.'

'So, I just wondered if you had an old white shirt hanging around, that you wouldn't mind donating.'

'Course. I'm wearing these double weave things these days,' he said, brushing at his chest. 'So I've got a few of the old cheaper type lying around somewhere.'

'He only needs one.'

'Last day, eh?'

'Last day.'

'You did it, Lind.'

'*He* did it.'

Mike stood, and walked towards the spare room, but then stopped. '*That's* all you wanted to talk about?'

Linda shrugged.

'You could've called me. I would've brought it round.'

'A hassle.'

'I'd do anything for you, Linda,' he said.

He gave her the shirt, they said their goodbyes, and he let her out of the flat. He listened to her footsteps on the stairs, and heard the front door of the building slam. He drifted into the kitchenette, and opened the fridge. The intercom buzzed again.

He picked up the receiver. 'Yep?'

'Mike, it's me,' Linda said.

'Oh. You all right?'

'Fine,' she said. 'Fine.'

'Okay . . .' he said.

'There *was* something else.' Her breath crackled through the receiver.

'What is it?'

'It's about Mum. It's about what happened.'

Mike waited for a moment, and then filled the silence himself. 'She was going to get better, wasn't she?' he said.

'Yes,' Linda said. 'I think she probably was.'

Mike took the receiver away from his ear for a moment. Through the open window of the flat, he could hear the scrape of his sister's shoes on the stone steps outside. 'You better come back up,' he said.

Lucas had always thought English was like a train. Word followed word, like an engine pulling a carriage. Consequences flowed from left to right. 'And then, and then, and then.'

Cassie had taught him there was no 'and then' in sign language. You didn't wait for the next word, for what came next, because it all happened simultaneously. Your right hand was a falling tree (your puffed cheeks told of its size), and your left hand was the man who stood beneath it. It all unfolded before your eyes, inevitable.

On the morning of his last day of school, he loped into the kitchen and smelled smoky bacon and toast, found his mum suddenly revived, beaming at him. '   ready?' she said.

'For what?'

She plucked the shirt from the ironing board and squeezed it at the neck like a piping bag. 'Uncle   don't ruin one of your good ones.'

She gave him the shirt, and then held him. He could feel the pressure in her body, the tears she was holding back. She pulled away. 'You made it, Lucas.'

'Not yet,' he said.

In his bedroom, he stood before the mirror in Uncle Mike's shirt, the yoke and collar of which had turned a sort of bone colour. He buttoned it over his vest. The cuffs had frayed. It almost fitted him across the shoulders, but not quite. His hair had begun to curl again. He needed a trim.

On the top deck of the school bus, the kids were already signing each other's shirts. They wrote emotional goodbyes, limericks and swear words; they drew breasts like bullseyes in green and blue. Duncan Youds untucked his shirt, and urged the girls to sign over his crotch. '   down there,' he shouted. 'Right down there. Ah, yeah!'

When they got off the bus, the air smelled of Hawaiian Tropic sun oil, and raspberry Mr Freeze. All over the school, groups of kids leaned against each other, pressing pens into shirts.

At form period, the pupils put music on the ghetto blaster. Lucas remained seated, while the others lounged across tables, or danced. Collages peeled from the walls of the form room. Lucas didn't do foreign languages, because they took him out for basic studies, but it seemed that French and Spanish lessons consisted mostly of cutting and sticking. On the walls were pictures of sandy beaches snipped from brochures, women in bikinis, and heartbreakingly beautiful swimming pools, unrippled. Lucas tried to focus on those bright blue rectangles of water, far away from school.

At the front of the class, Señor Potts, his form tutor, beamed at him proudly. Potts pumped his fist, triumphant that they'd made it to the end of the year. But the Rexel clock above him showed 9.25 a.m.

In biology, Mr Solomon brought in Mr Kipling Bakewell tarts (reduced for clearance), and took board-games out of the lab store cupboard. The girls wanted the handsome science teacher to sign their shirts, and the clamour gave Youds and his friends the chance to make their spastic faces across the room at Lucas.

Lucas turned away and stared at the door. He would've forgiven Cassie for abandoning him, if she had only walked through that door and said, 'Hi, Mario. Sorry I'm late.'

Iona sat down across from him with a battered old edition of Connect 4. Her long straggles of brown hair, which she wore tied up above the undercut, grew out of a black dye job, so that the natural colour seemed grey. 'You want to be red or yellow?' she asked.

Lucas nodded to the girls holding out their shirts to the teacher. 'Don't you fancy Mr Solomon?' he said.

'Huh?' Iona said. She looked over her shoulder, but had the good sense and manners to turn back to Lucas before she spoke. 'Oh. No. Erm. I fancy *Miss Webster*, from PE.'

'Right,' Lucas said.

The few people who had signed her shirt had taken some care: song lyrics, anarchy 'A's, and a wobbly-mouthed Nirvana smiley. Someone had drawn a dotted-line heart on her chest, with a scissor sign. CUT HERE AND REMOVE.

Lucas dropped a red coin into a slot at random.

Iona tapped his hand. 'What was the joke your mum told?' she asked.

'Pardon?'

'In "A Life in the Day". You said your mum told a joke, but you skipped over it.'

'That's because it doesn't work in sign language,' Lucas said.

'Yeah. So   the joke?'

Lucas sighed. 'Why was the cockerel sad?'

Iona shrugged.

'Because he only got laid once, and it was by his mother.'

Iona laughed, scandalised. 'Jesus, your *mum*   that?   mum told you a *mum joke?*'

'She can be very inappropriate,' Lucas said. 'Cassie was supposed to do the joke in speech, but . . .'

'Your support worker?   happened to her?'

'I don't know.'

Youds and his crew gurned at him. They'd been sniffing the gas taps, and the smell reached him now. Lucas felt like striking a match. Iona rubbed a yellow coin in her fingers, but then turned and hurled it at Youds. He ducked, and it hit him on the hand. He rose up, laughing. Then he made a 'V' with his fingers and stuck his tongue through it.

'   viously, he's never done *that* before,' she said.

Lucas shrugged.

Iona took out a blue marker pen. She put the fingers of her free hand to her chin and then moved them forward. *Please.*

She handed the marker to Lucas. He leaned over and signed her sleeve. MARIO.

She took back the pen, came around the side of the desk and gestured to his uncle's shirt. *May I sign it?*

She pretended to look hard for a space in which to write, and Lucas laughed. She did it like someone who knew sign language. Iona wrote low on his shirt, upside down so he could read it, one clause either side of the buttons.

NOBODY DIES A VIRGIN   LIFE FUCKS US ALL
           Iona   (and Kurt)

Lucas, fearing he might cry, looked away. A poster on the wall said that humans shared thirty-three per cent of their DNA with daffodils. Lucas thought of his uncle's catchphrase: *Show them what you're made of, Luke.*

At the end of the lesson, Iona accompanied him out of the science lab and into the corridor. 'You have history next, right?' she said.

Lucas nodded, and they walked on briskly. They turned right into another corridor, which was all windows. Lucas couldn't see Iona's face with the glare of the sun behind her, so he switched sides. Better.

'   you really don't know where she's   ?' Iona said.

'Who? Cassie? No. I sent her a text this morning. She has a mobile phone because her brother is deaf. But she didn't reply.'

Lucas liked the feeling of disclosing personal information about Cassie and her family. He liked the intimacy it suggested.

'I heard   she and her boyfriend had   away, or moved town or   ,' Iona said.

Lucas frowned. 'No,' he said. 'She doesn't have a boyfriend.'

'Oh. I think she does actually.   Suk Panesar saw   older guy in the Red Lion.'

Lucas shook his head. They bumped through a set of double doors, and into a much darker space, near the humanities block. 'She *told* me she didn't have a boyfriend,' he said. 'I mean, why would she lie?'

'Hey, I was disappointed, too. I thought, with that hair   broad shoulders   pretty, she might   . You never know. But it's always the same old story, isn't it?'

'No, it isn't,' he said.

'Okay.'

'You don't know what you're talking about,' Lucas said. 'It's fucking different. I don't just let things happen to me anymore. I *choose* what happens. *I* do!' He could feel himself losing control of the muscles in his throat. Iona's expression told him he was shouting too loudly.

'Lucas, I said okay. I'm sorry   need to freak out.'

'Leave me alone!' he roared, and then strode back in the direction they'd come from. He knew from films that Iona might be calling to him. But it seemed to Lucas that friendship was just a game of Pop-Up Pirate, and you were better off getting the shock of the ending over with as soon as possible.

As he turned the corner again, he saw Youds and company marching towards him. Was this it? Were they about to descend on him, as they had warned? He stood still, and signed to them.

Man is wolf to man. So watch out.

But the boys simply passed him by.

And that, in the end, was their punishment, whether they meant it or not. They ignored him. Everyone did. Youds and his gang had forgotten their promise to attack him, and the others had lost interest. He'd poured all of his attention into Cassie, and she had left him.

He didn't realise what had happened until it was too late. As the clock ran down on the final hours of school, he looked around at shirts entirely covered in names, the red and green and blue and black bleeding into each other. And Lucas's remained almost blank – just the one dedication, from a girl who now probably hated him. He tried to convince himself that he didn't mind, but he knew his mother would. He imagined her face as she opened the door to him in his almost unblemished shirt. All those years she had invested in his education, and this shirt would be the ultimate sign of failure. Lucas feared she might fall back into the miserable state in which she'd wallowed for the last few weeks.

The other kids sang, apparently. He lip-read the word 'baby', drawn out over four beats. The faint pulse of music reached him through the soles of his shoes. He pocketed a few marker pens, and excused himself to go to the toilet, but he wasn't coming back.

He took the path leading to the outdoor swimming pool, following the scent of cheap chemicals and stale sweat and pine sap. He climbed the small wall, and squeezed through the evergreens that surrounded the pool. Lucas sat down on one of the viewing benches and stared at the gorgeous blue of the pool water.

He'd never swum in the pool, because he did speech therapy instead: hundreds of hours of mouthing the noises that had led him here, today. God knows he'd learned his lines. In any case, since he could sign, Lucas was capable of keeping places within him (a park, a cinema, a living room with sun streaming through the patio doors). He could rebuild those places in the air, whenever he wanted. He should remember *this* place, when he next felt down.

He held up a finger on his right hand, to represent himself, and a finger on his left, for Cassie. She was there, somewhere within his signing space, but he couldn't gauge the distance. He couldn't imagine himself into her point of view. And now, because of what Iona had said, he had to accept the possibility of a third person between them. He took out his Nokia and typed a text in capitals, scrolling through each letter. HELLO. PLEASE TEXT ME. NOT A GOOD DAY HERE. DID I DO SOMETHING WRONG? He deleted the last sentence, and then sent the message.

He took the lids off the coloured marker pens, and sniffed them, wrinkled his nose. This was simply a necessary task, and he shouldn't get emotional about it. He considered his options: he could take the shirt off, but there wasn't a good flat surface, so he just turned the pen on himself. He started in the top left corner, and tried to match the pithy wisecracks with the names of his classmates, though he didn't know them well.

GOOD LUCK, DUDE! GREG.

GO LUCAS! LAURA.

KEEP IN TOUCH, MAN. YOUDSY.

The awkwardness of writing on his own body helped him to vary the handwriting styles. He drew faces and stick people, and fairly realistic eyes over the nipple area. He got a little carried away, made crosses for kisses on his arms, and began to elevate the praise and gratitude and friendship and love to the levels it might have been had he done absolutely everything differently.

The muscles in his wrist soon ached. He drew a chain around his neck, from which hung a big clock, like Flavor Flav, with the hands at half past three; above his heart, he scrawled a large 'M' for Mario. The task absorbed him so completely, he didn't even realise he was crying until he'd finished. Stupid. Pitiful. Cassie would have shouted at him.

After throwing the marker pens into the pines, he sat there for a while, eyes closed, the smell of warm chlorine in his nostrils. He remembered sheltering from a downpour in a dark seafront café with Nanna. They'd emerged from the cinema into a storm, and found beach pebbles washed up on West Street, a live fish writhing in the middle of the road. They ducked into the nearest place. The waiter lit a candle. Nanna signed to Lucas. *The sea is noisy. I'm sorry about the film.*

He had to lean around the clutter of table decorations to see her hands. Nanna called to the waiter. When he came, she placed upon his tray the two menus, the candle, the vase of flowers, the bowl of sugar, salt and pepper pots, and a wooden container filled with cutlery. She gave the waiter further instructions, and he left.

Lucas frowned at Nanna as she removed her coat and fixed her hair. *Wait*, she signed. A few seconds later, an ugly strip light flickered on, picking out the grime on the table and the damp on the walls, but allowing them, finally, to communicate.

There, she signed. *Better. Now, which cat did you like best?* She made the sign for cat with one hand, because the other was pressed deep into her midriff.

Lucas thought, now, about diving into the pool, breaking the plane. He thought, briefly, of things with which to weigh himself down. They said it wasn't a bad way to go, but he worried that nobody would find him until September.

He dragged himself up. Through a gap in the pines, he could see the school gate, and so, a few minutes early, he made his exit from secondary education.

The bus driver gave him a sidelong glance. 'Single to Ringdean,' Lucas said, and the driver smiled, as if Lucas's voice provided the answer to a mystery.

He took a seat upstairs and the bus pulled away. Down hollows, up rises, into the suburbs. Lucas imagined what he would say to Cassie, when he arrived at The Cut. *You left me for dead*, or, *I love you*. What if she wasn't there? He thought about her notebooks, which they'd filled with conversations. Perhaps he could sneak into the house, somehow, and get hold of those. But he remembered the Deaf pub night, and the poet who had signed, *We make bad burglars, and bad security guards*.

The bus stopped outside the shops, and Lucas descended. Across the road, The Cut seemed too busy, too bright. Cassie's mum patrolled the floor, and Lucas knew she would turn him away. So he lowered his head and walked down the side of the terraced row, looking for some sort of back way in. But there, coasting slowly next to the kerb, was Uncle Mike's Honda. The headlights flashed. Lucas stopped walking and sighed, exhausted, defeated, and struck with wonder. Sometimes, his tiny family were nowhere to be found, and sometimes they were everywhere at once.

Earlier that day, Cassie had sat on Mike's sofa with her fists squeezed tight. She wore a black vest, which left visible the luminous pink straps of her bra. Mike recognised the underwear, and felt a guilty clench in his dick.

'I knew it the minute I got here,' she said. 'I was like, Uh-oh, he's wearing his shoes indoors. He's being all clinical and decisive.'

'Cassie.'

'I want you to know something, Mike. A couple of things. Firstly, I'm not a symbol of some crisis you went through. I'm not a sign. I'm flesh and blood.'

'I know.'

'Secondly, you are not the only one who made a *bad decision*. I pretty much left my job because of you. Jesus Christ, did I pick the wrong man.'

Mike nodded. 'I couldn't agree more.'

'Bit patronising, Mike.'

'I guess in this sort of situation, it's hard to say the right thing. Last night, I had a long chat with my sister, and, well, I just feel like I need to spend more time with them. Linda and Lucas, I mean.'

'That's a terrible idea.'

'They're my family.'

'No, I meant that it's a terrible idea for *them*. They're better off without you,' Cassie said. 'I'd like you to drive me home, please.'

'Your stuff is in the bathroom.'

'I know where it is. I need to stop at the Co-op, if that's not too much trouble.'

'Course,' Mike said. He looked around for something to do,

but he was completely ready to go. He had the keys in his hand.

In the car, Cassie sat with her sports bag open on her lap, and occupied herself with organising her belongings. She took out the coral-coloured make-up bag he'd come to recognise from his bathroom, and slammed it, unzipped, into the well on the dashboard. Several items spilled out: a bottle of nail colour, a blister-pack of pills, and a perfectly spherical stone. She pulled down the passenger side visor and raised her eyebrows at the mirror, wiped off her eye make-up with a cotton pad, and threw the pad into the foot-well. Mike would miss those traces of her around the flat – the fog of Intensive Care and steam in the bathroom, the clogged-up spikes of her mascara brush.

He pulled up outside the Co-op. 'Shall I . . . I'll wait here,' he said.

'Fuck's sake,' she muttered, as she got out of the car.

Waiting at the roadside, Mike felt – as he often did now – an urge to visit Stephen. It was not an urge of the body – he didn't want to be beaten up. He wanted to talk, to tell Stephen about his parents. He wanted to hear about Hannah's preparation for university, and her exam revision. He remembered winter in Stephen's house, the colours of the glass light shade above the kitchen table.

When Cassie returned to the car, she dumped her bag of shopping on the back seat, and got in the front. Mike half-expected her to have bought alcohol, but when he twisted in his seat, he saw only a large plastic bottle of milk, and some apples.

'Let's go,' she said.

As usual, he parked around the corner from The Cut. He had never met Cassie's mum, had never stepped inside her home. Cassie pushed the car door open.

'I'm sorry,' Mike said.

'In a couple of months you'll remember me,' she said, stepping out onto the pavement and opening the back door to retrieve her shopping.

Mike turned to look at her. 'Come on,' he said. 'I'll always remember you.'

She laughed. 'I don't mean all *that* bullshit. I mean the smell.'

'Eh?'

Cassie unscrewed the lid from the four-pint bottle of milk and began to pour the contents into the upholstery of the back seats. Mike was too slow to stop her, so he just closed his eyes. He could hear the quiet glug of the liquid, and then the hollow plastic tumbling into the foot-well.

'Give it a few weeks for the milk to turn,' Cassie said.

Then she was gone. He watched her hurrying, hunched, out of sight. She'd left her make-up bag and all the crap on the dashboard, but she'd taken the apples. Mike picked up the soiled cotton pad, and shovelled the bag and the pills into the glove compartment. He reached over and pressed his hand into the back seat. Milk came up through the fabric. It ran along the camber of the upholstery and pooled in the seams. Being fresh, it didn't smell too bad, yet, but Mike buzzed the windows down anyway. He figured he would drive around for a while, let some air into the car.

As he pulled away, his nephew came around the corner. Mike's first instinct was to put his foot down, and drive off

297

before the boy spotted him. But Lucas looked half-mad, his curls turned up like little horns, his shirt daubed red and blue and green. Mike slowed down and flashed his lights.

Lucas saw the car, and stopped walking, as though Mike was some crushing, inevitable inconvenience, like a blocked drain or a flat tyre. Mike drove up alongside him. 'Hello, mate! What you doing? School's not finished yet, is it?'

'What?' Lucas said.

Mike leaned across and opened the door. 'Get in,' he said, pointing to the seat.

Lucas shook his head.

'Come on. Just sit for a minute'

Lucas's shoulders dropped. Really, he had very few options. He got in the car, closed the door, and sat there, staring straight ahead. Eventually, he sniffed. 'Stinks in here,' he said.

'He who smelt it, dealt it,' Mike said. He cut the engine. 'Has school finished already?'

'What?'

'School.'

'I tried school. Gave it a good go. It wasn't for me,' Lucas said.

'You got some signatures, though, eh?' Mike said, gesturing to the shirt.

'Oh, yeah. Loads. Very popular.'

'What are you doing out here?'

'Nothing much. What about you?'

'Same.'

Lucas nodded, and they looked out of the window for a while. 'When that milk goes off—' Lucas said.

'I know, I know.'

'You're clumsy.'

'Yep,' Mike said. He turned in his seat. 'Let's have a look, then. Hey, you've got some kisses, here.' Mike examined the signatures closely, the weird scrawls and drawings. 'Christ,' he said. 'Eleven years of learning, and some of these kids can hardly write.' He reached out for the shirt, but Lucas grabbed his wrist, hard.

'Woah. What's wrong, mate? What is it?'

'Stupid!' Lucas shouted, unbuttoning the shirt, and ripping it off, so that Mike had to lean out of the way of his elbows.

'What are you doing?' Mike asked. 'What's going on?'

'Just leave it, okay?' Lucas said.

Lucas breathed loudly, crumpled the shirt in his lap. He wore a vest, and Mike saw that the ink had gone through the cotton, and faint words covered Lucas's arms.

'I don't understand,' Mike said.

'No, you don't,' Lucas said. 'So forget it.'

Mike nodded. He reached back and pulled his leather jacket off the parcel shelf, gave it to Lucas. 'Here. You can wear this, if you like.'

Lucas examined the jacket, checked the label, and then shrugged it on. It hung loose at the chest.

'Suits you,' Mike said. 'You look like *Goodfellas.*'

'What, all of them?'

They stared at each other, the smell of milk-soaked nylon already beginning to sicken them. 'Listen, Lucas,' Mike said. 'I know I've been a bit of an idiot, the last few months. I lost the plot, basically. At first, I wasn't able to adjust to living on my own.'

'What?'

'I got involved in a couple of things that I shouldn't have.'

Lucas glanced away for a moment, and then stiffened. He picked up the perfectly round stone from the well in the dashboard. 'What's this?' he asked.

'Just a pebble.'

'Where did you get it?'

'Don't know. The beach, probably. Anyway. What I'm saying is that this . . . phase I've been going through. It's done. Finished. I've had a chat with your mum, and I'm going to make some real changes.'

Lucas weighed the stone in his hand. He squeezed it hard, as if any pressure other than one million years of sea tides could crack it.

'Are you listening?' Mike said.

'An older man,' Lucas said.

'What?'

'It was you. All this fucking time.'

'Lucas, what are you talking about?'

'Cassie. I'm talking about Cassie.'

'Oh. Hang on. Wait.'

'It's all the wrong way round.'

'Lucas, listen.'

Lucas hurled the stone and it ricocheted off the dashboard, hit the rubberised steering wheel and smacked Mike on the bone above his eye socket. His vision went white with the pain.

'Shit,' Lucas said. He reached out to Mike, but then pulled away.

Mike touched his eyebrow twice. The second time, his fingers were streaked with thin bright blood. 'Sake,' he said. He leaned forward, and cradled his head. The whole left side of his face had gone heavy and numb, and he thought he might throw up. The blood came fast between his fingers. He glanced at Lucas, who had turned towards the window, tensed up against his own feelings. He might have been crying. Without looking, he passed Mike the balled-up shirt, and Mike pressed it against the wound.

'Lucas.' Mike tapped his arm. 'Mate? Look. I'm okay.'

Lucas turned to him and nodded – a quick dip of the chin.

'I'll be okay,' Mike said, taking the shirt away from the cut, but then quickly putting it back again. 'I'm really totally fine.'

'That's just your opinion,' Lucas said.

'I'm sorry,' Mike said. 'I'm just sorry. That was what I was trying to say.'

'Do you need to go to hospital?'

'No. It's just a scratch.'

They sat there for a while, both trying to get into a position that wouldn't cause them too much pain. Mike retrieved his first aid kit from under the seat. He adjusted the rear-view mirror, and cleaned the cut, dressed it with Vaseline and cotton wool and tape, while Lucas tried not to look impressed. After that, Mike tapped Lucas's shoulder. 'Congratulations,' he said.

'Huh?'

'You finished school.'

Lucas blinked slowly. 'Yes.'

'What do you want to do? To celebrate. Apart from throw stuff at me.'

'Don't know.'

'Well. While you think about it, I'm going to drive for a bit, try and get some fresh air into this stupid dairy farm stinking car.'

He started the engine and pulled away, past The Cut, out of Ringdean, inland. He drove fast, taking the back roads, and they climbed through the Downs, fields of bright yellow whatever rising above on either side of the car. The sun glared off the flint villages. A church bell cracked the hour. The smells of pollen, and dirt, and dung, mixed with the milk smell in the car. Lucas sniffled, his eyelids drooped.

Mike drove back down through the trimmed golf courses to the coast road, and they shot through Peacehaven – past the pet stores, the Wimpey, and the mobile home site. Sometimes the cliffs were visible, sometimes the great big void of the sea.

Mike did not look at his parents' old house as they drove through Saltdean.

'I want to see Mum,' Lucas said.

'Eh?'

'I want to go home.'

'Good decision,' Mike said.

The inside of Paul's cabin was clean, but worn. A striped rug lay sun-faded in the shape of the window, and the old film posters on the wall had bleached beyond recognition. A small TV and video recorder sat on a writing desk. Linda and Paul stood next to each other by the open window, looking out on the mobile home park, its statues and washing trees. They couldn't see any people, though they could hear the sound of a path being swept, a television.

'You ever been to Rome?' Paul asked.

'I haven't been anywhere.'

'You go to the Forum, and it's all ruins, obviously. Column stumps and smashed up bits of wall. You have to use a lot of imagination to picture what it would have been like. But here . . .' He cast his arm over the site, with its green-tinged fountains, alabaster serpents and pissing cherubs. '. . . here, you get to see how it really would have looked in Antiquity.'

'You're funny.'

'I used to be. These days, not so much.'

'You were funny in the letters.'

'Was I? Sometimes I wish I'd never written them.'

'Don't say that.'

'Well. Maybe, if I hadn't written them, she'd still be here.'

Linda shook her head. 'I miss her so much.'

'She used to talk about you all the time,' Paul said.

'What did she say?'

'She was always telling me what you thought of the films. She thought you were the bee's knees. You and your brother. If I can tell you one thing before I curl up my toes, it's that.'

Linda closed her eyes. She didn't believe in voices from beyond the grave; she knew that Paul's memories were as close as she'd ever get to hearing her mum's thoughts again.

'How's your son?' he asked.

'Mum talked about Lucas?'

'Yeah. I met him once,' Paul said. 'That must be weird, sorry. I bumped into them in the park, one day, chasing leaves.'

'He's angry with me at the moment. Rightfully so, probably.'

'A mother's place is in the wrong.'

Linda smiled.

'Daisy taught me the alphabet, you know,' Paul said. 'Sign language.' Carefully, on his big hands, Paul finger-spelled a word. 'Ah,' he said. 'I don't know if that's right. I've forgotten it.'

'Me too,' Linda said.

'So how do you communicate with him?'

'By slowly smothering him to death.'

Paul laughed. 'You're just like your mum.'

The tears came then, blurring her vision of the cabins, and the cliff top, and the sea beyond.

Paul's hand hovered near her back. 'Oh God,' he said. 'I shouldn't have said that.'

'Nicest thing anyone's said to me for ages.' She pressed her palms against her eyes, riding the sobs. 'Did you look after her, Paul?'

'What?'

'Did you take care of her? When you were together?'

'I tried to,' he said.

'Did she have a good time with you? Did she have fun?'

'I think so. I think she did,' he said, breaking down himself now.

She might have held him, but she couldn't, quite. Not yet. On the windowsill stood a solitary Beswick fox, unmistakably the one from her parents' bedroom, with the hairline cracks from where Lucas had dropped it all those years ago, its head twisted round to monitor the pursuit of the huntsman and the hounds, who were long gone. Linda touched the cold, porcelain body.

'What will you do about your dad?' Paul asked.

'I can't think about it now. I'm afraid that if I see him, I might kill him.'

Paul nodded. 'I thought that once, too,' he said. 'Wouldn't do much good, though, eh?'

Linda shook her head. The silence was not without awkwardness, which gave her an idea. 'Paul,' she said. 'Would you like to go to the cinema?'

'You know what? I think I'm done with the cinema. At least for a while. You should go, though.'

'I haven't been for years . . .' Linda said.

'You should ask your son to go with you.'

Linda glanced at Paul, who was rocking gently on his feet. He looked exhausted.

'I don't know what's on,' she said.

Paul looked at his watch, the leather strap worn and discoloured. 'There's always something,' he said.

She got home a little while before Mike brought Lucas back. The two of them stood dishevelled on the path, Lucas in a vest and leather jacket, Mike using a balled-up shirt to dab at a leaking wound on his forehead. Linda embraced Lucas, and then stood back. 'All done?' she said.

'All done.'

She turned to her brother. 'What happened to you, Michael?'

'I tripped at work, or fell off my bike, or something,' Mike said.

'What?'

'Doesn't matter. I'm okay.'

'Do you want to come in?'

'Nah. I'm knackered. I'll call you, though.'

Mike tapped Lucas on the shoulder. 'You can keep the jacket,' he said.

'You can keep the shirt,' Lucas replied.

Mike ambled back to the car, hands in pockets, the shirt tucked under his arm.

'Hey, Uncle Mike,' Lucas said.

'Yes, mate.'

'Show them what you're made of, eh.'

Mike smiled, and Lucas stepped inside the bungalow, closed the door. Linda had tied up some celebratory balloons in the hallway, and Lucas bopped them gently with his fingers.

'Do you want to go and see a film, Lucas?' she said.

'What? I thought you didn't like the pictures.'

She shrugged.

'Okay,' he said.

'I'll get ready,' she said, but as she turned, Lucas touched her arm.

'Mum,' he said.

'Yes, love.'

He made a circle on the centre of his chest with his fist. She didn't know what it meant, and then she did. It came back. *Sorry.* She made the circle, too, as best she could.

Lucas waited in the hallway.

As a little kid, he'd played with his cars on the carpet, right here where he now stood, and watched his mum march purposefully out of the kitchen, breeze past him and open the front door to reveal his Nanna, beaming on the step.

Lucas, being deaf, had found this miraculous, as if his mother had somehow *conjured* Nanna, simply by opening the door.

She must have explained the concept of knocking to him shortly afterwards. She must have talked him through the qualities of sound – how it travels through objects and the air, how if you make enough noise, somebody will come to you.

But in any case, when he was seven – even though he *must* have known the truth – his mum had to stop him from opening and closing the front door every half hour, trying to bring his dead grandmother to the step.

He remembered clutching the rough fibres of the welcome mat as his mum dragged him back into the house. He remembered her face, stricken with grief. She'd said that Nanna was not coming back, and that Lucas was letting in the fallen needles from the trees.

He opened the door now, and looked out on the empty street: the larches across the road, the dull street lamp. Glancing down at himself, he saw where the marker pens had penetrated the shirt. Faint letters in red and blue and black and green covered his vest and his skin. It didn't matter. *This* was what he was made of: the things that had happened to him, the people who had ignored and befriended him, the people who'd left when he needed them, whether they wanted to or not. The people who'd stayed. He was made of memories, and of the things he couldn't remember, of the language they forced into his mouth, and the language they tried to rip out of his hands. He was made of the words scrawled all over his body, and the words that faded in the air.

Acknowledgements

Many people have helped with me with this book. I would like to thank:

Derek Neale and Fiona Doloughan.

David Swann, Karen Stevens, and Bethan Roberts. Julie Redfern. Keir Livock. Emma Sweeney. Naomi Austin. Parveen Dunlin, John Walker, and the members of my BSL class.

Laura Blackburn, Joanna Garber, Matthew Jones, David Rowland, Eddie Hogan and Blake Hogan. Véronique Baxter, Mark Richards, and all at David Higham and John Murray. Everyone at the University of Sussex Library.

Sally O'Reilly, Catherine Cole, and Gerard Woodward.

Special thanks go to Alice, Jesse, and particularly Emily Hogan. I dedicate this book to my family.